633 SQUADRON: OPERATION SAFEGUARD

633 SQUADRON: OPERATION SAFEGUARD

FREDERICK E. SMITH

ROBERT HALE · LONDON

ISBN 978-0-7090-8427-3

Robert Hale Limited
Clerkenwell House
Clerkenwell Green
London EC1R 0HT

www.halebooks.com

2 4 6 8 10 9 7 5 3 1

Typeset in 10/12½pt Palatino
Printed and bound in Great Britain by
Biddles Limited, King's Lynn

To my late beloved wife Shelagh, to whom I owe so much and who has inspired so many of my novels.

CHAPTER 1

IT WAS EXCEPTIONALLY chilly and quiet in Adams's confessional that March morning. The English spring was having one of its manic blips and the Mosquitoes were out on a routine mission. At the same time, waiting for the crews to return safely was always a strain for Adams, and it made him more conscious than usual of the acrid smell given off by the Nissen hut's coke stove. Although Adams had raked it and played about with its damper, it doggedly gave out more smoke than heat, resigning Adams to waiting until the resident chimney sweep, one Aircraftman Matthews, could remove the metal pipes and flush out their sooty contents.

He walked to a rain-streaked window, glanced out, then turned to his assistant, a slim, good-looking girl of twenty-two years. 'What do you think, Sue? Is it better to be cold or smoked to death?'

Fully aware why he was restless, Sue Spencer smiled. 'I think cold is less dangerous, sir.'

Giving a grunt of agreement, Adams pushed open the window and glanced out again. Sutton Craddock airfield was a dismal picture that morning. Pools of water were lying on its tarmac aprons and Mosquitoes under repair were looking like drenched birds on their dispersal points. Here and there ground crews, muffled up in pullovers, greatcoats and waterproof capes, could be seen working on them. The rest of the men, Adams knew, would be huddled in their dispersal huts, playing cards, smoking, and drinking mugs of hot, black tea around their stoves while they waited for their charges to return. The thought made him turn to Sue Spencer again. 'What about another pot of tea, Sue? I think we've earned one, don't you?'

Her eyes twinkled as she moved towards a sink and kettle. 'Have we, sir?'

Adams swung his arms around his body to warm himself. 'No, we haven't but we'll have one on credit. We'll be busy enough when the boys get back.'

Frank Adams was a complex man. Bespectacled, bulky of build, in his mid-forties, he was a man who found war obscene and had only allowed himself to take part in the 1939 conflict because of the atrocities the Nazis were carrying out against Jews and other ethnic minorities. In Adams's thinking, the only thing worse than war was the torture and murder of the innocent and because he had been unfortunate enough to be of military age at a time when both obscenities were paramount, he had been compelled to make his choice. In private life he was married to Valerie, a woman fifteen years his junior who, since the USA had joined the war, had begun to prefer fun-seeking American officers to an intelligent but more serious-minded husband.

But Adams's complexity did not end in his ambivalence towards the war. In many ways its objectives repelled him: the destruction of the enemy's resources, the wrecking of his cities, the killing of his civilian population. Even more deeply he felt dismay at the loss and death of his young colleagues in carrying out these distasteful tasks.

At the same time, because he had the imagination to conceive the brutal horrors of Nazi occupation, Adams envied the young crews whose daily missions over occupied Europe brought hopes to those enslaved millions. Had he been younger and physically fitter, Frank Adams might well have volunteered to fly, although how well his sensitivity would have fared in combat is open to speculation. As it was, his age and his defective eyesight allied to his probing mind had led him to become an intelligence officer, a role which ironically enough meant he was the first man at the airfield to investigate the grisly details of a young colleague's death.

At the moment he was watching a Mosquito on the eastern side of the airfield. A fitter had climbed into its cockpit and two drenched mechanics had jumped on its tail unit. The reason was clear a few seconds later when a dull cough was heard and black smoke plumed out of its engine exhausts. A second and third cough followed and then the throaty roar of a Merlin under test.

Adams's eyes turned back to the two mechanics who, heads bowed against the hail of spray being hurled back at them, were helping with their weight to keep the aircraft's tail from rising. Grimacing, he jerked a thumb at the steel-grey sky. 'If that cloud drops any lower they'll need to light the flare path when the boys get back.'

Sue Spencer was about to reply when they both heard footsteps on the concrete path that led across the front of the Nissen hut. A moment later there was a tap on the door and a young man in a rain-stained greatcoat appeared. Seeing Adams, he gave a smart salute. 'Good morning, sir.'

Checking his rank, Adams saw he was a pilot officer. 'Good morning. What can we do for you?'

'Are you Squadron Leader Adams, sir?'

Adams noticed he had an upper-class accent. 'Yes, I am. What's your name?'

'I'm Pilot Officer Chalmont, sir. I've just been posted here.'

Adams was unable to see his status because of his overcoat. 'What are you? Aircrew or ground staff?'

'I'm a pilot, sir.'

'I see. Did you report to the guardroom on arrival, Chalmont?'

'Yes, sir.'

'Then didn't they tell you to see the adjutant?'

'Yes, sir. I've seen him. And he sent me to you.'

'Did he say why?'

'Not really. He just said if I waited here I'd eventually meet the air crews.'

'So you haven't seen the CO yet?'

'No. It seems he's busy at the moment. I'm to see him later.'

'How long have you been travelling?' Adams asked.

'Only a couple of hours.'

'Have you been to the mess?'

'No, sir. I came straight from the adjutant to you.'

'Then you must feel like a cup of tea.' Adams pointed to one of the Nissen hut benches. 'Sit down and relax. Take your coat off if you like.'

Chalmont moved towards the bench. 'I think I'll leave it on, if you don't mind.' Pausing, he sniffed. 'What's the smell, sir?'

'That's our stove,' Adams told him. 'You don't know a good chimney sweep, do you?'

The young man grinned and shook his head. 'No, sir. Never gone in for that kind of thing.' He pulled out an expensive-looking cigarette case. 'May I smoke, sir?'

Although he was polite and obeyed military etiquette in every way, this was a self-assured young man, Adams thought. 'Yes, you can. No, thank you. I'm a pipe smoker myself. And my assistant doesn't smoke.' He turned to Sue Spencer. 'What's the situation with the kettle, Sue?'

'It's almost boiling, sir.'

'Good.' Adams turned back to the pilot officer. 'What's your background, Chalmont?'

'Educational or service, sir?'

'Both, if you like?'

'I went to Chesterfield and then Cambridge, sir. Then I joined the RAF. I did my training in Canada.'

I thought you were a public schoolboy, Adams reflected. He changed the subject. 'It's quiet in here at the moment because most of our crews are out on a mission. You won't recognize this place when they get back.'

'How long will that be, sir?'

Adams glanced at the huge clock at the far end of the hut. 'Around twenty minutes.' He indicated Sue Spencer, who was spooning leaves into a teapot. 'That's when my assistant and I get down to work.'

'Might I ask what the squadron's doing this morning?'

'We're attacking an important marshalling yard in France,' Adams told him.

'Might I ask why, sir?'

Adams shook his head. 'No, you can't. Most operations are classified these days.' Adams did not offer a reason. With everyone believing the invasion of Europe must come that summer, rumour had it that even Sutton Craddock's resident blackbirds had been ordered to keep their beaks closed. Instead he went on: 'We've got the entire squadron out today because we couldn't get fighter support. So one flight is giving cover to the other.'

The young man nodded. 'You carry short-barrelled cannon as well as stores, don't you, sir?'

'That's right. Our Mossies were specially adapted for our raid on the Swartfjord and we've kept them that way ever since.'

'That was a fantastic operation, sir. It must have been the most famous air strike ever made.'

Adams's expression was a mixture of pride and regret. 'Famous but terribly costly.' He almost went on to say it was like the rest of the squadron's missions but checked himself in time. 'You sound as if you've studied the squadron in some detail.'

Chalmont exhaled smoke. 'One hasn't to study it, sir. Everyone knows its record.' He paused, then went on: 'Mind you, you do keep some of your operations close to your chest, don't you? There are all kinds of rumours about a Norwegian operation you carried out recently. One says that you landed over there yourself. Did you, sir?'

Sue Spencer noticed Adams wince at the reminder of Operation Valkyrie. Recovering quickly, Adams showed his disapproval of the young man's curiosity. 'You ask too many questions, Chalmont. Why don't you wait until you're a fully fledged member of the team. You'll know more about our activities then.'

'I hope so, sir. But you sound as if I might not be accepted. There isn't a danger of that, is there?'

Noticing the sudden break in the young man's self-confidence, Adams shook his head. 'I wouldn't think so, although it hasn't anything to do with me. You are a new pilot, aren't you?'

'Yes, sir. This is my first posting.'

'You're lucky to be sent to this squadron. Do you know that?'

'Yes, sir. Although I did ask for it.' Seeing Adams's expression, the young pilot went on: 'My OTU had a kind of competition. The ones with the highest marks were allowed to give their preference. So I was able to name this squadron.'

Adams found himself wondering if this self-assured young man would feel the same way about the special service squadron in three months' time. There had been a time when, because of its fame, aircrews had queued up to join it. But since rumours of its heavy losses – due to the hazardous missions it was given – had spread round the airfields, it had earned the reputation of being a suicide unit and recruits were fast drying up. 'What made you do that?' Adams asked. 'Do you like special missions? Do you like excitement?'

Chalmont looked surprised at the question. 'Oh, no, sir. Nothing like that.'

Adams sensed a change in the young man. Until now his self-assurance had hidden deeper facets of his personality. Now they seemed to be coming to the surface. 'Then what is it?' he insisted.

The young man exhaled smoke. 'I lived in Spain before the war and saw what the Nazis did there.'

With his interest suddenly sharpened, Adams sat down on the bench facing the pilot officer. 'You lived in Spain? Where?'

'Guernica, sir. My father was in the diplomatic service.'

Adams gave a start. 'Guernica? Were you there when the Nazis bombed it?'

'Yes, sir. We saw it all. We lost some friends there.'

'I see,' Adams said. 'So now you want to pay the Nazis back. Is that why you've come to us?'

To his surprise Chalmont shook his head. 'Oh, no. Nothing like that. It's just that we saw too many innocent civilians killed. Your squadron is only used against military targets. That's why I asked to join it.'

Adams suddenly decided he was going to like this young man. 'What were you reading at Cambridge, Chalmont?'

'Art and English, sir.'

'Have you written anything?'

Chalmont nodded. 'A few things. Little things.'

'What sort of things?'

'A short story or two. A few articles and poems.'

Adams exchanged a glance with Sue who, teapot in hand, was also showing interest in the recruit. Adams leaned forward. 'Did the adjutant tell you what flight you would be in?'

'Yes, sir. He said it might be A Flight. Under Squadron Leader Harvey.'

Adams winced. Harvey. The irascible working-class flight commander to whom upper-class aircrews were anathema. To give himself time to think, he accepted a mug of tea from Sue and waited until she had passed a second one to Chalmont. Adams took a sip before speaking. 'Will you take a little advice from me, Chalmont?'

The young man lowered his mug. 'Of course, sir.'

'Then I shouldn't let it be known that you've written poetry.' Before Chalmont could reply, Adams went on quickly: 'It's difficult to explain why but some servicemen have a prejudice against writers and poets. They don't think they make good fighting men. You and I know it's different. History tells us that it has usually been the romantics who've been the first to man the barricades. But prejudice doesn't recognize this. So I'd keep your talents to yourself, at least for a while.'

To Adams's relief Chalmont showed no surprise or resentment. Instead he was smiling. 'I did meet some of that at Officer Training Unit, sir. So I do know what you mean.'

'Good man. Mind you, this doesn't apply to me. I love talking about literature and poetry. So if you ever feel like a chat about them, let me know.'

The young man's eyes were searching Adams's face as if seeing him for the first time. 'Thank you, sir. I'll remember that.'

'There's just one other thing,' Adams said. 'I wouldn't let anyone know your reason for wanting to join the squadron. Particularly your senior officers.'

'Why is that, sir?'

'In general, operational officers aren't keen on their men having likes and dislikes of your kind. It tends to make them uneasy.'

Before Adams could say more, the far-off drone of engines was heard. As Chalmont's eyes turned to the window, Adams nodded. 'Yes, I think it's them. But they'll be a few minutes yet. So finish your tea.'

CHAPTER 2

AS THE FIRST Mosquito circled Sutton Craddock, the airfield exploded into activity. Engines coughed into life, fire trucks and ambulances ran into their pre-set positions along the runway, crew transports began racing around the perimeter track. Brass-throated voices bawled out orders, a tannoy rasped harshly and then delivered an announcement, a green Very light soared up from the control tower. Sutton Craddock was preparing to welcome back its returning warriors.

The first Mosquito with feathered propellers swept over the Nissen hut and lowered itself on the wet runway. Spray, hurled back from its spinning wheels, almost hid it from sight before its brakes brought it to a halt at the end of the runway. As it turned to taxi to its dispersal point, a second Mosquito squatted down and threw back its own smoke-screen into the windshields of the fire trucks and ambulances that were keeping pace on either side of the runway.

Standing at the window, Chalmont glanced at Adams who, along with Sue Spencer, was watching the squadron's return. 'Have they had any losses today?'

Adams shook his head. 'No, thank God. We got their report after they crossed the coast. There's some flak damage but no injuries as far as we can ascertain.'

As more and more aircraft landed and taxied to their standbys, the transports were meeting them and picking up their crews. As Chalmont watched them Adams turned to him. 'It won't be long now before you meet your new colleagues.'

'I don't suppose you know who they'll be pairing me off with, do you, sir?'

'That's the CO's and the squadron commander's decision,' Adams told him. 'But I suppose there is a possibility you might crew with Mark Richards.'

'Is he flying with them today?'

'No. He's on leave at the moment.'

'What happened to his pilot, sir?'

Beside him Adams saw Sue Spencer flinch. Stevens, Richards's pilot, had been badly wounded by LWG fire during a recent operation. Showing immense courage he had flown all the way back to an emergency airfield in England before collapsing and dying. As he and Richards had been close friends, Richards had believed the young pilot had fought off death for his sake. The twin effects of watching his friend's pain and knowing that if he lost consciousness both of them would perish had been traumatic. Although Richards had denied any loss of morale, the Medical Officer had been humane and insisted on a long leave to help him recover from his ordeal.

Caught by Chalmont's question, Adams was struggling to think of a lie when Sue came to his rescue. 'I wonder what Millburn and Gabby will be arguing about today.'

Adams gave her a grateful glance before turning to Chalmont. 'They're our squadron comedians. Millburn's a Yank who got into the RAF via Canada at the beginning of the war. The Yanks keep trying to win him back but although he'd deny it to the death, Tommy's become more British than we are. Gabriel, his observer, is a little Welshman with big ears and a pointed nose, so he's nicknamed Gabby the Gremlin. Although they're a highly professional team in the air, they're either playing tricks on one another on the ground or chasing every comely lass in Yorkshire.'

At Chalmont's look of surprise, Adams wondered if in his evasion he had said too much about senior officers to a new posting. The truth was that Adams found it difficult to live up to military etiquette with all its pomp and circumstance and had always suffered problems in striking the right posture with junior ranks. The fact that it endeared him to the squadron's younger officers and other ranks had never crossed his mind. Self-critical to a fault, Adams felt that as he had accepted his present role and rank, he ought to play the part with a modicum of dignity.

Across the airfield the last of the crews had climbed down from their aircraft and were boarding the transports. As the first of the Bedfords began speeding back along the airfield perimeter, Adams nodded at Sue Spencer. 'I suppose we'd better get ready.'

As she nodded and retired to one of the large tables that ran down the centre of the Nissen hut, Adams glanced at Chalmont. 'I don't suppose you've ever attended these debriefings we have after an operation?'

'No, sir. Although I've been told about them, of course.'

'Then this is your chance to see a live one. It'll also give you a chance to see your new colleagues. Sit over there and keep your eyes open.'

As Chalmont walked over to a chair that stood alongside a large wooden filing cabinet, there was a squeal of brakes outside, followed by laughter and the loud chatter of voices. As the door was flung open, a voice with an American accent sounded above the din. 'Come on, you guys. It's conscience time. Admit your sins to your Father Confessor.'

A few minutes later the hut was packed with milling men carrying helmets and face masks and NAAFI girls handing them tea and biscuits. Smoke from dozens of cigarettes mingled with the smell of oil and wet uniforms. As the first crewman moved forward to the large table, 633 Squadron in the form of Adams began running over the profit and loss accounts of its latest mission.

The AC2 halted outside the office door. 'This is it, sir. A Flight commander's office.' Then his voice dropped. 'You sure you want to see him just now? His kite got hit today, so he'll be in a filthy mood.'

Chalmont hesitated then shrugged. 'No, I'm told I have to see him.'

The informality of 633 Squadron was evident in the AC2's voice. 'Then better you than me, mate. Best o' luck.' Giving a half salute, the AC2 walked off down the corridor.

Chalmont adjusted his tie and tapped on the door. A gruff voice shouted something. Unable to decipher it, Chalmont pushed open the door and entered. In the split second that followed, his eyes took in an image of a small room with filing cabinets, wall posters, a radio, and a scowling man behind a desk with a pile of papers in front of him. Although the man was seated, Chalmont recognized him as the tall, raw-boned squadron leader he had seen at the debriefing session an hour before. Highly decorated, he was wearing the same worn uniform he had been wearing then. Beside him was a large black mongrel dog. It stirred on seeing Chalmont and half rose. The low growl it gave was followed by a gruff command from the seated man. Glancing at him, the dog sank down again.

The same gruff voice halted Chalmont in his tracks. 'What do you want?'

Chalmont came to attention. 'The squadron commander told me to report to you, sir. I'm Pilot Officer Chalmont.'

Frank Harvey's deep-set eyes moved over the young pilot's impeccable uniform. 'Are you now?' he grunted. Then recognition appeared on his rugged face. 'You're the young bugger who was sitting in

Adams's confessional, aren't you? I wondered what you were doing there.'

'I'd been sent there, sir. Afterwards I saw Wing Commander Moore and he sent me to you.'

Harvey scowled. 'Then he should have known better.' He nodded at the pile of papers on his desk. 'Doesn't he remember the bloody forms I've still got to fill in?'

Chalmont decided it was a question best left unanswered. Instead he asked one of his own. 'I understand the operation went well, sir? Congratulations.'

The self-assurance of the question clearly took Harvey by surprise. 'Who's posted you here, Chalmont?' Before the young man could reply, Harvey picked up his desk telephone. 'Betty? Yes, it's me. I've got a new kid in here. Named Chalmont. Has Ian sent in his documents yet? He has? What do they say?' There was a short pause, then a subtle change in Harvey's voice. 'All right. Bring 'em in right away, will you?'

Replacing the phone, he transferred his gaze to Chalmont. 'So you're a sprog, are you, Chalmont? We're not used to 'em here. Most replacements come from other squadrons. How did you manage it?'

Remembering not to mention his Guernica experience, Chalmont explained. He received a grunt from Harvey. 'So that's what the OTUs are doing these days, is it? What the hell made you choose us?'

Before Chalmont could reply, a pert Waaf entered the offices with a file in her hand. As she handed the file to Harvey, she gave Chalmont a smile that said much about the contents of his documents.

Harvey took the file from her. 'Give Teddy Young a ring, Betty, will you? Tell him I'd appreciate it if he'd come to my office right away.'

The girl nodded, gave Chalmont another smile, then disappeared. As Harvey opened the file and began reading, the young pilot eyed his face. Bony and muscular, it was as craggy as the Yorkshire fells from whence the man came. After a minute he glanced up at Chalmont. 'What's this school you went to? Chesterfield. Is it a public school?'

'Yes, sir.'

The sound Harvey made was remarkably like a sniff. 'And you went to Cambridge afterwards.'

'Yes, sir.'

'What's all this about Spain?'

'My parents lived over there for some years, sir.'

'What was your daddy? A diplomat?'

'Yes, sir.'

With an expression that some might describe as distaste, Harvey moved to more familiar territory. 'Why did you ask to be posted here?'

Remembering Adams's warning once again, Chalmont moved carefully. 'It's a famous squadron, sir. Most crews would like to be on board.'

Harvey's gruff voice leapt at him as if the Yorkshireman had been waiting for the chance. 'That's bullshit, Chalmont. Most men have more sense. And if they haven't, they bloody should have. So what's your reason?'

'That is my reason, sir. Sorry.'

'Then it must have been a hell of a school you went to, Chalmont. Didn't they teach you common sense?'

If Harvey had meant to disconcert the young man, he failed. 'I can't remember that, sir. I suppose they did.'

As Harvey scowled there was a tap on the door and a powerfully built, ginger-headed flight lieutenant with a row of ribbons appeared. 'You want to see me, Frank?'

Harvey nodded. 'Yes.' He waved a large disparaging hand at Chalmont. 'This is a new kid we've got. Named Jeremy Chalmont.' Harvey spoke the name as if he had a touch of toothache. 'He says he volunteered to join us. Can you believe it?'

Teddy Young, an Australian from his love of horse-racing down to his sense of humour, grinned. 'They come all shapes and sizes, Frank. Some guys like death or glory.' He turned to Chalmont. 'Welcome on board, kid. I'm Teddy Young. The only guy on the squadron with a decent birth certificate.'

Chalmont looked impressed. 'Are you the Australian who got back from the Swartfjord operation, sir? The only pilot who flew back?'

Young glanced at Harvey. 'There's fame for you, Frank.' His gaze moved back to Chalmont. 'I'm B Flight commander, kid. Are you posted here on your own?'

'Yes, sir. From OTU.'

'He asked to come here,' Harvey repeated. 'Makes you wonder if he shouldn't see the MO.'

Young grinned. 'There isn't any insanity in your family, is there, kid?'

Chalmont smiled. 'I've never heard of any, sir.'

'Never mind. There's always a first time.'

As Chalmont smiled again, Harvey gave him a scowl. 'All right, Chalmont. You've had your fun and you've let me take a look at you. Are you fixed up for quarters?'

'Yes, sir. I'm to billet with a navigator called Richards.'

'Richards? He's on leave at the moment. All right. Piss off now and I'll let you know later who you'll be crewing with.'

Chalmont drew himself to attention, saluted the two officers, and left the room. As the door closed, Young turned back to Harvey. 'A self-possessed young bugger, isn't he?'

'Aren't they all?' Harvey asked, passing him the younger man's documents. Young took a quick glance at them and then grinned. 'I get it now. He went to your old school. Did you have a chat about old times?'

The Yorkshireman scowled. 'I never could stand those cocky young bastards. Full of crap and bullshit and thinking they know it all. Just like you bloody Aussies. What about you having him? Think of the fun you'd have when he teaches you to speak the King's English.'

The Australian grinned again. 'But I'm not having him, am I? Ian's sure to crew him up with Richards now that Richards has lost his pilot. That's probably why he's sharing Richards's billet. Number four in your flight, my old mate.'

Knowing he was right, Harvey scowled. 'I don't get on with his sort. Can't we do a swap? Ian will probably agree if we both ask him.'

'Not a chance, matey. He's just the guy you need. He'll bring a bit of class into your flight. By the way, did you know Richards was back?'

Harvey showed surprise. 'I thought he still had a week to go.'

'He has but as his family are over in Canada he hasn't any home in the UK. So I suppose he'd rather be back with us lot.'

Harvey frowned. 'That doesn't mean he's going back on ops, does it?'

'No. The MO insists he finishes his full leave first. So he can spend the next week getting pissed in The Black Swan. Or having it off with the local popsies. Why don't you ask Millburn and Gabby to introduce him to some of their bints? God knows they have enough of them.'

Harvey grinned. 'I don't think they'd be the right type for Richards.'

'Why not?'

'I'm told Richards's mummy and daddy taught him to stick to good girls. It's something to do with religion.' Harvey made a last effort. 'Why do I get all these odds and sods? If he's teamed up with Chalmont there'll be two oddballs in the same kite. Let's talk to Moore, Teddy. You can handle 'em better than me.'

Young threw the Yorkshireman a cigarette. 'Not a chance, mate. I'm happy with my team.' He changed the subject. 'Do you know Davies is here?'

Harvey gave a start. 'No. Who told you?'

'Adams. Apparently he arrived by car when we were out. He's been closeted with Pop Henderson ever since.'

'Does Adams know what he wants?'

'Not yet.'

Harvey's rugged face had darkened. 'It'll be another stinker. What does that little sod ever want but blood and glory?'

Young hid a smile. The clash of personalities between the rugged Yorkshireman and Air Commodore Davies was a private joke in the squadron. In spite of Davies's affection for the squadron he had created, it did not prevent him giving it missions of almost suicidal proportions when he felt the war effort required them. Harvey, on the other hand, while obliged to carry out the air commodore's missions, made a point of attacking every minor brief in the battle orders if he found they carried an unnecessary risk to the men in his flight.

None of this militated against combat efficiency – no one drove his men harder than Harvey if he believed every effort had been made beforehand to keep risks down to the minimum – but it did mean he and Davies often clashed heatedly in the preliminary briefings before an operation began.

Harvey's behaviour derived from his background and character. In Harvey's world you took care of the young men who trusted and followed you and did everything in your power to deserve that trust.

But there were other, perhaps less laudable, reasons for Harvey's dislike. In the past Davies had always chosen his squadron commanders from 'upper crust' aircrew officers. Ian Moore was a typical example. Born into money and privilege, Moore had been brought in by Davies to lead the squadron after the shattering losses in Norway when almost everyone else had thought the promotion should have gone to Harvey. Although Moore's leadership and Harvey's courage during Operation Rhine Maiden had eventually healed the breach between the two men and made them the closest of friends, Davies's choice had done nothing to endear him to Harvey. In the Yorkshireman's eyes, Davies reeked of the old breed of officer who believed no one but a 'gentleman' could be a brave and successful military leader.

'So you haven't any clues why Davies is here?' Young asked.

Harvey gave him a pitying look. 'Me? I'm always the last bugger in the squadron to find out what he's up to.'

It was difficult for Young to be serious for long. 'Perhaps he's after Hitler. Perhaps he wants us to raid that Eagle's Nest in Bavaria.'

'I wouldn't put it past the little sod. Mind you, he could be here to give me the shove. It must have hurt him like hell when Ian made me a flight commander.'

Laughing, Young swung his long legs to the floor. 'You haven't said yet why you wanted to see me. Was it only about this new kid?'

Harvey frowned. 'I thought you might do the decent thing and take him over. But if you won't, what about giving him a few lectures on the squadron's demands and tactics. I'm no good at that kind of thing and bullshit's your second name.'

Young grinned. 'Me?'

'Of course. You're an Aussie. In any case, as the kid says, you're the only one who flew back from the Swartfjord. He'll take notice of you.'

Young picked up Chalmont's file again and turned over a page. A moment later he gave a whistle. 'The kid's got some record. Top in just about everything.' Then he gave a start. 'Hang on. He hasn't had leave for seven months. So why can't he have leave too? Then both he and Richards will be nice and fresh when they go into that flight of yours.'

Harvey glanced at the file again, then nodded. 'You're right. OK, if Ian approves it he can have his leave. That'll get him out of the way for a week or two while you prepare his training.'

Young grinned again. 'Flight commanders train their own kind, matey. You forgotten that? All part of King's Regulations.'

'What the hell do you know about King's Regulations, you bloody Aussie,' Harvey grunted. 'Piss off out of here before I chuck these forms at you.'

CHAPTER 3

THE SMALL MAN lying on his bed with a blanket drawn over him raised his head as the billet door opened. 'That you, Millburn? Shut the door. It's bloody charpy in here.'

Millburn shrugged off his greatcoat and threw it on a chair. 'Stop moaning about the weather. Welsh gremlins like you ought to be used to it. I'm the one who should be grumbling.'

Gabby gave a sniff and changed the subject. 'What did Harvey want? Had it anything to do with Davies?'

'No. A new kid's been posted here. One of your public school types. Frank wants me to give him a talk on tactics.'

Gabby gave another sniff. 'You? What do you know about tactics? Does Frank want to kill the poor sod?'

Millburn grinned. 'Frank knows gold when he sees it, boyo. He knows I'm the one guy with the gen to teach these kids.'

'That's the biggest joke I've heard this year, Millburn. You fly by the seat of your pants. And I'm the poor bastard who has to fly with you.'

Millburn's grin spread. 'You should watch that jealousy, kid. It could shrink your libido.'

'Jealous? Of you, Millburn? That'll be the day. What is the kid, anyway? A chauffeur like you or a real airman?'

'A chauffeur. I tried to palm you off on him but Frank didn't think it fair on the lad. Not until he's got more experience in knowing Blighty from Krautland.'

'Funny, funny,' Gabby grunted. 'You'd be in the shit without me, Millburn. Slap bang inside one of those Stalag prisons. But stop arsing about. Do you know what Davies is doing here?'

'No. He's taken Moore with him and is locked in Pop's office. That's all I know.'

Gabby grimaced. 'Then it's one of those crazy missions of his. It has to be.'

Millburn lit a cigarette and dropped into a chair. 'Not necessarily. He could be planning to drop you into Krautland and doesn't want Jerry to know. A gremlin like you could wreak havoc with Superman's plans.'

Gabby scowled. 'Can't you ever be serious? When are we going out in that car of yours again? I keep thinking about that Wren I met the other week. The one with the tall friend with blonde hair. If I don't make it soon I might lose her to one of those big matelots who're always prowling around Scarborough.'

'Can't you ring her?'

'Not this week,' Gabby muttered. 'She said she had a week's leave and was going to her parents'.'

Millburn's good-looking face lit up with understanding. 'Of course. Why didn't I think of it before? Gremlins can't do it until it's full moon, can they? That must be tough, kid. Really tough.'

Gabby threw him a look of disgust. 'Why don't you switch over to the Yanks, Millburn? They're dumb enough to keep asking for you.'

'It wouldn't be right, kid. The war has to come first. Take me away and your outfit would fall to pieces.'

'That's another laugh, Millburn. You're only tolerated because you're a Yank and our lot don't want to upset Roosevelt. But why the hell did I get you? Didn't anyone think about me?'

'They did, my little Welshman. They took pity on you and gave you a real pilot. So where's your gratitude?'

Gabby tried again. 'So you've no idea what Davies is doing here?'

'Not a clue. Unless he's taken pity on that Scarborough popsie and is arranging for you to be on duty during full moon. Come to think about it, that would be a real kind gesture. Gremlins can be ugly little bastards in bright moonlight.'

Groaning with disgust, Gabby flung himself back on his bed and turned his face from the grinning American. 'Why did I get you, Millburn? Why does someone hate me up there?'

Henderson had guessed Davies was making no courtesy call when the SP with side arms appeared outside his door. 'What are you doing here?'

'Warrant Officer Bertram sent me, sir. On Air Commodore Davies's orders.'

'Air Commodore Davies? Is he here?'

'Yes, sir. Came by car fifteen minutes ago.'

'Then where is he?'

'He was talking to Mr Bertram when I left, sir. I don't expect he'll be long.'

Giving the SP a puzzled frown, Henderson withdrew into his office again. Henderson, a middle-aged, broad-shouldered Scot was a professional airman and the squadron CO. Nicknamed somewhat affectionately 'Pop' by his men, Henderson viewed visits by Davies with mixed feelings as they were usually the prelude to a dangerous mission.

Like Adams, he had the same contradictory feelings about Davies. On the one hand he admired the air commodore for his vision in creating a special service squadron and for the man's drive and tenacity. On the other hand he felt that at times he committed the squadron to dangers beyond the call of duty, as had happened during the Black Fjord operation and other missions since. As a professional, Henderson was fully aware that war called for such dedication and sacrifice and it was leaders like Davies who could swing the balance between defeat and victory. At the same time Henderson had never been able to decide how much personal ambition lay behind Davies's decisions. Possibly both, the Scot thought. The two objectives were not incompatible.

Henderson's thoughts were broken by the sound of dual footsteps along the corridor outside. There was a brief pause as Davies's somewhat high-pitched voice could be heard talking to the sentry. Then the door opened and two men entered the office.

One was Davies, a small man whose sprightly movements and energy belied his age. His enemies – and they were many because fellow staff officers were jealous of his squadron and his success – said he resembled and acted like a cocky sparrow at some times and a belligerent fighting cock at others.

His companion, a wing commander, was a taller, much younger man with wavy, fair hair and the slight puckered scar on his right cheek caused by a bursting flak shell. His uniform, adorned with the DSO and Bar, the DFC and the American Congressional Medal of Honour, was an impeccable fit. Although Ian Moore's enemies – and in his case they were few – might mutter that anyone with his wealth could afford the luxury, they would miss the point entirely. Moore's appearance was an expression of his personality, the signature of a man who believed in keeping the wrappings of a parcel neat and secure so that the contents could not spill out and disintegrate. As he moved forward with Davies, a slight limp could be detected, the result of another injury incurred in combat.

Davies's voice was disturbingly hearty. 'Morning, Jock. Sorry for the unexpected visit but as I had to call in at High Elms this morning, I thought I'd pop in to see how things were going with you after that Valkyrie affair.'

Relaxing slightly, Henderson pointed at the two spare chairs in the office. 'Won't you sit down, sir?'

Nodding, Davies began removing his greatcoat. 'I'm told the job went well this morning.'

'Yes, it did, sir. And no casualties either.'

'So I believe. Good show.' Pausing, Davies shivered and shrugged his coat on again. 'It's charpy in here, isn't it?'

'It's a cold morning, sir.'

Davies glanced round the office and saw an unlit coke stove in one corner. 'Why isn't that lit?'

'The fuel regulations are in force, sir.'

'So?'

Henderson coughed. 'I'm supposed to set an example, sir.'

Davies stared at him. 'Good God, man. You're cutting things a bit fine, aren't you?'

'I think it's better this way, sir. And I don't feel the cold anyway.'

Davies gave a grunt. 'That's because you're a Scot. And you've got a bit of meat on your bones. It's poor bastards like me who suffer.' His tone changed. 'I suppose you're enjoying these little routine jobs?'

With the possibility Davies was thinking up some major mission, Henderson thought it would do no harm to gild the lily. 'We are, sir. We needed a break after that Valkyrie job.'

Davies grinned. 'It was a bit hairy, wasn't it?'

Henderson's voice could have a touch of Highland brogue at times. 'Hairy is one way of putting it, sir. For our part we're putting the pieces together and getting rid of the frostbite. One thing is for sure, however. It's comforting to be standing on dry land again.'

Davies nodded. 'I can't deny that. When they started shelling the lake, I thought we were finished. How is Adams coping? He put up a bloody fine show in Norway. You know I wanted to put him up for a decoration?'

'Yes, sir. You told me. But he wouldn't have it, would he?'

'No, he wouldn't. He wouldn't tell me why either.' Davies glanced at Moore. 'I had to ask Ian. Stupid reason, I thought. But Adams is an odd sod, isn't he?'

'He's a brave one, sir. I never believed he could cope with those conditions.'

'Did any of us? I thought if he had a medal, it might help his status with that wife of his. She's a social climber, isn't she?'

Henderson exchanged a glance with Moore. 'I think she's a bit more than that, sir. But in any case Frank isn't the kind to buy favours from anyone. People have to take him as he is or not at all.'

'I suppose you're right. Anyway, he got the chance.' Davies changed the subject. 'You know I wanted to give you all a rest after Valkyrie but the powers-that-be wouldn't let me.' Davies's voice sank, explaining to Henderson the reason for the SP at the door. 'We have to use every kite we've got on these interdiction raids. I don't need to tell you why, do I?'

Although certain the enemy knew as much as he did, Henderson appeased by lowering his own voice too. 'You don't know the date of the invasion, do you, sir?'

Davies frowned. 'If I knew I wouldn't be allowed to tell you, Jock. The only thing we can be sure of is that it's coming sometime this year. That's why I'm not allowed to give your boys a well-earned rest.'

Expecting another of Davies's special jobs, Henderson was looking more cheerful now. 'I don't think we expected a total rest, sir. As long as you haven't another Valkyrie in mind I think we can cope.' He glanced at Moore. 'Do you agree, Ian?'

The young squadron commander smiled. He had a cultured, laconic voice. 'Yes, I do. Routine operations are quite a change from ice and mountains.'

Davies made a sound that was suspiciously like a sigh. 'I wish it was that simple but it isn't. This damned invasion is making all kinds of bedfellows. Have you heard of anyone called McBride?'

As both men shook their heads, Davies went on: 'I hadn't until today. He's one of SOE's special agents. A big tough character who works with the Maquis and other resistance groups in Europe. He feels a special service squadron like yourselves would be a huge asset to him.'

Henderson looked startled. 'You aren't passing us over to him, are you, sir?'

'No, I've managed to stall things so far. But as he has got Air Vice Marshal Coningham's ear, I'm afraid it's not going to be long before he gets hold of you. Only until the invasion, that is. After that I'll have you back again.'

Henderson was looking horrified now. 'Until the invasion? That could be months away.'

Davies was looking genuinely sympathetic. 'I know it isn't good news, Jock, but if Coningham gives his assent I won't have any choice. But let's not look on the black side. If I can get enough jobs for you linked to the invasion he might change his mind.'

'Is that what you intend doing, sir?' Moore asked.

Davies turned to him 'Yes. Fortunately I don't think Brigadier Simms likes McBride, so he has promised to do all he can to help us. So don't be surprised if you get jobs linked to the Resistance in the days ahead. You will feel better if the orders come from me than from this SOE character, won't you?'

Henderson had never felt he would say such a thing but he did and meant it. 'Much better, sir.'

'Good. Then that's one point cleared up. Now what about Harvey? Are you happy with him?'

Henderson looked puzzled. 'Yes. Of course I am. Why?'

Davies turned to Moore. 'What about you, Ian? Are you happy with Harvey?'

'Very much so. He's one of the most experienced men we've got.'

'I'm not talking about his experience. I'm talking about his personality. Don't you find him an awkward bastard to deal with?'

'Not at all, sir.'

Davies scowled. 'Friendship can deny faults, Ian. You're not letting it cloud your judgement, are you?'

When he was certain of his facts, Moore could be as immovable as the next man. 'Not in any way, sir. I couldn't ask for a better flight commander. His men will follow him anywhere.'

Giving a grunt, Davies tried another way. 'What about his temper? I hear he's losing it much more than he did. Is that right?'

Moore gave a short laugh. 'His temper? Harvey's done nearly three tours. If he blows his top now and then, so do we all. The truth is, sir, he ought to be given a rest. I thought you intended to the last time we spoke about it.'

Davies showed testiness at the reminder. 'There's nothing I'd like better than to give him a rest. It would take him out of my hair, for God's sake. But I can't do it while this present flap is on. At the same time I have to be sure Harvey's the right man for a flight commander. This talk of bad temper worries me.'

Knowing nerves was only Davies's excuse to berate Harvey, Moore met the challenge head on. 'Who's told you this, sir?'

'No one in particular,' Davies evaded. 'It's just one of those rumours that get about.'

'It's not a rumour in this squadron, sir. In fact it's pure rubbish. If

Harvey has any worries it's about Anna Reinhardt. She's been over in occupied Europe for over eight months and there can't be a day when Frank isn't thinking about her. That's all that's wrong with him. Apart from the thing we're all suffering from these days.'

Davies frowned. 'What's that?'

Moore's blunt reply made both men stare at him. 'Fear. When the war looked as if it were going on for ever, we were certain we weren't going to live through it. So we accepted it and lived with it. But now that it looks as if it might end this year or next, we're starting to worry we might get killed before it's over. That's the secret fear every soldier, seaman and airman is living with these days.'

Knowing Moore's record for bravery was a byword in the service, Davies's expression was a picture. 'You too?'

Moore turned to face him. 'Why not? I'm no different from the rest of them.'

There was a moment of silence in the office, then Davies shrugged his shoulders. 'So you're happy to keep Harvey as A Flight commander?'

'More than happy, sir. Until you give him the rest he has been promised.'

'Damn it, Moore, I will give it him when I get the chance. I've told you that. And if you're so bloody obstinate about it, then we'll leave the command structure as it is. Satisfied now?'

'Yes, sir. Thank you.'

The comparative mildness of Davies's reaction to Moore's implied criticism surprised Henderson for a moment. Then he realized Davies must have guessed that Moore as well as Harvey was in love with the courageous German girl, Anna Reinhardt, who had risked her life so often for the Allied cause. His suspicion was endorsed by Davies's next words, added almost as an afterthought. 'Talking about Anna, Brigadier Simms has hinted she might be returning to England soon. Let's hope he's right.'

Henderson did not miss Moore's look of relief. 'Will that be before or after the invasion, sir?'

Scowling at Moore's use of the forbidden word, Davies lowered his voice again. 'I can't say that. You know Simms. At times he can be tighter than a bull's arse in fly time. But I got the impression it'll be just before the invasion.'

For one who seldom showed emotion, Moore's disappointment was noteworthy. 'Then it could be months before she's back. Don't they realize the danger she's in?'

27

It is doubtful if Davies would have made his concession to anyone but his favourite squadron commander. 'Ian, the southern counties are chockablock with troops and equipment. So many they'll be falling into the sea if they send any more. So it's as clear as a duck's arse it can't be delayed that long.'

With at least half the cat out of the bag, Henderson could not help trying to pull out the remainder. 'That must mean the summer, sir. Or the first spell of fine weather.'

Davies gave him a sarcastic glance. 'Don't be so sure of it. Maybe they'd like a big storm to throw everyone up high and dry on the enemy beaches.'

Henderson ignored his sarcasm. 'What are your views, sir? Are we going to pull it off?'

Davies's tone changed. 'We must, Jock. We can't afford failure because God knows what would happen then. The Yanks might get fed up and give priority to the Pacific theatre and it's even possible the Russians might sue for peace. Frankly, for Britain I think it's a matter of life or death.'

In the silence that followed, the roar of an engine under test could be heard. It was Henderson who broke it. 'So we can take it that our orders will still be coming from you, sir, not from this McBride character and the SOE?'

Davies nodded. 'Yes. For the moment the structure remains the same. So if you've problems getting replacements let me know. I can't promise to get everything while this flap's on but I can kick a few arses here and there.'

Henderson hid a smile. Since Davies had met and worked with General Staines, the American three-star general who commanded a wing of B17s, it had become noticeable he had unconsciously picked up a few American expressions. 'I'd appreciate that, sir.'

'Good.' Davies picked up his cap. 'Then I'll get back to Group.' He nodded at Moore. 'Congratulations again on that job you did today, Ian. It was first-class.'

'Thank you, sir.'

Davies turned back to Henderson. 'Keep up the good work, Jock. With things hotting up, you never know. There might be another big job one of these days. In which case we'd want you in first-class condition again.' He waved Moore aside as the young commander moved to open the door. 'I'll see myself out. Bye.'

The two officers saluted him, then waited as his hurried footsteps disappeared down the corridor. Henderson walked to the door, dismissed the SP, then turned to Moore. 'What was all that about, Ian? A bleat about Harvey, a check on our serviceability, or a tip-off we might soon have to take orders from some macho SOE bastard? I like Simms but this McBride character doesn't sound my cup of tea. I don't think Davies likes him either.'

Moore nodded. 'It doesn't sound that way. Mind you, it could be he resents the idea of someone borrowing his squadron. He is very proud of it.'

Henderson sat down somewhat heavily into his chair. 'Let's hope he's wrong. It's bad enough his giving us jobs like Crucible and Valkyrie but at least he's an airman and knows his business. God knows what jobs some aggressive SOE officer might give us.' Henderson reached in a nearby cabinet and drew out a bottle. 'After all that I need a dram, Ian. Have one with me.'

CHAPTER 4

THE MESS WAS quiet that night when Adams entered. In the time-honoured way after a successful operation, the crews and the executive officers had gone over to their favourite pub, The Black Swan, to celebrate, and the mess contained only those whose duties precluded their absence or whose tastes led them to prefer a quieter environment.

Adams's reason was the former. With many debriefing forms to authenticate, he had been compelled to return to his confessional after dinner to complete them and it was past nine o'clock before they had been ready for dispatch to Group headquarters. Feeling like a little company before retiring, Adams had made for the mess in the hope of seeing one or two of his friends there. Unable to spot Moore or any of his closest colleagues, he was about to withdraw when he spotted a couple chatting at the bar. One was Chalmont but Adams's poor eyesight required him to move closer before he could confirm his suspicion and recognize the other man as Richards.

Chalmont caught sight of him approaching. 'Hello, sir. Can I get you a drink?'

'That's kind of you, Chalmont. Just half a pint, thank you. I see you've already met Richards?'

Chalmont met the eye of the mess steward and put in his order before turning back to Adams. 'Yes, sir. They've put us in the same billet.'

'That's good.' Adams turned to the second man. 'How did your leave go, Richards?'

Richards made a slight grimace. In appearance he was a contrast to the blond Chalmont, being slimmer in build and less fair-skinned. Although of the same height, he had dark hair, distinctive features, and quick, nervous movements. In the beginning Adams had thought he came from Jewish stock but since had discovered he was Welsh in origin. He had also discovered that the young man's parents had emigrated to Canada some years before the war, which meant Richards had no home to visit when on leave. This information had come to Adams second-hand. Although Richards had always done his job well, he was an introvert by nature and if he found his domestic position a lonely one, he had never been heard to complain about it. Being something of an introvert himself, Adams respected his reserve but at the same time wondered if the trauma he had suffered when his pilot had died had done more inner damage than a more extrovert personality might have suffered.

'It was all right, sir, thank you,' Richards said. 'But I got a bit bored towards the end of it.' He had a pleasant, accent-free voice although now Adams knew his nationality he believed he could detect a lilt of Welsh in it.

'But it isn't ended yet,' Adams pointed out. 'You've still got a week left, haven't you?'

Richards gave a shrug. 'I'd rather spend it here, sir. I can always have a day or two in Scarborough or Bridlington if the weather improves.'

Adams was surprised that Richards had been allowed to return before his leave was over. Military regulations being what they were, a man on leave was not supposed to consume service rations during that leave. Adams could only suppose – correctly as it turned out – that their medical officer, a well disposed man in Adams's estimate, had had a quiet word with the adjutant and a blind eye was being turned on the young man's presence.

Having heard by this time of the arrangements made for Chalmont, Adams turned to him. 'As you've now been given leave too, perhaps Richards will show you some of the local sights. Unless you're going home, that is.'

Chalmont nodded. 'We've just been discussing that, sir. As Richards hasn't anywhere to go, I've suggested he comes home with me. My people won't mind at all.'

'What a good idea.' Adams glanced at Richards. 'Are you taking him up on it, Richards?'

The navigator drew on his cigarette. 'It's tempting, sir.' He glanced at Chalmont. 'But are you sure your parents won't mind?'

'Not a bit. I'll phone them later but there's no problem. They'll be glad to have you.'

'Then that's fine.' Adams said, taking his glass of beer from Chalmont. 'A man needs a home when he's on leave. Where do your parents live, Chalmont?'

'Just outside Hereford, sir.'

Adams pulled out his tobacco pouch and pipe. 'It's nice country round there, even in this weather. You'd be a mug not to accept, Richards.'

'I suppose I would, sir.' Richards turned to Chalmont. 'OK. Thanks. When shall we leave?'

'Tomorrow if we can. But it depends how the trains run.'

'Inquire in the guardroom,' Adams said, striking a match. 'They've got all the gen about buses and trains.'

The train gave a tired whistle and heaved itself forward again. Like the rest of Britain's rolling stock in 1944, it was as exhausted and run-down as its people. It was also crowded, as all trains were, with passengers standing in both the compartments and in the corridors.

Chalmont and Richards were two of the servicemen standing in a corridor with their cases at their feet. Outside the weather had relented at last and a pale sun was attempting to escape from an anaemic sky.

The two young airmen were chatting amicably. As Adams had noticed the previous evening, they seemed on the same wavelength in spite of Chalmont's more privileged background. At the moment Chalmont was answering Richards's questions about his family.

'No, Father retired at the beginning of the war. I think he's sixty-six or -seven now. Mother's younger. Late forties. She's the powerhouse in the family. My elder brother, Jack, is in the navy. My sister, Hilary, lives at home but works in the local hospital. She can be a bit dynamic too. Far too bossy for my liking.'

'How long were your parents in Spain?'

'Ten years.'

'So you were there right through the Civil War?'

'Not me. Most of the time Jack, Hilary and I were at school in England.'

'Then how did you come to be in Guernica when it was bombed?'

'Hilary and I were on vacation from school and because Father wasn't allowed leave at that time he fiddled it so that the Foreign Office paid for our visit. It didn't seem a big deal at the time because we were well north of all the fighting. I think it was Mother who pushed Father to go for it. If he hadn't pulled it off it might have been a year or longer before they saw us again.'

'And the town was bombed while you were there?'

'Yes. In one way we were lucky. Our house was outside the town.

But the town itself was razed. It was the first air raid we'd seen. When it was over Mother tried to organize help for the wounded. Hilary and I weren't supposed to go into town but we did. There were bodies everywhere. Screaming kids, some without arms or legs. Hilary hardly spoke a word for days afterwards. Mother was so worried about her that she returned to England with us.'

'But Hilary is all right now?' Richards asked.

He did not notice Chalmont's brief hesitation. 'Oh, yes. She got over it.' He glanced at his wristwatch. 'Another half hour and we should be there.' His voice changed, became curious. 'Tell me about Adams. He's a friendly character for a squadron leader, isn't he?'

Richards nodded. 'Yes, he doesn't fit the mould at all. I think he's still a civilian at heart although he's got a hell of a service record. Did you know he's been over to Norway?'

'Norway? You mean before the war?'

'No. Just a few weeks ago. Haven't you heard about that raid we did in Norway in February?'

Chalmont stirred with interest. 'You mean Operation Valkyrie? You weren't on that job, were you?'

Richards nodded. 'I'd only been posted to the squadron a couple of weeks earlier, so I was still in its operations reserve. But because they wanted us at full squadron strength, I and a couple of other crews were drafted into it.'

The respect Chalmont was now showing was in conflict with his self-assured manner. 'I hadn't realized you were on that job. What was it like?'

'Pretty hairy. Particularly when the Jerries started to fire on the ice.'

'You were there to bomb a cruiser, weren't you? When it reached a deep part of the fjord? Why was that?'

Richards shook his head. 'We were never told. We assumed it was because of its cargo so that it couldn't be salvaged. But we were never told what the cargo was.'

'And you've never found out since?'

'No. But it must have been hellishly important because our orders were to sink the cruiser at all costs.'

Chalmont was intrigued. 'What the hell could it have been? Haven't you any idea?'

'There are rumours it was the same stuff that the squadron destroyed in the Swartfjord but, as no one knew what that was either, it isn't much help.'

Chalmont was clearly fascinated. 'Who thought of the operation in the first place? Landing on a frozen lake sounds crazy. Weren't you scared?'

Richards grimaced. 'Me? I thought we were finished, particularly when Jerry found us.'

'Christ, I'd have shitted myself. All the aircrews I've spoken to thought it crazy to risk the squadron like that. So you don't know the reason?'

'No. Only that we were told at the briefing that it was probably the most important raid we'd ever make.'

'What the hell could it have been for?' Chalmont mused. When Richards shook his head, he went on. 'Where did Adams fit into all this?'

'It was his idea in the first place so he was allowed to go over first to make arrangements with the Norwegian partisans to prepare the lake. He did a hell of a job later on. At one time he had to kill a five-man patrol of Germans to prevent the squadron being found.'

Chalmont gave a start. 'You're joking. He doesn't look as if he could kill a mouse.'

'He did it, just the same. If he hadn't none of us would have got back.'

The blond pilot whistled. 'That's incredible. I liked him on sight but who would believe he could do a thing like that?'

'I think he surprised everybody. Davies – that's the air commodore who created the squadron – wanted to give him a medal but he refused it. The boys say that's because he doesn't want reminding about the men he killed.'

Chalmont made a face. 'I'll treat Adams with more respect the next time I see him. You're sure he's not an ace pilot as well?'

Richards laughed. 'They say he'd like to be one. Did you notice his assistant, Sue Spencer?'

Chalmont grinned. 'Are you kidding? She's gorgeous.'

'She's got a story behind her too. She used to be engaged to a pilot called St Claire, a concert pianist in peacetime. He was shot down while doing a job for the SOE and hidden by the Belgian partisans, in particular by a girl around his own age. But the Gestapo knew he was hidden somewhere and tortured the girl to give away his hideout. When she refused they killed her. Eventually the escape network got St Claire back to England but everyone found he was a changed man.'

'You mean because of the Belgian girl?'

'That's right. For some reason I've never known he was allowed to fly over Europe again. But whereas previously he'd been an even-tempered man, now he wanted to kill every German he saw. It got so bad that eventually Henderson had to post him away. Some think it's only for psychiatric treatment and that he'll be back. He's certainly one of our best pilots.'

'How did Sue take all this?' Chalmont asked.

'I don't think she's ever got over it. Mind you, they're still engaged so it might turn out all right in the end.'

The train was slowing again. 'One more station and it's Hereford,' Chalmont said. 'It'll be good to see the family again.'

'You are sure about this?' Richards asked. 'I can always stay in a bed and breakfast or a pub and meet you in the mornings.'

'Stop worrying, for God's sake. They're looking forward to having you.' Chalmont smiled. 'Particularly as you've got the job of navigating me back from Jerryland. That ought to make 'em give you five-star treatment.'

They reached Hereford fifteen minutes later. Chalmont led Richards on to the platform. 'Let's find a cab.'

Richards gave a start. 'A cab? Can't we take a bus?'

Chalmont clapped his shoulder. 'No, we can't. This is my treat and in any case Father's paying for it. So let's go home in style.'

CHAPTER 5

THE CAB DRIVER drove down the gravel drive and pulled up outside a large detached house. Chalmont fished into his pocket for money. 'Thanks, driver. Keep the change.'

The cabbie touched his cap, then drove off. Chalmont led Richards up a flight of stone steps to a porticoed entrance. He was reaching for a brass knob to pull when the door swung eagerly open and a tall, handsome woman in her late forties appeared. Her arms went around Chalmont for a moment before she addressed him. 'Hello, darling. So the train was on time for once. How lovely to see you again.'

As she was welcoming Chalmont, Richards saw a couple standing behind her. One, wearing corduroys and a smoking jacket, was an elderly man with thinning white hair. The other was a tall, slim girl in her early twenties. As Lucinda Chalmont drew back to allow her husband and daughter to greet Jeremy, Richards gained a better view of the girl. In turn she glanced at him as Chalmont and his father shook hands.

Richards could not define his emotion as the girl's eyes ran over him. The face that sent odd quivers down his spine could not be called beautiful in the conventional sense. It had too much strength and character. Nor could her glance be called friendly. Her mouth was unsmiling and her eyes contained no warmth or welcome. Indeed, without knowing why, Richards imagined a trace of hostility in them. Yet the total effect excited Richards more than the face of any girl he had seen. With her jet black hair, her white skin and her composure, she was like some El Greco painting of a woman who despised men for their lusts and at the same time excited them by her unattainability. While not a man usually disturbed by attractive women, Richards had the feeling he had fallen in love with this girl before she had even spoken to him.

It took a nudge from Chalmont to make him realize Lucinda Chalmont was addressing him. 'So you are Jeremy's new friend, Mr

Richards. I'm so glad you were able to come with him. We would have met you at the station if we could have obtained petrol for the car. Come and meet my husband and my daughter, Hilary.'

Richards shook hands with her and then with her smiling husband, whose greeting was equally affable. 'Glad to have you, Richards, particularly as you are a friend of Jeremy. Make yourself at home while you're here.'

Thanking him, Richards was then introduced to the girl. Her hand-shake was firm but like her voice it contained no warmth. 'Jeremy tells us you are his new navigator. Is that right?'

Richards was feeling an inexplicable shyness. 'Yes. It seems so.'

'It seems so? Don't you know?'

Richards felt his cheeks turning warm. 'Our flight commander tells us we'll probably be teamed together but I think it needs confirming by the squadron commander.'

'Don't you think he will confirm it?'

'I expect so. Otherwise we wouldn't have been given leave together.'

The girl showed impatience. 'It seems pretty certain to me. Have you flown together yet?'

'No. We shall start training when our leave expires.'

Mrs Chalmont, noticing the young man's embarrassment, took Richards' arm. 'We're delighted to have you, Mark. It is Mark, isn't it?'

'Yes, Mrs Chalmont.'

'Then what about a cup of coffee after your long journey? Or would you rather be shown your room first?'

Richards hesitated, then indicated his holdall. 'I'd like to get rid of this if I may.'

'Of course. And you can freshen up at the same time.' Lucinda turned to Chalmont. 'I've given Mark the room next to your old one, Jeremy. I think he'll be comfortable there.'

A minute later Richards found himself following Chalmont up a large, curving flight of stairs. Chalmont glanced back. 'Everything all right?'

'Yes. I like your parents. They're very friendly.'

'So they should be. You're their guest. Sorry if Hilary seemed a bit sharp but that's her way.'

Richards wanted nothing better than to talk about the girl but Chalmont gave him no opportunity. 'I thought the folks looked older since I last saw them. Particularly Father. But I expect he has plenty to do around the house since the war took away the servants.'

'Did you have many?'

'No. Only a housekeeper and a gardener.'

They had now reached a large landing lined with doors. Chalmont pushed one open and waved Richards inside. 'This is yours. All right?'

Richards took in a large, handsomely furnished bedroom with a large bay window. 'All right? After service billets and boarding houses? This looks like something from heaven.'

'It's a pity we didn't meet earlier or you could have spent your entire leave here. What have you been doing for five weeks anyway?'

Richards shrugged. 'Wandering around. Getting a room here and there. Being bored to death if the truth were known.'

'That's a shame. But never mind. Do as Dad says and make the best of it here. We've got some good walks nearby and the pubs aren't bad either. We can try one after dinner if you like?'

Richards wanted to ask if Hilary would join them but embarrassment held him back. 'Yes. I'd like that.'

'All right then.' Chalmont moved to the door. 'I'll leave you to wash up. See you in half an hour.'

Richards nodded. When the door closed he went over to the bay window. Although the light was beginning to fade he could see a large kitchen garden below with a row of poplars at its far end. To the right was a lawn and as he stood there a golden retriever suddenly ran on to it, chasing a ball that had been thrown for him. Watching with interest, Richards saw a girl wearing a sheepskin jacket appear. As the dog ran back to her with the ball, Richards saw the girl was Hilary and felt his heart miss a beat.

He stood watching her as she played with the dog. The heavy sheepskin jacket she was wearing could not hide the grace of her movements. He watched her until the movements of the frolicking dog made her turn towards the house. Richards had not believed she could see him but the fading light must have caught his window because he saw her face lift towards him. Feeling almost as if he were guilty of an indecent act, he drew back quickly but felt certain he had been seen.

Not daring to glance down again, he withdrew and sank on the bed. To his astonishment he felt his pulse was racing. At that moment Richards could not decide whether he was glad or sorry to have accepted Chalmont's invitation to stay with his parents.

Dinner was served ninety minutes later. The habits of a lifetime were evident. Douglas Anthony Chalmont had changed into a dinner jacket and looked every inch the diplomat as he presided at the table. Lucinda

Chalmont looked equally distinguished with her thick, iron-grey hair brushed back and her black evening dress set off by a single necklace of pearls. The only one of the three who had not changed was Hilary. Whether her reason was contempt for the family ritual or the fact she did not feel the guests deserved the compliment, Richards could not guess, but she was still wearing the same afternoon frock she had worn on his arrival.

Yet to Richards she could not have looked more attractive. No doubt to celebrate her son's leave, Lucinda had set lighted candelabra on the table and it would have been difficult to imagine any light that could have enhanced the girl's striking appearance more. It lent an added sheen to her black hair, toned her white, unblemished skin, and gave an added lustre to her dark, composed eyes. Richards, who was seated opposite her, was finding it more and more difficult to keep his eyes from her.

It was soon clear from Douglas Chalmont's conversation that Jeremy was a favourite in his parents' eyes. 'So you've got the squadron you wanted, son. Congratulations.'

Lucinda Chalmont sounded less enthusiastic. 'Isn't it the squadron the newspapers are always writing about? The one that carries out spectacular raids?'

Chalmont's expression suggested he saw no point in denial. 'It is a special service squadron,' he confessed. 'That's why they've been given unusual jobs and had such publicity. But they're lucky in having Mosquitoes to fly. It's the safest aircraft in the RAF. So that's a huge bonus.'

Lucinda's reply told Richards she was not easily diverted by her son's reassurances. 'They didn't offer much protection during that Black Fjord in Norway, did they?'

'That was a one-off operation,' Chalmont lied. He glanced back at Richards. 'Isn't that right, Mark?'

Richards did his best to support him. 'Yes. The Mosquito is a safe aircraft, Mrs Chalmont. It can fly higher and faster than almost any enemy fighter. And because it's made of wood it can even absorb flak better than metal aircraft. Most aircrews envy us for having them.'

'But it still drops bombs on people, doesn't it?' The unexpected comment came from Hilary. 'Like any other bomber in the RAF.'

Surprised at the question, Richards mistook its meaning. 'Oh, yes. In fact it carries a huge bomb load for its size. And with the cannon we carry it can take on any enemy fighter. It's a remarkable aircraft in many ways.'

'And that makes you proud of it? Because it carries bigger and better bombs?'

Richards was floundering now. 'I'm sorry. Shouldn't I be? Don't we need better aircraft than the enemy if we're to win the war?'

Richards never knew what the girl would have replied had not Douglas Chalmont broken in quickly. 'That's enough, Hilary. Mr Richards is on leave and I'm sure he doesn't want to talk shop while he's here.'

Hilary's dark eyes moved from him to Richards. 'Is that true? Don't you want to talk about your job?'

Richards gave an apologetic glance at Douglas Chalmont before replying. 'I don't particularly mind. I'm sorry if I sounded too enthusiastic about the Mosquito. But she is a fine aircraft.'

'So you've said. She carries bigger and better bombs than other aircraft of her size. And that makes you proud of her. I've got the picture.'

The confused Richards was saved from answering by Lucinda. 'That's enough, Hilary. Your father doesn't want any more talk about the war tonight. And neither do I.'

Hilary shrugged. 'I thought we were fighting a war for free speech. Aren't we?'

'That's a silly remark, Hilary. Don't be so argumentative or you'll make Mr Richards wish he'd never come to stay with us.'

The girl's dark eyes moved back to Richards. 'Am I making you uncomfortable, Mark?'

Richards, who had no idea what was going on, tried to make his lie sound convincing. 'No. I didn't build the aircraft. So I've no axe to grind.'

Hilary gave her mother a triumphant smile. 'You see. Mark isn't a bit embarrassed.'

Seated alongside Hilary, Jeremy Chalmont had been showing increasing anger. Now it broke out. 'For Christ's sake, Hilary, you never give up, do you? Stop badgering Mark. He's no more to blame for this war than you are. So shut up and let him get on with his dinner.'

For a moment it seemed that the girl would snap back at him. Instead, after a glance at Richards's embarrassed face, she made a gesture of reconciliation. 'I suppose Jeremy's right. I'm sorry if I embarrassed you, Mark.'

With no idea what the scene was about, Richards managed a shrug of his shoulders. 'That's all right. I wasn't offended. Why should I be?'

For a moment it seemed that Hilary had an answer to his question. As if anticipating it, Lucinda broke in with a laugh of relief. 'There. A storm in a teacup. Nothing more.' Clearly pleased with Richards's behaviour, she indicated his wine glass and turned to her husband. 'How about some more wine for our guest, darling?'

At that moment, with a barely audible murmur of apology, Hilary rose and left the room. Seeing Douglas Chalmont was about to recall her, Lucinda motioned him to sit down. As he frowned but obeyed her, Lucinda turned to Richards. 'You must forgive her, Mark. She works in a hospital and has seen so many war casualties that it has made her something of a pacifist.'

'She thinks they might be moving her up to York soon,' Douglas Chalmont broke in. 'She'll see even more casualties up there, I would imagine. Isn't Yorkshire full of airfields apart from your own?'

Noticing Lucinda wince at the reminder, Richards felt her husband could have shown a little more tact. Nevertheless, thinking he understood Hilary better, the young navigator relaxed. 'I understand. sir. No, I don't blame her at all. Haven't we all had those feelings at one time or another?'

Lucinda studied his young face for a moment then glanced across the table at her son. 'I like your friend very much, Jeremy. I want you to bring him with you every time the two of you get leave.'

CHAPTER 6

THE TWO MOSQUITOES were darting through the Scottish hills like a couple of swifts. As the leader dipped down and almost slashed the upper branches off a forest of pines, its follower dipped down also and sent the uppermost branches reeling in the slipstream of its propellers. As the leader hugged the side of a glen, dipping and weaving to follow its contours, its double followed as faithfully as a pencil following its trace on paper. As the two aircraft darted into a steep valley and the roar of their engines reverberated like thunder from the surrounding hills, Gabby, in the leading Mosquito, grinned at his pilot.

'Harvey sent the kid out with the wrong man, Millburn. He's better at this low-level stuff than you are. Why don't you admit it?'

Millburn, eyes intent on the stream below and the pines that were streaking past, gave him a glare. 'Don't talk bullshit, you little fart.'

Gabby glanced back, then gave a chortle. 'But it's true. He's gaining on us. He's got your number, Millburn.'

Seeing Gabby was right, Millburn waited until the end of the valley leapt towards him, then swung T-Tommy to port until its wings were vertical to the blurred ground below. As the Mosquito catapulted out into a large loch, Millburn lowered T-Tommy down until the water was ruffled by his engines' slipstream. Unable to take his eyes off the water at such ultra-low level, he gave Gabby a shout. 'Where is he now?'

The violent manoeuvre had caught the following pilot by surprise but in a couple of seconds he had recovered and his Mosquito was skimming the water towards T-Tommy again.

'He's behind you again,' Gabby yelled. 'Coming up on your tail, boyo.'

Millburn was not a man to be churlish about a fellow pilot's skill. 'All right. The kid's good. Bloody good. Harvey's got someone a bit special here.'

Gabby grinned. 'Are you going to tell him that?'

'Sure I am. He's a lucky guy.'

'It's not what he wants to hear. The tyke's down on public school kids.'

'That's too bad. He's going to hear it anyway.' Millburn drew back on his control column and pointed to a range of mountains ahead. 'We'll give it another fifteen minutes, then make for home.'

In the following Mosquito, Richards felt himself relaxing as Chalmont alongside him followed T-Tommy to a safer height. If low-level flying was a strain on pilots who knew one moment of distraction could cause a fatal crash, it was worse for their navigators who were entirely at the mercy of their pilots' powers of concentration. Moreover, it was only weeks since Richards had suffered the ordeal of sitting beside a dying man and knowing that if the pilot lost consciousness he would die with him.

Yet confidence in his new pilot was already growing in Richards. As Millburn ahead had discovered, Chalmont's reflexes and flying skill were well above average and to some extent explained to Richards why the pilot had been granted his wish to join 633 Squadron. Because of its role as a special service unit, designed to take on missions of exceptional importance and difficulty, Davies required aircrews of high quality and was notorious for his efforts to steal such crews from other squadrons. While known among his 633 crews as The Bantam or The Little Fart, his agnomen among other squadron COs was the less affectionate one of The Poacher. So it was possible, Richards reasoned, that the ever alert Davies had done some kind of a deal with the OTUs to send their best cadets to his unit.

With the two Mosquitoes now flying at 1,000 feet, Richards judged it safe to chat with his pilot. 'That was terrific, Jeremy. Did you do much low-level flying at your OTU?'

Chalmont shook his head. 'Not more than most. But I've always enjoyed the excitement of it. I'm told you lot are specialists.'

Richards nodded. 'We do often get operations that require us flying beneath Jerry's radar. That's why Harvey sent you out on this practice. But obviously you don't need it.'

Chalmont shrugged. 'I don't mind. I'm enjoying it.' He nodded at T-Tommy a hundred metres ahead. 'That Yank isn't bad either. I thought he'd tear the wings of his Mossie when he came out of that valley.'

'He's one of the best,' Richards told him. 'Crazy at times but a terrific pilot. The guys love him and expect he'll be a flight commander one of these days. If he survives, that is.'

'What about his navigator, the Welshman?'

'Gabby? He's just as crazy. They're a legend in the squadron. And

among the local girls too. The story goes the hospital's so full of preg-
nant women that the local MP wants them both neutered.'

Chalmont grinned. 'You've got some odd sods in your squadron.
What do you think of Harvey?'

'Harvey? He's the best. Tough, honest, and totally reliable. You
couldn't have a better flight commander.'

Chalmont threw Richards a glance. 'Yet Adams warned me to tread
carefully with him. And he wasn't exactly friendly at my interview.'

Richards nodded. 'That's because of his background. He comes from
northern working class and I suppose they didn't get much of a deal
from this country before the war. They say he was hoping to be made
squadron commander after the Black Fjord operation but Davies gave
it to Ian Moore instead. As Moore's one of the wealthy upper-class
types, that didn't exactly help Harvey's feelings, although they seem
the best of friends now.'

Chalmont had not missed the implications of Richards's portrait of
Harvey. 'So he's got it in for me because of my public school background?'

'I wouldn't be surprised,' Richards confessed. 'But whatever else he
is, Harvey looks after his crews and he respects good pilots. So once he
gets Millburn's report, you should be all right.'

A voice came over the R/T at that moment. 'Red Two, I want you to
practise that climbing turn of ours again. You know the exercise, to
circle and cover each other's tail while we make for cloud cover. I'll
lead the way when we reach that second loch ahead. OK?'

As Chalmont replied and concentrated on a manoeuvre that time
and again had saved the squadron when outnumbered by enemy
fighters, Richards's mind wandered back to Hereford and Hilary.
Believing after the dinner-table scene that her hostility was not personal
to him but only a result of her pacifist beliefs, he had asked Chalmont
to find out if she would join the two of them in the pub one evening.

When she refused, Chalmont had told him impatiently he was a fool
to bother with her. But Richards was infatuated and on the last day of
his leave he had plucked up the courage to ask her personally if she
would go with him and Chalmont to a dance the WVS were running in
Hereford.

Again she had refused but this time he felt her refusal lacked the
hostility he had sensed on their first meeting. Disappointed and aware
he might not see her again for months, if ever, Richards had overcome
his shyness and asked if he might write to her. She had looked amused
as well as surprised. 'What on earth for?'

It had not been easy to give a reason. 'I've no one here to write to as the other men have and it would be something to look forward to.'

Her laugh and her look had mocking undertones. 'You poor thing. I thought the girls loved you bomber crews. Can't you find one of them to write to?'

'I've never wanted to write to anyone before,' he confessed.

Her forehead had puckered slightly. 'Then why do you want to write to me?'

'I don't know. I just do, that's all.'

'Isn't that rather silly?'

His earlier embarrassment had returned. 'Is it? I'm sorry. I shouldn't have asked.'

His clumsy apology had changed the expression in her eyes. 'You must think me a cold bitch. Do you?'

He shook his head. 'No. Not at all.'

'Well, I am,' she said. 'Hasn't Jeremy told you?'

'No. And I've never asked him.'

'You haven't spoken about me to Jeremy?'

'No. Only if you would go out with us, that's all.'

She seemed to come to her decision then. 'Very well. Write if you want to. But don't expect quick replies. The hospital keeps me busy and I'm a rotten letter writer in any case.'

He could not hide his pleasure. 'Thanks. I won't smother you with them. Just one now and then.'

That had been all and two hours later Douglas Chalmont had ordered a taxi to take the two airmen to the station. Hilary had joined her mother and father at the front door to see them off and her farewell as the taxi drove away had seemed a perfunctory one beside the affectionate gestures of her parents. Yet Richards had imagined her dark eyes had followed the taxi longer than either of the others as it made its way along the sweeping drive to the gateway.

Another R/T command broke into his thoughts again. 'OK, guys. That's enough. Follow me home.'

An hour later they were in Adams's confessional being briefed by Adams. Millburn followed Adams's glance at Chalmont, who was chatting to Richards near the door of the Nissen hut. He nodded at Adams's question. 'The kid's good, Frank. Harvey's lucky to get him.'

'Is that what you're going to tell Harvey?'

'Too true I am. The tyke had better forget his prejudices. He's got a winner in this kid.'

Adams was showing some relief. 'I'll see he gets your report. How does Richards seem? Do you think he's fully recovered?'

Millburn shrugged. 'It's hard to tell on an exercise like that. But I reckon he's got over it. He and Chalmont seem to hit it off together OK, which is what matters.'

Adams smiled. 'Like you and Gabby do.'

Millburn scowled at the diminutive Welshman who was chatting up Sue Spencer.

'Are you kidding? The little clown nearly took me to Norway this morning.'

Adams smiled again. 'Not according to the reports of the target spotters. They say you were bang on time.'

Millburn gave a sniff. 'Even gremlins have to get it right now and then. And the little sonofabitch has a lucky streak. You have to say that about him.' He turned back from Gabby to Adams. 'Better keep an eye on Sue while he's around. These gremlins have some sneaky ways. Look at the way he's talking to her. Doesn't it look sneaky to you?'

Adams laughed. 'I think Sue can look after herself. Even against gremlins.' He gathered up his papers. 'Thanks, Tommy. That's all I need. I'll see Harvey gets this report.'

As Richards finished emptying his suitcase and slid it beneath his bed, he noticed Chalmont setting a photograph on the top of his locker. It was a framed picture of his parents and was followed by a photograph of a girl in a swimsuit with a mass of blonde hair. Realizing Chalmont had noticed his interest, Richards felt obliged to make a comment. 'Is that your girl?'

Chalmont made a wry grimace. 'I'd like to think so. But she's got plenty of admirers.'

'What's her name?'

'Rosalind. I met her at the OTU.'

'Was she a Waaf?'

Chalmont nodded. 'A corporal. What about you? You're not married or engaged, are you?'

'No. I was going out with a girl before I joined up but she met a naval officer a year later and that was that.'

'And you've met no one since?'

'No one I fancy.'

Chalmont laughed. 'You sound like my sister. Too choosy.'

Richards could not have had a better lead in to the questions he wanted to ask. 'Hilary hasn't any boyfriends, then?'

'Hilary? Who would want a cold fish like her?'

Richards frowned. 'I thought her rather attractive.'

Chalmont stared at him. 'In spite of the way she behaved? Are you serious?'

'Yes. I don't blame her disliking civilian bombing. You don't like it either. Isn't that why you asked for this squadron?'

Chalmont ignored the question. 'Do you really fancy her?'

'Yes. As I said, I thought her very attractive.'

Chalmont had all the blindness that nature, perhaps wisely, gives to siblings of a different sex. 'Attractive? Good God. Why didn't you tell me? I'd have put in a word for you.'

'She has promised to write to me occasionally,' Richards confessed.

'She has? When did she promise that?'

'Just before we left. I asked if she would.'

Chalmont was showing genuine surprise now. 'And she detests bomber crews. You must have what it takes to get a promise like that.'

'She did say I must write to her only occasionally,' Richards confessed.

'Even so, it's a hell of a promise for Hilary to make. You must have thawed the ice somewhere. Men have won medals for less.'

'I don't suppose you have a photograph of her, have you?' Richards asked.

'No, but I can probably get you one. Like me to try?'

Richards had never liked Chalmont more than at that moment. 'Would you?'

'In my next letter home, old boy. In fact I'll phone my parents tonight and ask 'em to send one. How's that?'

'That's great. I'll really appreciate it.'

Chalmont checked his appearance in a cracked mirror on the wall of the cubicle, then turned with a grin to Richards. 'Mind you, I might not be doing you any favours. I can't think what kind of letters she'll send you. As likely as not they'll only be lectures about bomber crews and their villainy.'

Richards began to lay out the blankets on his unmade bed. 'I'll take a chance on that.'

Chalmont moved towards the door. 'Aren't you coming for a pre-lunch drink?'

'I'd rather get unpacked first,' Richards told him. 'I'll be along in a few minutes.'

Chalmont shrugged. 'All right. See you there.'

As Chalmont closed the door and disappeared, Richards spread out the last blanket and then lay back on his pillow. If he had been called to explain why he wanted a few minutes on his own he would have been embarrassed to give his reason, which was to digest the things Chalmont had told him. Was Chalmont right in thinking that Hilary's promise to write to him had been a major concession? To date he, Richards, had wondered if family interest had been her reason. After all, he was her brother's navigator and it made good sense that he should be kept in as good a mental state as possible.

But Chalmont's words had seemed to deny such a suggestion. Unless Chalmont completely misread his sister – which seemed more than unlikely – Hilary's decision to reply to his letters had been reached without an unrelated influence of any kind. Although Richards knew it was only a small gesture in itself, it was one he clung to in the days that followed.

CHAPTER 7

I T WAS TWO weeks before Harvey called Chalmont and Richards to his flight office. Paying attention to Chalmont rather than his navigator, the rugged flight commander was showing little enthusiasm as he picked up a piece of paper from his desk. 'I've got your training reports here, Chalmont. Normally we give new crews longer before sending them into action but as Flight Lieutenant Millburn says you appear to have picked up our ways quite well it's been decided you're ready to join us. That's from today.'

Chalmont was looking pleased. 'Can I ask what flight we'll be in?'

The gruff answer came from somewhere at the back of Harvey's throat. 'Yes, I've got you, Chalmont. In A Flight.'

'Good, sir. Thank you.'

Harvey leaned forward. 'What's good about it, Chalmont?'

In his imperturbable way the young officer showed surprise. 'Everyone speaks well of your flight, sir.'

Harvey scowled. 'Don't give me that flattery crap, Chalmont. Everyone knows I'm a bastard if anyone puts a foot out of line.' His deep-set eyes turned on the navigator. 'Isn't that right, Richards?'

Richards decided it wasn't the right moment to grin. 'Yes, sir. They do.'

'Too bloody true they do,' Harvey grunted. 'And you two bear it in mind. You follow my orders to the letter when you fly with me. None of that playing the hero and diving off to attack a nice, juicy target. We're a team and we operate like a team. All right?'

As both men nodded, the sound of a Mosquito taking off on an air test and roaring over the flight office could be heard, suspending conversation for a moment. It brought Chalmont's question as the sound died away. 'When is our first operation, sir?'

Harvey's eyes swung back on Richards. 'You haven't done a very good job on this fresher, have you?'

Richards started. 'Sorry, sir. I don't understand.'

'We paired him off with you because you've been with the squadron some time and know the ropes. Tell him we don't ask too many questions here. He'll get the answers when it suits us and not before. All right.'

Richards nodded. 'Yes, sir. I'll tell him.'

Harvey's voice changed in tone. 'The MO says you're in good shape again. Is he right?'

'Oh yes, sir. I wasn't too bad before but I'm fine now.'

'Good lad. Keep it up and look after this sprog here. I've got the feeling he might take some time to get used to our ways.'

Chalmont had noticed the softening of Harvey's voice as he addressed Richards. He also realized Harvey's eyes had returned to him as he was speaking. Without thinking he answered the belittling remark. 'Why is that, sir? Procedures are much the same on any bomber squadron, aren't they?'

Harvey's laugh was harsh. 'If you believe that about this squadron, then you really are a sprog, Chalmont. Talk to Richards and a few of the other lads and you'll find out why. Now piss off, both of you, and report in the flight office after breakfast tomorrow.'

The operations room was crowded three mornings later. The smoke from dozens of cigarettes was rising and making the models of enemy aircraft suspended from the roof look as if they were flying through cloud. On either side of the large Nissen hut posters covered the walls with such strictures as 'Beware The Hun In The Sun', 'Get Your Finger Out', and the ubiquitous 'Careless Talk Costs Lives'. The chatter of the crews, with the navigators carrying wallets on their knees, created an atmosphere of both youthful gaiety and suspense. Although like so many other light bomber squadrons, 633 was having at the moment to carry out interdict operations as a prelude to the invasion of Europe, its role as a special service unit always carried the possibility that some new and perilous mission might be on the cards. The result added a subtle difference to a normal daily briefing.

The platform at the far end of the room, backed by a huge map of Europe, was occupied by a row of chairs and small tables reserved for specialist officers whose task was to give the crews the meteorological, navigation, armament and other essential details relevant to their mission. Below the platform, occupying the front benches, were the senior crew members, with Harvey, Young and Millburn prominent among them.

A sudden shout of 'Attention!' ended the chatter and brought the entire assembly to its feet. A moment later Henderson, Moore and a gaggle of specialist officers, with Adams among them, marched down the aisle between the benches towards the platform. As the officers climbed to their allotted places, another bellow of 'At Ease!' allowed the crews to take their seats again.

It was Henderson who took the limelight first, cutting short the few whispers that had broken out. 'No, lads, you needn't look so worried. You're not being asked to breech Jerry's Atlantic wall yet. Instead we've got a wee job for you that you'll find interesting as well as useful. So relax while your squadron commander gives you the gen.'

There were a few cynical as well as rueful smiles among the longer-serving members. Aircrews had long learned that COs and particularly staff officers were masters of both humour and understatement. As Chalmont was to learn later, the absent Davies was supreme at the art of making a perilous assignment sound like a holiday trip abroad. Henderson was not quite in the same league but his avuncular presence and his slight brogue could still calm fast-beating hearts.

'The job we've got, lads, is to help the French Resistance. As you know they're busy blowing up trains and bridges all along the coast, which will help our army when the time comes. And how do we do this? By dropping 'em arms and explosives. Lancasters and Stirlings have been doing this for some time but because they're slower than us and so much bigger they're a better target for ground fire. Whereas we can nip in and drop our load before the Jerries know we're coming.'

Someone gave a stage whisper at this point. 'Like hell we can.'

A stentorian roar followed. 'Silence!'

Richards's whisper to Chalmont was better muted. 'The voice is the SWO. We call him Bert the Bastard.'

The two men were sitting on a bench behind Harvey and Teddy Young. Before Chalmont could reply, Henderson continued as if nothing had happened. 'It'll be a piece of cake. Low level to France and in and out when you get there. But I'll leave your squadron commander to give you the battle details.'

Moore took his place on the platform a few seconds later. Impeccably dressed as always, he brought a subtle change to the atmosphere in the Nissen hut. This was the crews' operational leader, the man who took the same chances as they took, the man whose decisions had proved time and time again to be correct. Apart from an occasional cough, there was silence as crews listened to his cultured voice.

'Our biggest problem on this operation is going to be timing. Aware of the danger of being harassed in the rear when the invasion starts, Jerry has greatly increased his ground patrols in both France and Belgium. This has made it even more dangerous for resistance groups when they try to pick up airborne supplies: only a week ago an entire party were annihilated by enemy fire. So we've developed new tactics with them. These include dropping supplies at night. So accurate navigation and timing are going to be very important.'

A hand rose from the front bench and the crews heard Harvey's voice. 'Skipper, I don't understand why we're being used. Mossies aren't built to drop supplies. They're much too fast for the job. Why not Hudsons or even C47s?'

A murmur of assent went round the room. Showing no irritation at the interruption while at the same time making it clear he did not favour the operation himself, Moore nodded at Harvey. 'I take your point. We are too fast and our bomb bays aren't really suited for the job either. But Lancs and Stirlings have been suffering high losses recently and a brass hat somewhere has decided that Mosquitoes might be the right kites for the job. I suppose a second reason could be our experience of low-level flying at night. Supplies dropped from high level or even medium level can drift miles in windy weather. Whereas we can go in low and pinpoint our dropping area.'

'Can we?' Harvey still sounded dubious. 'What about high buildings, bridges, electric cables and the rest?'

Moore nodded again. 'That has been taken into account. Our resistance group have chosen a spot free of all obstacles but trees. They've also got torches to illuminate the boundaries of the dropping area. Providing we keep to our timing and our navigation is spot on, there shouldn't be any problems.'

A second hand rose and Richards recognized an American accent. 'Why is the timing so important, skipper?'

'Jerry's the reason for that,' Moore explained. 'He has motor patrols running down the feeder roads at set intervals and our group couldn't find a dropping area far enough from one to avoid detection. So it's vital we arrive, drop our loads, and get away before the next patrol arrives. It's vital because if the detection area is spotted, the supplies won't only be lost but the resistance group could be captured or killed.'

Another hand rose. 'Are we getting any cover, skipper?'

'On a night mission, Preston? No. You'll be on your own once you've dropped your stores. We don't want any collisions. That's why it will be important that every navigator keeps his own charts. I don't want anyone landing in Denmark or Sweden.'

As laughs broke out, another question came. 'When do we go, skipper?'

'Tonight, Roberts. So go easy on the lunchtime booze. Two pints is the limit today.'

As a groan ran round the hut, Moore smiled. 'Any more questions before I turn you over to your executive officers?' When none came he motioned at the officers seated at tables behind him. 'Then come up and get all the gen. Providing you keep to it you should all be home and tucked up in bed soon after midnight.'

There was a rumble of benches on the wooden floor as crews moved to the executive officers to be given the co-ordinates, timing, and other details of the operation. It was forty minutes before Chalmont and Richards left the room and made for their billets. Richards glanced at Chalmont. 'What do you think?'

Chalmont shrugged. 'It doesn't sound too bad, does it?'

'Not if we can find the dropping zone. And the partisans aren't found and captured before we get there.'

'Finding the place isn't your worry, is it? Isn't Moore leading us there?'

'That's the plan but I'm hoping the Met people are right about the darkness factor. If darkness comes before we arrive we might have trouble following Moore. He can hardly put on recognition lights, can he?'

Chalmont grinned at Richards. 'I've every confidence you'll get us there. If you don't it'll hardly lose us the war, will it?'

Richards smiled back. 'I like your way of putting things in the right perspective.'

'I probably owe that to my father. He taught me never to allow a problem to turn into a crisis.'

'Until Guernica,' Richards suggested.

A cloud crossed Chalmont's face. 'Until Guernica,' he admitted.

CHAPTER 8

THE MOSQUITOES WERE flying as low as cormorants seeking an evening meal. Behind them the sun was a molten crescent about to dip into the crimson sea. Ahead the sky was rapidly darkening, hiding the perilous coastline that Richards knew lay ahead. On either side, flying in echelon to avoid one another's slipstream, sleek aircraft gently rose and fell. A scene from an artist's brush, Richards thought. Full of colour and movement and yet serene and painfully beautiful.

It was not the first time Richards had experienced this emotion. Returning from raids on certain evenings when the sky above was tinted green and gold and shafts of dying sunlight had turned clouds into castles of gold, he had found himself asking the same question. How could such beauty exist in a world of barbarism? Why did God taunt men with such beauty and serenity and then as quickly supplant it with cruelty? What was the purpose behind it? At such times Richards envied his colleagues, who seemed free of such questions and could find any solace they needed with women, in the mess or in The Black Swan. Religion, Richards had long decided, was a cruel burden for a man to carry in wartime.

Although born with certain religious instincts, Richards had found no mental conflict when his age had made him eligible for military service. Apart from a strong sense of patriotism he had also seen the Nazis as bullies and murderers and it had seemed every decent man's duty to contain them and liberate the innocents who suffered under their tyranny. To this end he had been proud to be one of the new crews sent to 633 Squadron after the squadron's appalling losses in the Black Fjord. At the time he had not given much thought to the bombing of civilians but since Chalmont's arrival and the subsequent meeting with Hilary he had suddenly become aware how lucky he was to be in a unit devoted only to military objectives. In an oblique way this had made him feel closer to Chalmont than to any pilot he had flown with before.

Sitting alongside him in the Mosquito's snug cockpit, Chalmont was being given no time for extraneous thoughts. In common with all the pilots on the operation, every cell in his mind was occupied with the job in hand. Flying in formation at ultra-low level required concentration of the highest order. Every aircraft ahead or alongside had to be watched for the slightest deviation, every swell of the waves below was a reminder that water had the solidity of concrete when hit at high speed. To watch all the dangers and instantly react to them, a pilot hardly dared blink his eyes, much less allow his thoughts to wander.

Allowed more freedom than his pilot, Richards saw a green flare shoot out from a Mosquito ahead and sizzle for a few seconds in the water. With ultra low level meant to deny the enemy radar picking up their approach, radio silence was equally necessary. Richards tapped Chalmont's shoulder. 'Guns, Jerry. Moore wants us to check our guns.'

Chalmont nodded and his thumb moved to his gun button. On either side Mosquitoes slid almost imperceptibly away from one another to clear the sky ahead. A few seconds later Richards heard the massive clatter of S-Suzy's 20 mm cannon and felt her shudder and recoil.

The formation closed again but only for a minute. Then a red flare was seen shooting out and fizzling in the sea. Knowing its message, Richards felt a familiar tightening of his throat. 'Enemy coast ahead,' the flare said. 'Follow me in line astern.'

The value of 633 Squadron's regular training became evident now. Mosquito after Mosquito, avoiding collision only by long-practised manoeuvres and the reflexes and skill of their pilots, dropped back until they were extended over the water like a line of thick rope.

The reason for the tactic became clear a couple of minutes later. Ahead in the gathering gloom a line of tracer could be seen shooting up into the sky. The coasts of the occupied countries were lined with enemy defences whose purpose was to shoot down any Allied aircraft before they could penetrate Europe and carry out their missions. Although more and more guns had been added to the defences as the war had progressed, inevitably some entry points were stronger than others. This was one reason intelligence officers like Frank Adams interrogated crews on their return from operations. For to keep losses down it was important that every new gun post was recorded and logged for the benefit of future operations.

Tonight, however, the responsibility of finding a relatively safe entry point lay with Moore's navigator, Hopkinson. Although more guns and searchlights were opening up and searching the sky like fiery swords, their lack of success suggested Hopkinson had taken careful note of Adams's advice at the briefing.

One by one the Mosquitoes streaked over the coast and although some rocked from the nearness of bursting shells and tracer drilled a line of neat holes through Millburn's starboard wing all the aircraft crossed the coast safely.

But the danger of the operation had only just begun. Every crewman knew that the surprise factor was now over. Not only would the gun crews be radioing messages to Luftwaffe controllers about their entry but the German Observer Corps would be tracking their route every yard of the way. It was no exaggeration to say that within a minute of the Mosquitoes crossing the coast, phones would be ringing in the offices of German night fighter squadrons and enemy crews would be grabbing their parachutes and racing towards their aircraft. At this point in the war German defences were numerous and highly efficient.

There were also natural perils to face. With the sun having now dipped below the horizon, darkness was closing in fast and hills and power lines difficult to pick up even with the sharpest eyes. It left Moore no option but to lead his Mosquitoes up to a 1,000 feet while he addressed his navigator. 'What's our ETA, Hoppy?'

Hopkinson, a wiry, sharp-faced cockney with a short-fused temper but reputed to have the finest eyesight of any man in the squadron, stared out of the cupola. 'No more than ten minutes, skipper. The field's not far from the coast.'

Moore nodded. 'Let's hope they've got their torches ready. And that Jerry hasn't any suspicion of what's going on.'

Back in S-Suzy, as the need for intense concentration eased, Chalmont turned towards Richards. 'How am I doing?'

Richards grinned back. 'You're doing fine.'

'Do you think Harvey'll be pleased with me?'

'Satisfied,' Richards corrected. 'Harvey's seldom pleased. But he might give you seven out of ten.'

Chalmont made a comical face. 'Seven! Watch it. It might go to my head.'

Richards liked the man's sense of humour. 'No danger of that. Not with Harvey around. That's why you don't find any inflated egos in our flight. He's too quick to stick pins in them.'

Chalmont nodded at the bomb release quadrant alongside Richards. 'What height were you told to drop the stuff?'

'It depends on the wind. We're to get our instructions from the ground. If there's little or no wind we can drop it from seven hundred.

If there's wind we go low and forget about parachutes. Apparently the stuff's packed so it won't damage on impact.'

Chalmont glanced up at the rapidly fading sky. 'What about night fighters? Do you think they can reach us in time?'

'If they do, let's hope we've dropped our load first.' Richards pointed to a bulb on S-Suzy's dashboard. 'Keep an eye on our boozer. It'll tell us if one's getting within range.'

CHAPTER 9

I N THE FADING light, Pierre Levrey tried to check the time. Unable to see his watch for the branches of the bush around him, he pushed them aside with his Sten gun and stepped out on the verge of a narrow deserted road that ran alongside the line of trees. A hundred yards to the south two felled trees could be seen blocking the road. Beyond them, half hidden in the fading light, two parked lorries waited. As Levrey lifted his arm to scan his wristwatch, a hoarse voice made him start. 'Pierre! Is that you?'

A second later, Levrey caught the acrid smell of cheap tobacco. '*Oui*, Jean. What's your problem?'

A man stepped from the line of bushes at the far side of the road. Jean Arnaud was a Frenchman thin to the point of emaciation with hollow cheeks and lank black hair. A stub of his rolled cigarette dangled from his thin lips. Born in the slums of St Nazaire, a man with a hatred of authority, Jean Arnaud fitted into the Maquis like a cartridge into a rifle breech. Although he appeared too frail to support its weight, he was carrying a bazooka over one thin shoulder. His accented voice was as razor sharp as the knife he carried in his belt. 'Are the men all in position?'

'*Oui*. On all sides of the field.'

'Will the English be on time?'

'Why not? They usually are.'

'They are when it suits the bastards.' While he loathed the Fascists, Jean Arnaud had no great love for the English either, with their landed gentry and their monarchy. 'They'd better not be late tonight.'

Pierre Levrey, powerfully built with a square face and a thatch of brown hair, took a glance down the road but saw nothing. 'What are you worried about? That new Boche garrison in Etienne?'

'Aren't you? They might have some glory-seeking bastard in charge who decides to change the timetable. Isn't that what sodding new brooms always do?'

'Jean, we've got the young kid Jacques keeping an eye on the garrison. He'll let us know if he sees anything suspicious.'

Arnaud spat out his disgust. 'You shouldn't have put on a kid like that. He'll be more interested in looking at girls than at the Boche.'

Another gust of wind drowned Levrey's reply. As it died away Arnaud stiffened. '*Entendez!*'

Levrey listened but could hear nothing for the rustle of leaves. Then he heard the far-off drone of an engine. The sound was carried away by the wind a few seconds later but it was thirty seconds before both men relaxed. Arnaud's glance was a rebuke. 'It could have been the Kubelwagon patrol.'

'Or the English aircraft,' Levrey pointed out.

'No, those bastards will be late tonight. I've got a feeling they will. We should have set up another road block further up the road. Then we'd have had a chance to get the supplies away before troops could reach us.'

'We couldn't let the English make the air drop if the Boche knew about it,' Levrey protested. 'They'd never have trusted us again.'

Arnaud spat out his cigarette stub. 'You think they're doing it for us? We're the Joes, the bloody expendables. Our job is to engage the Boche and get killed while they come ashore at the invasion smoking their expensive cigarettes.'

Levrey smiled. 'You're too cynical, Jean. No one's making you fight and kill the Boche. You're doing it because you enjoy it.'

The man gave a feral grin. 'You can say that again. In fact....' Then he gave a start. 'The road. Look!'

Levrey turned sharply to glance down the northern stretch of road. At first he could see only a shadow in the fading light, then he saw it was a cyclist pedalling furiously towards them. He stepped out on the road to gain a better view. Arnaud joined him. 'It's that kid of yours, Jacques. Something's wrong.'

A few seconds later the cyclist braked alongside them. Sweat was beaded on his young face. Breathless from his exertions, he took a few seconds to speak. 'The garrison ... I came right away....'

Arnaud gripped his arm. 'Have they changed their time?'

Still panting hard, the youngster nodded. 'That mechanic at the garage told me ... you know ... the garage that works for the Boche....'

The claw-like hand of Arnaud's bit into his arm with feverish strength. 'What time are they coming? Did you find out?'

'No. He didn't know that. Only that he heard two of the patrolmen talking about a changed roster.'

Arnaud glanced at Levrey. 'Didn't I tell you?' he gritted. He pointed back along the road that the cyclist had taken. 'Get another man and make for that bend. In case the bastards get here before the air drop.'

Levrey hesitated. 'But shouldn't we warn the English first? Foix is over there with his transmitter. I'll go and tell him. Then I'll follow you.'

Arnaud jerked him back. 'No. If things go wrong, Foix must not transmit to the English until the last minute.'

Levrey stared at him. 'Last minute. What does that mean?'

'It means they mustn't be warned until the Nazis have reached this bloody field and are picking up the supplies themselves. We must get those supplies, Pierre. That means we can't risk frightening the English off. In any case, do you want the Boches to latch on to our transmission? Let the English come. If the patrol comes later than we thought, everyone will be happy.'

'But what if it comes early and Foix doesn't warn them? The English might have heavy losses.'

'So what?' Arnaud spat. 'They can spare a few aircraft. But it won't happen if a patrol doesn't come or we can silence it before it uses its radio.' His voice rose as Levrey still hesitated. 'For Christ's sake, man, don't you want that equipment? Get moving, for God's sake.' He turned towards the young cyclist and laid a bazooka rocket on the road. 'Hide your bicycle in the bushes, then bring this and a Sten gun with you. *Tout vite!*'

Obeying, Jacques threw his bicycle into the bushes, collected a Sten from a nearby partisan, and then scampered after him. Realizing Arnaud could be right, Levrey called for another partisan to join him. A moment later the two men ran after Arnaud and Jacques, who by this time had reached a sharp bend in the northern road.

Although Arnaud's shallow chest was heaving painfully by this time, he continued running until the party reached a spot where trees lined the road on both sides. Panting hard, he turned to Levrey. 'This'll do. You two take that side and we'll take this. If a patrol comes make certain they're well within range before you open fire. We mustn't give 'em time to use their radio. OK?'

Levrey nodded and he and his fellow partisan ran across the road. Picking a site behind a tree, Arnaud winked at the eager youngster beside him and took from him the bazooka rocket. On the other side of the road, hidden behind a knoll, Levrey was condemning himself for his earlier argument. Arnaud was a ruthless bastard but as usual he was right. After all, the Boches' new timetable might allow for a later patrol than the partisans had allowed for, in which case the stores could be dropped and collected without the Boches ever knowing about the operation. On the other hand, if the worst happened and a patrol did come early, it should be possible for some stores to be gathered and spirited away in the old farm trucks before enemy reinforcements could be brought up. Supplies were desperately needed and surely the English would have enough sense to abandon the operation if ground fire grew too hot.

Deciding he had been too precipitous in his judgements, Levrey was settling down in the damp grass and thinking about a cigarette when he heard the distant sound of an engine again. Although the rising wind kept drowning the sound, its tone when it returned told him it was a road vehicle and moving in their direction. As he listened he saw a glow appear among the trees half a mile or so away. Half a minute later it turned into a narrow beam of light that probed the fields on either side of the road. Alarmed, he nudged the partisan alongside him, then ran across the road and dropped alongside Arnaud. 'Do you hear it?'

Arnaud had another rolled cigarette in his mouth. 'I hear it, *mon ami*. You see I was right, *n'est pas?*'

Levrey was in no mood to argue. 'What do you think it is?'

Arnaud's response, instead of showing alarm, was that of a man who welcomed the approaching danger. 'I think they have not only changed their timetable, they have changed their transport. It's not a motorbike and sidecar this time or a Kubelwagon. I think it is an armoured car.'

'Then how the hell are we going to stop it?'

Arnaud patted the bazooka beside him. 'With this, *mon ami*.'

'But you've only got one rocket. Can it do enough damage?'

'It can if I aim it well. But it might not kill all the crew. You must help me to do that.'

'But what about the air drop? Shouldn't Jacques run back and tell Foix? At least we should warn the English.'

Arnaud's reply was as decisive as a slashing knife. 'Non. If we are lucky we can destroy the car before they can use their radio. If we are not, the English might be able to drop their supplies before the Boches' armour gets here. How long is it before the English are due?'

Levrey peered down at his watch. 'Thirteen minutes.'

'Then let us hope they are on time. The Boches might see the fire from their burning car and come to investigate.' As the wind dropped, the sound of the slow-moving patrol car could be heard again, nearer this time. Knowing the conflict was only minutes away, Levrey nodded at the excited Jacques and whispered in Arnaud's ear. 'Don't you think you should send the boy back to the others? We don't want him killed or injured.'

There was an immediate protest from the youngster, whose sharp ears had picked up his words. Arnaud grinned at Levrey. 'There's your answer. It's right he should see a few more Boches killed. It'll make him all the keener to help us in the future.'

Unable to hide his distaste, Levrey saw the patrol car's searchlight was probing a bend in the road less than 300 yards away. Arnaud tapped his arm. 'Get back before they can see you. And remember this. You kill every man who jumps out after I fire. We must have those supplies.'

Watching the searchlight until it swung away and probed a field, Levrey ran across the road and dropped alongside the tense partisan, a farm labourer named Moreau. 'Arnaud thinks he can stop it with his bazooka. We must pick off all survivors. So get ready.'

The sound of the patrol car grew louder. Its swinging searchlight made it difficult to identify but its shadowy shape gave Levrey the impression of a large armoured vehicle fully equipped to take care of itself. As it moved steadily nearer, the thud of Levrey's heart and the windswept leaves above hid the distant drone of aero engines. When the vehicle was close enough for its searchlight to illuminate the trees above him, Levrey felt his mouth turn dry and knew he was afraid.

CHAPTER 10

OPKINSON WAS THE first to see the wink of a light at one o'clock. He reached for an Aldis lamp. 'There they are, skipper. Shall I give 'em the call sign?'

Moore nodded. 'Yes, but that's all. We don't want Jerry to latch on to them. They're taking a big enough chance as it is.'

A minute later Hopkinson caught Moore's arm. The single light ahead was still winking. 'They say we'll have to drop at low level,' Hopkinson told him. 'The wind's over fifteen knots.'

Moore shrugged. 'Pity but it can't be helped.' Knowing the enemy defences would now be fully alerted, he addressed the squadron. 'Gunboat Leader to Red and Blue Sections. Target sighted at one o'clock. Orbit when over target and drop your stores at low level in numerical order. Section Leaders confirm.'

Back on S-Suzy, Chalmont and Richards heard the affirmative voices of Harvey and Teddy Young. Chalmont turned to Richards. 'Won't that tell the Jerries we're dropping equipment for partisans?'

Richards shook his head. 'Hopefully no. That's why Moore used the word stores. Jerry will know we call bombs stores, so he'll assume we're attacking some French target around here.'

The single winking light was dead ahead now. Reading it himself, Richards turned to Chalmont again. 'We need to watch out for trees on all sides of the field. And there are power lines two miles west of it.'

Chalmont nodded. Although there was still light at 1,000 feet, the ground below was growing darker by the minute. The deepening gloom was accentuated by a trail of sparks south of the target as a freight train steamed towards the coast. Richards pointed at it. 'That's what our air attacks are doing. Forcing Jerry to do all his troop and freight movements at night.'

Chalmont asked the question all servicemen were asking one another. 'Do you think the invasion will come this summer?'

Richards shrugged. 'They tell me there are so many troops and tanks down in the south the birds haven't room to land. They can't leave it much longer or the island might sink.'

The winking light was close now. At another order from Moore the Mosquitoes began to climb and form a huge circle above the field. By this time they were well separated. With the luminous light on the western horizon fading fast, the danger of collision was increasing by the minute.

As all the crews knew, Moore would be the first to venture down. Had it been daylight, neither he nor his crews would have seen much danger in the basic operation. But at night it was possible that the partisans, ignorant of the limitations of high-speed aircraft, were underestimating the danger of obstacles. In addition, the winking lights were no proof in themselves they were in friendly hands.

Whatever the degree of risk, it was typical of Moore to sample it first. A brief order came and then A-Apple was seen diving downwards towards a square of faint lights that had sprung up along all sides of the dropping zone. Inside A-Apple, as the darkened square drew nearer, Hopkinson's grumble reached Moore. 'They could have chosen a bigger field, couldn't they? I don't like the sound of those bloody trees.'

Knowing his man well, Moore smiled. 'Don't worry, Hoppy. I won't leave you dangling from a French poplar.'

Hoppy grimaced. 'I hate poplars. They always make me think of cemeteries.'

Moore laughed. 'Forget cemeteries and drop the supplies when you think we're low enough. Don't rely on the altimeter.'

Hopkinson nodded, his hand on the release. The ground was coming up fast now as the Mosquito's true speed became evident. As the field, enclosed by black walls of trees, came sweeping towards them, even the battle-hardened Cockney felt his muscles tense. Like every man in the squadron he knew this was an inappropriate role for the Mosquito with its high speed and sensitive controls. In Hopkinson's eyes, the use of Mosquitoes to arm resistance groups was proof in itself that the invasion was coming that year and every effort possible was being made to soften up the enemy.

For a veteran like the Cockney, however, collision was the lesser of his fears. Stories had reached the Allies over the years of enemy troops capturing partisans, torturing the code from them, and then waiting with guns trained while the Allied aircraft landed their agents or flew in low to drop their supplies. More often than not the results were fatal for the unsuspecting airmen.

It was a possibility that made Hopkinson hold his breath as A-Apple flashed over the trees on the western side of the field and entered the danger zone between the dimmed lights. When no deadly tracer came lancing out, Hopkinson relaxed and pulled back the bomb release. A second later two large black bundles with unfurled parachutes fell from its bomb bay. Kicking like a horse relieved of its burden, A-Apple headed towards the eastern boundary and the road where the farm trucks were waiting.

But the danger was not over yet. Suddenly A-Apple's two engines gave a scream of protest as her nose rose sharply. Pressed back into his seat, Hopkinson gave Moore a startled glance. He received his reply a few seconds later when Moore steadied A-Apple and resumed his climb to the orbiting Mosquitoes. 'Didn't you see them, Hoppy? Those trees on the rising ground? East of the road.'

Saddled with the reputation for having the best eyes in the squadron, Hopkinson felt double shame. 'No, I didn't. But why didn't those stupid sods warn us?'

'They wouldn't look dangerous from the ground. The hill's shallow and it's a few hundred yards from the field.' Moore switched on his R/T. 'Your turn, Red Zero. But watch for rising ground east of the target. It has trees, so bank away and climb before you reach it. OK?'

With the crews suitably warned, Harvey dived down and dropped his supplies. As he began climbing back and Red One, his wingman, made to follow him, Hopkinson turned to Moore. 'Can't we speed things up a bit, skipper? Jerry's night fighters can't be far away.'

Moore knew he was right but with the last of the twilight gone, the risk of collision had to be balanced against interception. 'We'll leave things as they are for the moment, Hoppy. With luck we might make it.'

Levrey squeezed himself down into the damp grass. The patrol car was so close now that he could hear the crunch of its tyres on the uneven road. As its searchlight swung over him, a night bird gave a squawk of protest and flew away with a clatter of wings.

Beside him he heard a whisper from Moreau. 'How many men? Can you see?'

Levrey hoped his whisper did not betray his fear. 'No. But there can't be more than half a dozen. Don't fire until Arnaud does.'

The searchlight swung back again, revealing a tenuous evening mist that was settling over the fields. As it etched every leaf on the bush ahead of him, Levrey cringed. Surely they must be seen. And because we are lying here with Sten guns, he thought, at any moment a machine gun will smash the life from us and all our defiance will be for nothing. When the searchlight swung away once more, Levrey could not believe his good fortune.

The searchlight was right in front of Levrey now, its blinding light sweeping back and forth and mesmerizing him. Then, quite suddenly, there was a sudden hiss, a massive explosion, a brilliant flash, and then a medley of shouts and screams. The searchlight that had dominated the countryside blinked out, to be replaced by the blazing wreck of an armoured car. Silhouetted against the leaping flames, the dark figures of soldiers, some with their uniforms ablaze, could be seen leaping down to the road.

All fear had left Levrey now. It was kill or be killed. Shouting to Moreau, he leapt to his feet and began spraying bullets at the half-stunned soldiers. As he released the trigger for a moment, he heard the clatter of a Sten gun opposite and knew some of the soldiers must have leapt out on Arnaud's side of the road.

With Moreau joining in the slaughter, it was quickly over. By this time the flames from the burning patrol car were twelve feet high. Painted red by the fire, looking like some malevolent jinnee, Arnaud edged round the heat and prodded at the bodies by the roadside. When one German stirred and gave a groan, Arnaud fired a four-second burst into his body. His thin lips drew back at Levrey's protest. 'Don't fret for him, *mon ami*. Think what would have happened to you if you'd been captured.'

Now the fight was over, Levrey wanted to vomit. As he fought the nausea, he heard the crackle of bursting cartridges within the patrol car. As heat and danger drove them all back, Arnaud gazed up at the sky from which the sound of patrolling Mosquitoes could now be heard. 'What will the English do when they see this fire? Will they panic and run back to their island or will they be men and go on to drop the supplies?'

'They won't run away,' Levrey told him. 'But they might wonder what to do next. They won't want to put our group in danger or for the equipment to fall into German hands. After all, none of us know what the garrison will do when this patrol car fails to radio back.'

His words alerted Arnaud. He swung round on Jacques, who was eyeing the carnage around the blazing patrol car with both horror and fascination. 'You've got the youngest legs here. Run to Foix, tell him what's happened, and tell him to send a message to the English flyers.

Until they hear otherwise they must continue dropping their supplies. Do you understand?'

The boy nodded and ran off. Seeing Levrey's expression, Arnaud gave his pitiless grin. 'It goes right down to the wire, *mon ami*. What other way is there?'

Until Red Four, flown by Paddy Machin, was diving down to the reception field, the orbiting crews had no warning of the happenings below. Their chief concern, apart from the risks of collision, was the likelihood that German night fighters might reach them before the air drop was completed. It was only when S-Suzy was banking round on the western crescent of the wide orbit that Richards gave a start and pointed down. 'What's that?'

Chalmont banked steeply to follow his gaze. 'It looks like a burning vehicle of some kind. On the road that leads to the field. Better tell Moore.'

Richards switched over to R/T. 'Gunboat Leader. Red Six here. There's a vehicle on fire on the feeder road. Do you want us to take a look?'

In A-Apple, Moore's reply was positive. 'No. Remain in orbit until you're given the all clear.' Moore turned to Hopkinson. 'Get on the blower and ask their radio operator what's going on.'

It was over two minutes before Hopkinson received a reply. 'They've got a message a German patrol car's been blown up. No troops have arrived so they think it's safe to continue the drop.'

Moore's hesitation lasted only a second. He addressed his radio again. 'Gunboat Leader to Red Five. Down you go.'

In S-Suzy, Richards turned to Chalmont. 'Did you hear that? We're continuing the drop.'

Chalmont nodded. 'I expect it was their people who ambushed the patrol.'

Richards was trying to see the vehicle but with S-Suzy at the far side of the orbit now, the fire was little more than a flickering point of light in the dark countryside. As S-Suzy banked again a shape looking no larger than a bat could be seen crossing the twinkling lights of the reception field. 'Red Five's just finishing his drop,' Richards announced. 'Are you ready?'

Chalmont nodded and S-Suzy began her dive. As she was levelling off on her approach run, a sudden, strangled voice came over the R/T. 'Look out, skipper. Bandits ... I'm hit and ...' The voice ended abruptly as a bright flash lit up the sky for a moment. It was followed by a burning wreck that slithered down and exploded among the fields below.

Moore's reaction was instantaneous. Equipment could be quickly replaced. Trained crews could not. His order crackled on pilots' radios. 'Gunboat Leader to all crews. Avoid all combat whatever the situation. Abort mission, drop stores, and make for home. At the double.'

Harvey and Young, the two section leaders, added similar orders. There was no panic among the orbiting Mosquitoes but there was no hesitation either. Fighting enemy aircraft in daylight on equal terms was one thing. Fighting them without possessing their radar 'eyes' was like a blind man facing a sharp-eyed enemy. The orbit of aircraft broke and with eyes fixed on their boozer bulbs that indicated the nearness of an enemy fighter, crews obeyed their leaders' orders.

The one exception was S-Suzy. With the dropping zone less than a minute away, Chalmont was wondering whether rather than waste his stores he should continue and drop them where they were needed. Although the dim lights ahead had now been extinguished when Moore's message had spread to the partisans, Chalmont felt certain he could identify the field. Richards, however, had no such doubts. 'What are you doing? Didn't you hear our orders?'

With S-Suzy down to 400 feet, Chalmont could not take his eyes off the dark shapes that were rushing towards him. 'It won't make any difference, will it? Only a few seconds.'

Afraid of distracting him, Richards decided Chalmont was probably right and a few seconds more could hardly matter. In fact both men could not have been more wrong. Having guessed by this time the purpose of the Mosquitoes, the Me–110 Staffel leader had decided his best chance of catching one was near the field where lights had been seen earlier. He was rewarded when his radar operator gave a shout. 'I've got one on the Emil, skipper. Ahead at eleven o'clock.'

The Me–110 tilted slightly, then steadied. 'Get me closer, Hans. Closer.'

At this point neither Chalmont nor Richards were aware of their danger. It was only after Richards had dropped his stores and Chalmont was drawing back on his control wheel that Richards gave a warning shout. 'Jerry! The boozer!'

Glancing at the dashboard, Chalmont saw the indicator bulb had begun pulsing redly. Startled, he banked more steeply but the pulsating light continued. Beside him Richards twisted round in his seat, struggling to see the threat that had latched on to them.

Back in the Me–110 the Staffel leader was making life or death calculations. The Mosquito could outrun him. That he knew. But on a night so moonless it probably could not see him when they were both so close to the ground. So he would guess its escape route and catch it again before its speed could leave him behind. Accordingly he swung the ME around and banked in a circle above while he issued orders to his radar operator. 'Don't lose him, Hans. Stick to him like glue.'

In S-Suzy the boozer had gone dead, alarming both men because it was known that the German AI equipment had to be switched off when close to its prey to prevent it being damaged. For thirty seconds or longer they expected the deadly impact of cannon fire. When it failed to come and the boozer began flickering again, they believed the immediate danger had passed and their superior speed should now carry them out of danger.

Ten seconds later the bulb went dead again, this time assuring them they were out of range of their attacker's radar eyes. Richards was about to congratulate Chalmont when suddenly S-Suzy shuddered as tracer drove into her body and flashed past her starboard wing. As Chalmont instinctively banked away from the burst of fire, his cry reached the equally alarmed Richards. 'How could he catch us? We're supposed to be thirty knots faster.'

What neither men knew was that the Staffel leader's radar operator had succeeded in keeping them on his screen while his pilot had gained altitude on them. Now by diving on them he was able to match the Mosquito's speed. And with the Mosquito now forced to take evasive action against an enemy it could not see, the odds were hugely stacked against its survival.

Like a blind man trying to avoid the thrusts of a sword, Chalmont banked and threw S-Suzy about until Richards believed her wings would shear off. Deciding their only chance was to reach sea level and hope his pursuer would hesitate to follow him for fear of collision among the waves, Chalmont began his dive, only for two luminous lances of tracer to strike his bomb bay and force him level again. Wondering if his pursuer was playing cat and mouse with him, Chalmont realized he was playing no game when, with a series of explosions, huge sparks flew from his right engine, followed by a hideous scream as its propeller shattered. As he switched the engine off, Chalmont believed all hope had gone for himself and Richards. The shattered engine with its cowling gone was glowing red in the darkness, making S-Suzy a prey for any night fighter in the sector.

It was then the firing ceased and a gruff voice came over the R/T. 'Red Six. How bad are you?'

The breathless Chalmont managed to find his voice. 'We've lost an engine, sir. But I can still fly her.'

'Then get the hell out of here. Millburn and I are giving you cover. Go.'

Beside Chalmont, Richards sounded like a man who had fought fifteen rounds against a world champion. 'Harvey! He's come back for us. Didn't I tell you he's a hell of a man?'

Chalmont had no strength left to answer. Drenched in sweat, numbed by the ordeal, he fought to nurse the battle-damaged S-Suzy across the Channel while Richards searched his map for an emergency airfield.

CHAPTER 11

DEFIANCE WAS WRITTEN all over Harvey's craggy face as he entered Moore's office the next morning. Although by this time the two men were the best of friends, matters of procedure and protocol could still stir up old enmities when Harvey suspected he was under criticism. Knowing his man well, Moore waved him to a chair before any comments were passed. 'Sorry to keep you from your breakfast, Frank, but I wanted a few private words before we get mixed up with those young barbarians in the mess.'

Harvey remained standing. 'Aye, I guessed as much. What's your bleat? That I disobeyed your orders when I went back for those kids?'

In situations that could easily explode, Moore's coolness was legendary. 'I want to talk about it, yes. But there are other things too. I take it you've made a full report of all that happened to Adams?'

'Of course I have. And I've mentioned that I disobeyed your order. Did you think I wouldn't?'

Moore smiled. 'Just the opposite. You can be an awkward bastard at times, Frank, but you've never been a liar.'

With Moore talking his language now, some of Harvey's defiance fell away. 'Ian, I'd no choice. Not after I'd sent those kids down and then saw that ME had latched on to them.'

'Is that what alerted you?' Moore asked. 'The tracer?'

Harvey nodded. 'Lacey happened to look back and spotted it. Otherwise we wouldn't have known. Neither of the kids put out a distress call.'

'I'd wondered about that,' Moore said. 'We mustn't forget to ask them when they get back. Do you want to talk to them or shall I?'

Harvey's smouldering resentment at the behaviour of his new pilot burst out at last. 'It's up to you but either way I'm going to give Chalmont a bollocking. If the young sod had obeyed our orders I wouldn't have had to risk losing Millburn and Gabby.'

'Or yourself and Lacey,' Moore reminded him. 'You took a hell of a chance, Frank. Don't do it again. I can't afford to lose my flight commanders.'

Harvey's expression this time was less defiant than sarcastic. 'I shouldn't let that worry you. Davies can't wait to give me the push so Adams's report'll be just what he needs.'

Moore ignored the remark. 'You'll have heard that both the men are coming back today?'

Harvey nodded. 'I got the message last night. Apparently they'd a hairy landing at Holmsley and both were a bit shaken up. But the MO cleared them and Holmsley are flying them back this morning.'

Moore rose to his feet. 'Don't be too hard on them, Frank. Richards had a bad experience only a few weeks ago and Chalmont is a new boy. They'll have learned a lot from last night. Now why don't you get along to breakfast?'

Harvey paused at the door. 'Are you coming?'

'In a few minutes. I've just got a couple more jobs to do.'

Early though it was, Moore found Adams and Sue were in the confessional. Having only received his reports from the tired crews late the previous night, Adams had been left with no choice but to complete his work on the morrow. He was just sorting out his reports prior to sliding them into folders when Moore appeared in the doorway. 'Morning, Frank. Sorry to bother you this time in the day.'

'That's all right, Ian. What can I do for you?'

Moore approached his table. 'I've just found out that Harvey included in his report an admission that he deliberately disobeyed my orders when he went back to help Chalmont and Richards. Is that right?'

Adams nodded. 'Yes, and it's put me in a spot. According to Millburn and Gabby he saved these kids just as last year he saved young Peter Marsh. It's that protective thing in him, Ian. He has this feeling of responsibility towards his crews.'

'I know,' Moore said. 'And so do his men. Tell me. Has he reported Chalmont and Richards for disobeying orders?'

Adams showed surprise. 'No. His report just says they were going down under orders to the dropping zone when the MEs arrived.'

Moore laughed. 'The deceitful old bugger. Frank, I want you to omit that report he made about himself. Scratch it out, rub it out, do whatever you will but get rid of it. I don't want Davies to see it.'

Across the room Sue Spencer had heard his request. Her eyes dropped quickly to her reports as Moore glanced at her but not before her appreciative smile had given her thoughts away.

Adams was showing relief but also with some apprehension. 'There's nothing I'd like more, Ian. But I am supposed to record everything I'm told.'

'I know that. You'll be breaking orders. And I'm breaking orders telling you to do it. It's a week for breaking orders. Everyone's doing it. So why not us?'

There were times when Adams's spectacled face could look impish and this was such a moment. 'You're right. Why not?'

Moore clapped him across the back. 'Not a word to Harvey or he'll think I'm turning soft.'

Richards glanced up from his desk as Chalmont entered the billet. 'What's the MO say?'

Chalmont shrugged. 'The same as Holmsley. It's just a stomach sprain. He's put me off duty until the weekend.' He glanced at Richards's desk. 'Who're you writing to? Hilary?'

Showing some embarrassment, Richards nodded. Chalmont reached his bed and dropped on to it. 'What are you telling her? How lucky we are to be alive?'

Richards gave a half laugh. 'I don't think that's the thing to tell her, do you? But we are lucky, aren't we? If it hadn't been for Harvey....'

Chalmont nodded. 'He's the last one I'd have expected.'

'It's not the first time he's done it,' Richards told him. 'One of his men was trapped last year with his exhaust shrouds blown off. Knowing he was a sitting target, Harvey gave him cover although he must have known he would be first to go when an attack came.'

'What happened? Were they attacked?'

'Yes, they were. Both kites escaped but only because they found cloud cover in time.'

Chalmont gave an appreciative grimace. 'Maybe we're lucky to be in his flight after all. I had my doubts after my interview. You know he wants to see us at 1500 hours?'

'Yes. An SP called in and told me. That'll be to bawl us out for not obeying orders. I suppose that's the least we can expect.'

Chalmont made a gesture of protest. 'Hang on. You wanted to obey them. Remember that when we see Harvey.'

Richards threw him a cigarette. 'I didn't argue, did I? No, we're in this together. I prefer it that way. Otherwise they might split up our team.'

About to protest again, Chalmont hesitated, then pointed at the letter Richards was writing. 'While you're on the blower to Hilary tell her that her brother approves of his navigator. Although I can't guarantee it, it might just get you another Brownie point or two.'

Smiling in appreciation, Richards continued with his letter. As Chalmont lay back and closed his eyes, details of the previous evening sprang back at him. Tracer streaked across the dark screen of his eyelids, red-hot pieces of metal screamed into the hidden recesses of his mind. Jerking open his eyes, he discovered his heart was pounding like a drum and his entire body was drenched in sweat.

Forcing himself to calm down, he lay wondering if Richards was undergoing the same delayed reaction. He wanted to ask him but the sight of Richards still writing his letter changed his mind. He would ask some other time. Yet he knew a discussion of the experience would help diminish the worst of its memories.

He found his escape a moment later. He would write a short story using the incident for its main structure. Without knowing it, Chalmont was proving himself a born writer by his need to translate personal experiences into a form that was a deliverance as well as a palliative.

Noticing him reach for a writing pad and pen, Richards raised an eyebrow. 'Don't tell me you're going to write to Rosalind?'

For a moment Chalmont was tempted to tell the truth. It would be a comfort to share his love of words and literature with a colleague. Then, remembering Adams's warning, he changed his mind. He did not know Richards well enough yet. He pulled a face at the navigator. 'You're making me feel guilty. I've just remembered I haven't written my parents for over a week.'

CHAPTER 12

ILLBURN THREW OPEN the billet door, then gave a grunt of disgust. 'I should have known, shouldn't I? Gremlins can't face honest daylight.'

With the early English spring unable to decide on its appropriate role, a cold wind was playing round Sutton Craddock airfield that day and only too willing to sweep into any room to investigate its contents. Gabby, awakened by Millburn's contempt, found a draught chilling his indignant face as he rose from his blankets and peered at the American. 'What's the matter with you, Millburn? Don't they shut doors in America?'

Grinning, Millburn entered the billet and sealed off the draught. 'So our Welsh gremlin is in a bad mood today. What's your problem, boyo? Did our little venture last night upset you?'

Expression indignant, Gabby pushed himself higher up in bed. 'That's something I want to talk to you about, Millburn. We could have been killed. Do you realize that?'

Millburn dropped on the bed alongside him. 'But we weren't, were we? So what are you bellyaching about?'

'Bellyaching? I want to know why every time a hairy job comes along we're given it. Harvey could have asked any one of a dozen guys to go back with him but he chose us. Why?'

'That's easy. We're the best. Aren't you pleased?'

Gabby's dishevelled face glared at him. 'Pleased? Asked to fly among a pack of ME's sniffing for blood? You think I'm crazy?'

'You disappoint me, boyo. I thought you'd be honoured to be asked to help a couple of kids who'd got themselves in the brown stuff. They have thanked us, by the way. The new kid, Chalmont, came over to me at breakfast.'

'So he bloody should,' Gabby muttered. 'And what's there to be honoured about? I've had nothing but nightmares since we got back about being blindfolded and a pack of MEs chasing us with pitchforks.'

'So that's what it was,' Millburn said. 'I did wonder.'

Gabby eyed him suspiciously. 'Wondered what what was?'

'Your wriggling and shuffling about in bed. I thought you were dreaming about Betty Grable.'

'It's not funny, Millburn. You've got to talk to Harvey and tell him to stop using us.'

'How can I do that?'

'Tell him you've got headaches or piles. Tell him your nerve's cracking. Tell him I've got BO or diarrhoea. Tell him any bloody thing but get us off the hook.'

'You know the reason for that, don't you?'

'For what?'

'You being smelly. Gremlins always get smelly when there's no moon. Wait until it comes back and you'll be bearable again.'

Gabby dropped back on his pillow with a groan. 'Why did I get you, Millburn? Who hates me up there?'

Used to Gabby in his dark Celtic moods, Millburn played the one card guaranteed to revive him. 'When are you going to see that Wren? The one with the gorgeous blonde friend with the Veronica Lake hairstyle.'

Gabby sniffed maliciously 'You fancy that blonde, don't you?'

'I wouldn't say no, boyo. Why don't you try to ring the other one and make a date?'

'It wouldn't be any good,' Gabby muttered gloomily. 'Since she's been back she's either been with that friend of hers or surrounded by dozens of hairy matelots.'

'OK, let her be with her friend. Does it matter?'

Gabby scowled. 'Of course it matters. It's bloody finance. I can't afford to take 'em both out together and anyway what would be the point? They stick together like Siamese twins.'

Millburn grinned. 'I reckon a real man could pull 'em apart. Why don't we try it and take my car into Scarborough?

Gabby gave a start. 'Could we get the petrol?'

'I've still got half a tank. It'd get us there and back.'

For a moment Gabby's suspicions returned. 'What's the catch, Millburn? When I asked to borrow the car last week you were as mean as a dog with a bone.'

'There's no catch, boyo. You've got the contact and I've got the car. Let's get things organized and have a good time. What do you say?'

By this time Gabby was wide awake. 'When?'

'When you can arrange it. As soon as you can.'

Revived, Gabby swung his skinny legs out of bed. 'Maybe Harvey did the right thing after all. Maybe you need the odd shock or two to realize what a tight bastard you can be.'

Millburn's eyes twinkled. 'You think I'm improving?'

Gabby was going no further down the path to reconciliation. He reached for his trousers. 'Don't get any wrong ideas, Millburn. You've still a hell of a long way to go.'

Harvey glared at the two men standing at attention before him. 'Well, what excuse have you got? Don't tell me you haven't cooked one up by this time?'

The two men looked at one another. In the silence that followed, Sam, lying alongside Harvey's desk, gave a yawn and stretched himself.

It was Chalmont who spoke first. 'We haven't one, sir.'

Harvey eyed him suspiciously. 'You disobeyed the orders of your squadron commander and myself and you hadn't a reason. Is that what you're saying?'

'No, sir. I'm saying we hadn't an excuse.'

Harvey's scowl grew. 'Don't play word games with me, Chalmont, or I'll stamp on you so hard you'll end up a stain on the floor.'

Richards broke in quickly. 'He's not doing that, sir. He's just telling you we haven't an excuse.'

Harvey's glare rested on him for a moment, then swung back on Chalmont. 'If you haven't an excuse then why the hell did you disobey a direct order?'

'We were no more than a mile from the dropping zone, sir, so I felt we might as well drop the stores. We knew the partisans needed them urgently.'

'*You* felt,' Harvey repeated.

Chalmont nodded. 'Yes, sir. It was my decision.'

Harvey glanced at Richards. 'Is this true? Weren't you involved?'

Richards frowned in embarrassment. 'I can't remember what I said, sir.'

Chalmont shook his head. 'He said we should abort. It was I who disobeyed the order.'

Harvey's eyes returned to him. 'So you believed you knew better than your squadron commander?'

Chalmont shifted uncomfortably. 'No, it wasn't that. We were just so near the dropping zone that it seemed good sense to finish the job.'

'Do you still think you were right?'

'No, sir. Not now.'

Harvey's voice rose. 'You were more than wrong, Chalmont. You risked the life of your navigator and might have caused the death of one of my best crews. Do you realize the risk Millburn and Gabriel took for you?'

'Yes, sir, I do. I've already thanked them.' Before Harvey could respond, Chalmont went on: 'We're grateful to you too, sir. You saved our lives.'

Harvey scowled. 'If I did, more bloody fool me. I've no time for clever young buggers who think they know it all. Why didn't you signal when you were attacked?'

Chalmont looked surprised by the question. 'It never occurred to me, sir.'

Harvey glanced at Richards. 'What about you? You're not new to the squadron. You know it always tries to help its crews if it can.'

'I never thought of it either, sir,' Richards confessed. 'I suppose we were too busy trying to get away from that ME.'

'You didn't do a very good job, did you? One engine taken out and half your tail shot off. A perfectly good kite out of action for weeks. You do realize that Wing Commander Moore ought to punish you both?'

Richards showed surprise. 'Isn't he going to, sir?'

'No, he's left it to me.' Harvey glanced back at Chalmont. 'What does the MO say about your injury?'

'I'm supposed to rest until the weekend, sir. But I'm fit enough to fly if you want me to.'

He received a look of disgust. 'Right now that's the last thing I want. Mossies like ours are in short supply. Get over to Mr Adams and tell him he's got a couple of assistants until the weekend. He tells me he has hundreds of photographs that need sorting and filing.'

Both men looked astonished. Chalmont was the first to recover. 'Is that all, sir?'

Harvey scowled. 'Why? Do you want a court martial instead? Because that's what you'll get if you don't keep your arses clean in the future. Have I made myself clear?'

'Yes, sir. Very clear.'

'Then get over to Mr Adams right away. Tell him he's to work you to the bone. Mornings, afternoons and evenings. All right?'

The two relieved men drew to attention and saluted. As they left the office and closed the door, Chalmont turned to Richards. 'I don't believe this. No proper punishment? Am I dreaming?'

Although showing equal relief, Richards displayed less surprise.

'He probably thinks we got a big enough fright last night. Now do you see why he's so popular with his men?'

Inside the office, Harvey was leaning down and patting the half-asleep Sam. 'You've got it made, haven't you? Not a care or a problem in the world. I'd swop places with you any time, you lucky old bastard.'

The mess was two-thirds empty that night when Adams entered; 633 Squadron was used to losses but Emerson and Yates had been popular crewmen and while it was traditional not to emphasize a loss, it was also traditional not to ignore one either. In normal circumstances men might have been seen debating or arguing at the bar but tonight the few members present were sitting quietly at tables and drinking as soberly as they were talking. Fully aware of the reason and mentally applauding it, Adams spotted Harvey and Teddy Young sharing a table and made towards them. 'Might I join you two for a moment?'

Pushing Sam aside, Harvey slid a chair towards him while Young signalled to a mess waiter. 'What will you have, Frank?'

A moderate drinker in ordinary circumstances, Adams hesitated. 'Just a half, thanks, Teddy. I can't stay long.' As Young gave the waiter his order, he went on: 'I'm sorry about Emerson and Yates, Teddy. That was foul luck.'

Young's nod gave nothing away. 'They call it fate, Frank. Their luck ran out. At least they got their message to us in time.'

Adams had often wondered how he would have behaved if fate had allowed him to lead men into life-and-death situations like these two flight commanders. 'Thank God for that, Teddy. At least it gave the rest of you the chance to get out.' Then he caught Harvey's expression. 'Well, nearly everybody.'

'Anybody but a stupid college kid,' Harvey grunted. 'How are they both doing? I hope you're working their arses off.'

'Of course I am, 'Adams lied. 'All the same, I thought you let them off lightly.'

Harvey scowled. 'I ought to have taken the skin off Chalmont. He was the sod who disobeyed the order.'

'That's what he told me. He doesn't think it fair Richards should be punished too.'

Young made a face as he glanced at Harvey. 'You've got a dinkum boy there, mate. I didn't think any of you Limeys could be that honest.'

Harvey grinned. 'That's only because you Aussies don't know the truth when you hear it.' He turned back to Adams. 'I know you like the kid but telling the truth won't save him from getting killed. Or getting others killed. I think he's the wrong type for this job, Frank. Maybe they stuffed him so full of facts and figures at his college that he thinks he knows better than the rest of us. Whatever it is, I'm keeping an eye on him in the future.'

Adams took off his glasses and rubbed them. 'What does Moore think of him?'

For a brief moment Harvey's old prejudices showed. 'Ian won't worry about his background. They come from the same Bond Street shop. But he doesn't like crews who disobey orders any more than I do. So the kid had better watch himself.'

Adams replaced his glasses. As he picked up his beer, Sam pushed himself from the floor and nuzzled against him. Looking pleased, Adams bent down and rubbed the dog's ear. 'Hello, old feller. We're still friends, are we?'

'He hasn't forgotten how you looked after him when I was in hospital,' Harvey said. 'Dogs don't forget things like that. You should get yourself a dog, Frank. There's no better company.'

Adams nodded. 'I will one of these days.' Glancing at his watch, he drained his beer. 'I suppose I'd better get back.' He glanced at Teddy Young as he rose. 'Thanks for the drink, Teddy. Sorry I can't stay and get you one. Perhaps tomorrow.'

The two flight commanders watched him leave the mess. Young turned to Harvey. 'What was all that about? Any idea?'

Harvey nodded. 'Yes. He came to thank me for not clobbering Richards and Chalmont.'

'But why would he do that?'

Harvey shrugged. 'Because he's Frank Adams. He's like a father to these kids. He's also got a soft spot for Chalmont.'

'Why?'

'I'm not sure. Unless it's something to do with the kid's background. You know he spent some time in Spain during the Civil War when his father was a diplomat over there. Frank tells me he saw the bombing of Guernica.'

'Guernica? What was that?'

Harvey gave a moue of disgust. 'Trust a bloody ignorant Aussie. Guernica's a Spanish city, bombed by Hitler's air force during the Spanish Civil War. Hundreds of civilians killed and the first time an open city had been bombed. So there was a hell of a fuss about it. Someone did a painting of it although I can't remember his name.'

'OK. But why would that have an effect on Adams?'

Harvey shrugged. 'Perhaps it hasn't. Perhaps it's something else. Whatever it is, maybe it's one reason why I went soft on the kid. If Frank Adams likes someone, he can't be all bad.'

Young grinned. 'You like Frank Adams. Right?'

'Right. They don't come any better. Or more lonely.' Then, already ashamed of his moment of sentiment, Harvey raised a hand to the watchful waiter. 'Let's have another. All this goodwill's making my throat dry.'

CHAPTER 13

ADAMS DECIDED TO take Chalmont over to the squadron's favourite
pub the following morning. With Richards on the duty roster for
twenty-four hours, it was the first chance Adams had of chatting
to the young pilot on his own, and with Sue volunteering to man the
confessional for a couple of hours, Adams took his opportunity.

He found Chalmont seated at the desk in his billet, a writing pad
before him. Seeing Adams in the doorway, he lowered his pen and rose.
'Hello, sir. What can I do for you?'

'This isn't an official visit,' Adams told him. 'I just wondered if you
would like a pre-lunch drink in The Black Swan. Have you been over
there yet?'

'No, sir. We seem to have been too busy since I arrived.'

Adams could not blame him for his look of surprise. Adams was
fully aware that protocol did not encourage squadron leaders to invite
mere pilot officers out for a drink. He covered his embarrassment with
a nod at the writing desk. 'Mind you, if you're busy we can do it some
other time.'

Chalmont hastily picked up the writing pad. 'No, sir. It's nothing
important. I'd like to go over with you.'

Adams watched the young pilot slip the writing pad into his suitcase before straightening his tie and reaching for his cap. Adams
waited to ask his casual question until the two of them were
approaching the guardroom. 'How are those short stories of yours
coming along? Have you written any more since you arrived?'

Chalmont hesitated, then nodded. 'Yes, I have, sir. I finished one two
nights ago.'

Adams was gratified the young pilot showed such trust in him.
'Well done. What is it about? The war?'

'I'm afraid it is, sir.'

'Why be afraid of that? All wars should produce writers. Are you
pleased with it?'

Chalmont pulled a face. 'Not really, sir. It seemed all right when I was working on it but I was disappointed when I read it the next day.'

There was the click of heels and rifle as the sentry on the camp entrance came to attention. Returning the salute, Adams led Chalmont out and pointed down the road that ran by the airfield. 'That's our target for today.'

He was indicating an old country inn that stood alongside the road. 'I'm surprised Richards hasn't had you over by this time. Most of the boys prefer it to the mess.'

'I think he's like me, sir, he doesn't drink much. And we have been kept busy since I arrived.'

Adams gave him an amused smile. 'If neither of you is over fond of booze you're to be congratulated. Most of our aircrews can't get enough of the stuff.' He continued as if it were the same sentence. 'Don't worry if you find yourself dissatisfied with your writing. There's always a loss between the golden thought in the mind and its transfer through muscle and sinew to paper. I understand all writers and artists experience it. It's something that can't be avoided.'

The look he received was a mixture of respect and relief. 'How do you know that, sir?'

Adams gave a self-deprecating laugh. 'I've read about it. I've also experienced it when I've tried myself to write now and then. And the stuff that's come out is awful. Mind you, that's perhaps due to the original thought being pretty awful too. I'm no artist, Chalmont, but I can understand the problems artists have.'

Chalmont's expression made it very clear he had never expected to have such a conversation with a squadron leader. 'Have you written anything I can read, sir?'

Adams shook his head. 'Nothing that's here with me. But you could let me read your short story. Will you do that?'

There was no hesitation this time. 'Do you mean it, sir?'

'Yes. I'd like to read it. Give it to me when we get back. It'll be better reading than the AMOs I get every day.'

They had now reached the old pub. Solidly built, with a grey slate roof, whitewashed walls and surrounded by a picket fence, it was served by two gravel paths, one leading through a small garden and past a large crab apple tree to a private porch, the other to the public bars and the saloon. At the other side of the road the squadron hangars and the control tower could be seen towering over the long wooden fence that surrounded the airfield. Adams jerked a thumb at the airfield as he led the young pilot down the path that led to the porch.

'They couldn't be much closer to us, could they? No wonder they've become part of the squadron's tradition.'

Chalmont glanced at his watch as they entered the porch. 'Aren't we early for a drink, sir? Or don't they keep to normal pub times?'

An oaken door stood before them. As Adams reached for the heavy iron knocker that served as a bell, he gave Chalmont a wink. 'The local bobby does keep an eye on them but he can be a bit short-sighted at times. But you're right; we are too early for the bar this morning. That's why I'm using the private entrance.'

He swung down the heavy knocker twice and waited. A few seconds later Chalmont heard a bolt being withdrawn and saw the door swing open. The girl that appeared was big and handsome with dark hair and bold features. Wearing a black sweater that accentuated her large breasts, she had an apron tied round her waist. Her face lit up on seeing Adams. 'Hello, Frank. You want to see Joe? Come on in.' Turning, she gave a shout. 'Joe. Frank's here.'

Adams turned to the young pilot alongside him. 'Maisie, meet Jeremy Chalmont. A new pilot of ours. Chalmont, this is Maisie. A good friend in the nicest possible way to all our men at the station.'

As Chalmont held out a hand to the girl, her dark eyes flickered over him appreciatively. Liking what she saw, Maisie lifted her other hand to her hair. The barmaid of The Black Swan, Maisie was a girl whose feminine instincts were triggered automatically whenever a good-looking man came into her orbit and it was obvious she found Chalmont very good-looking. 'Pleased to meet you, Mr Chalmont, I'm sure. Are you a friend of Frank's?'

To avoid embarrassment to Chalmont, Adams broke in before the young man could answer. 'He's a new posting, Maisie. He hasn't been to the pub before and as I wanted to see Joe I thought I'd bring him with me.'

Maisie flashed Chalmont one of her special smiles. 'Then come in, both of you.'

She stood to one side as the men entered. Although she seemed to press herself as far as she could against the side wall, Chalmont noticed her breasts brush against him as he followed Adams inside. Generous to a fault, Maisie was never one to deny her lads a bit of entertainment even if she was selective in her final choice. Closing the front door, she pushed by Chalmont again and pointed at a door at one side of the hall. 'Go into the private lounge, Frank, while I go and see what Joe's doing.'

Following Adams, Chalmont found himself in an oak-panelled room with mullioned windows. Smoke-blackened beams crossed a low, white-washed ceiling. With the thick walls defying sounds from outside, the atmosphere was that of a bygone age. Chalmont made the point to Adams. 'I can see why this place is so popular. It breathes age and tradition.'

Adams was clearly pleased with the compliment. 'I thought you'd like it. Wait until you see the bar. It's covered with photographs of our old crews. There's even one of Grenville there.'

Chalmont gave a start. 'The Black Fjord leader?'

'That's right. And the men who flew with him. Joe Kearns keeps this pub like a museum.' Then his tone changed. 'Here he is now.'

A man wearing braces and shirtsleeves had entered the room. Joe Kearns was in his middle fifties with a countryman's ruddy face and white, thinning hair. His voice, genial in tone with a North Yorkshire accent, betrayed his pleasure at seeing Adams. 'Hello, Frank. Good to see you again, lad. Who've you got with you this time? Some relation?'

Adams introduced Chalmont. 'No, he's a new recruit, Joe. I brought him over to see this lovely old pub of yours.'

Kearns held out a calloused hand. 'Good to meet you, sir. I hope we'll see lots of you in the days ahead.'

Chalmont was still trying to come to terms with hearing a squadron leader addressed as lad. 'Thank you, sir. I hope I shall too.'

Kearns eyed the young pilot more carefully as he released his hand. 'You're not related to Wing Commander Moore, are you?'

'I, Mr Kearns? No, not in any way. Why do you ask?'

'Just that accent of yours, sir. You sound a bit like him.'

Adams was smiling. 'They had the same kind of education, Joe. It tends to show, doesn't it?' He changed the subject. 'Are we too early for a cup of tea or coffee?'

Kearns' eyes twinkled. 'You're not too early for a dram of whisky if you feel like it, lad. I had a delivery two days ago and there's a bottle put aside for special guests.'

Adams glanced at Chalmont. 'Feel like a small whisky, Chalmont?'

'It's a bit early for me, sir. But I'd like a cup of tea if I may.'

Kearns turned to the doorway where Maisie was taking in all that was being said. 'Will you do the honours, lass?'

Maisie directed another smile at Chalmont. 'The kettle's on, Joe. Just give me a couple of minutes.'

As with a swirl of her skirts Maisie vanished into the kitchen, Kearns turned back to Chalmont. 'That girl's crazy about you lot. When you go out on an operation she's not fit to live with until you get back. Ask Mr Adams here.'

Adams nodded. 'It's true. She waits until she hears the engines and then runs to the front gate and waves at every plane that comes in to land. She's been doing it so long that the crews don't feel they're safely home until they see her at the gate.'

'I must look out for her the next time we go out,' Chalmont said.

Kearns' eyes twinkled again. 'I should, sir. Because from the way she was looking at you just now I think you might get a special wave.'

Maisie brought in the tea five minutes later. 'Shall I be mum?' she asked Kearns.

'Aye, if you will, lass.' As Maisie busied herself with milk and teapot, Chalmont produced a packet of cigarettes and offered them round. When Maisie declined and both men shook their heads, Kearns tapped the stem of a pipe tucked in his shirt pocket. 'Thanks, sir, but both Mr Adams and me are pipe smokers. At least we are when the baccy's available.'

The comment brought a chuckle from Adams, who fixed the younger man with his bespectacled eyes. 'Chalmont, what you are going to see now is a classified military secret. Betray it and you're facing an instant court martial. Do I make myself clear?'

The puzzled Chalmont nodded. 'Yes, sir. Very clear.'

Adams finished in his tunic pocket and drew out a small package, which he handed to the smiling innkeeper. 'Three Nuns,' he told Chalmont. 'Pipe tobacco if you haven't heard of it. Joe's favourite and the services seem to have collared it all. So now and again Joe and I do a little black marketing. He saves a little whisky for me and I get an extra ration of the Nuns for him. I know we'll never win the war this way but it makes life a little easier while we're trying.'

Chalmont could not keep his face straight. 'It seems a splendid arrangement to me, sir.'

Adams glanced at Kearns. 'You hear that, Joe. Our young friend approves of our subterfuge. You were right. He did receive an excellent education.'

By this time Maisie had filled the cups and was passing them round. The glance she gave Chalmont as he took his cup from her made the young pilot blush. Kearns took a slap at her as she walked past him. 'Go and get those glasses polished, lass. We'll be opening the bar in half an hour.'

The two airmen left the pub fifteen minutes later. Adams nodded back at it as they made for the camp entrance. 'You wouldn't think it but that girl was heartbroken last year when Gillibrand was killed.'

Chalmont gave a start. 'Wasn't he the Canadian who won the VC?'

'That's right. It was when Jerry attacked the airfield. He was the only pilot who managed to take off and he deliberately crashed into one of their aircraft that was about to bomb the control tower. You used to be able to see the scar in the adjacent field where Gillibrand crashed and was killed. Some believe he saved the squadron from extinction by that act. He certainly made the Swartfjord raid possible.'

Chalmont was listening in fascination. 'And Maisie was engaged to him?'

Adams smiled. 'If men like Gillibrand are ever engaged. She certainly worshipped him. I think that's why she's so devoted to the squadron. She flirts with the boys because she is Maisie but underneath it all Gillibrand is still her man.'

Entering the airfield, they reached Chalmont's billet. There the young pilot handed Adams a script folded inside a large envelope. 'Has anyone else seen this?' Adams asked.

Chalmont shook his head. 'No, sir. I've taken your advice.'

Adams nodded. 'I think you're wise. Good. I shall look forward to reading it. And anything else that you write. They'll be safe with me.'

'Thank you, sir. And thank you for taking me over to the pub. I appreciate it.'

'That's all right, Chalmont. I enjoyed it too. Now I'd better get back to my office or Sue'll start thinking I've had too much of that whisky Joe keeps for me.'

'She knows about it too, does she, sir?'

'Sue? How can you work with a woman without her finding out everything about you? But she's a good lass, as Kearns would say, and keeps it all to herself.'

'You're lucky, sir.'

'Yes, I think I am, Chalmont.' Tucking the envelope carefully under his arm, Adams started for the confessional. 'Take care of yourself and keep your stories coming. The world's going to need the truth when this war's over.'

CHAPTER 14

EAN ARNAUD CAUGHT the arm of the man beside him, blew out the
paraffin lamp, and ran to the door. Gripping his Sten gun, he carefully drew the door back, pausing each time its hinges creaked.
Behind him his two companions, hardly daring to breathe, had
ducked down from the table where they had been working and were
now crouched on the floor. The rising wind, which had been seeking
ingress into the deserted building for the last half hour, now made a
triumphant entry and sent a pencil from the table clattering down.

The door creaked a last time and the dark shape of Arnaud slipped
outside. Whispering to his companion, Pierre Levrey half rose and
ran to the entrance. Listening intently, he heard nothing at first but
the swish of leaves and branches. Then he heard voices, distant at
first but growing louder. As tight as a coiled spring, he gave a muted
warning to his companion, who picked up his own Sten and ran to
his side. The voices were louder now, rising and falling in the wind,
and coming from the railway track that ran through the wood behind
them. As they listened one voice rose, as if saying farewell. A moment
later footsteps were heard and a man could be heard humming as he
approached the doorway. Levrey gave a laugh of relief. 'It's OK. It's
Arnaud back.'

As they lowered their guns and stood back, Arnaud entered the
room. 'All right, *mes amis*. You can relax.'

'Who was it?' Levrey asked.

Arnaud closed the door. 'An old guy. Taking his dog for a walk
along the rail track.' Arnaud gave his ferocious chuckle. 'He got a
bigger fright than I did.'

'Did he see your Sten?' Levrey asked.

'Naw. I hid it in a bush before I went over to him. I told him I was a
railway inspector checking the state of the station.' Arnaud glanced at
Foix, the third member of the trio. 'You can light the lamp, *mon chou*.
There's no one else out there.'

Foix moved back to the table and struck a match. As the lamp's yellow glow spread outwards it revealed a dilapidated room with two long padded benches running along opposite walls and a large circular metal stove in the centre of the floor. A pinewood table stood alongside the unlit stove and sepia photographs of coal-fired trains, one print with its glass shattered, hung askew on the stained walls. A clock with a shattered face shared a wall with them and a blanket hung over a large window devoid of glass. Once, passengers bound for Soissons had waited in the room but since Allied air raids had devastated the French railways, the commuter station had been long abandoned.

Levrey was not looking reassured by Arnaud's confidence. 'How can you be sure he won't say anything when he gets home?'

Arnaud gave his feral grin. 'Anyone who keeps a dog when food's rationed is a halfwit. No, the old fool won't say anything. He was only too glad I wasn't a Boche.' He glanced at his watch, then at Foix who was now seated at the table with a portable radio transmitter before him. 'How long before London transmit?'

Foix was replacing earphones round his neck. He glanced at his watch. 'Eleven minutes.'

'You know what you have to tell them?'

The radio operator, a stockily built man, showed irritation. 'You told me often enough. 17.30.'

'Make sure they repeat it back. I'll keep watch outside in the meantime. But let me know when they come through.'

As he closed the door behind him, Foix glanced at Levrey. 'He's not as sure of that old man as he pretends.'

Levrey nodded. 'I know that. But he'll take any chance to harm the Boches.'

'How the hell did he get into our group in the first place?'

'Someone over in London arranged it. Someone called McBride. I think they like his methods over there.'

'I'm buggered if I do,' Foix muttered. 'Killing the Boches is one thing. Enjoying it is something else.' When Levrey made no reply, the radio operator went on: 'It doesn't stop there either, does it? You do realize what will happen if London agree to this scheme of his?'

Levrey frowned. 'Of course I know. But what can we do if London make the arrangements with de Gaulle? They must surely know what they are doing.'

The pulse of Morse sounded in Foix's earphones five minutes later. Catching the radio operator's eye, Levrey called Arnaud back into the room. 'It's London. Right on time.'

As eager as a jackal with prey, Arnaud moved to the table. 'What do they say?'

Foix held up a silencing hand as the Morse continued. When it ended he glanced up at Arnaud. 'It's on: 17.30 hours on Sunday.'

Arnaud smacked a clenched fist into his palm as he swung round on Levrey. '*Bien, mon ami.* They've agreed.' He turned back to Foix. 'Tell them we'll be ready.'

With Arnaud operating the hand-driven generator, Foix sent his message while Levrey ran outside and wound in the aerial. Returning, he handed the coil to Foix. 'How long have we got?'

Foix was hastily packing his radio and its parts into its neat travelling case. 'It depends where their D/F vans are tonight. If they're in this area we've only got a few minutes.'

Levrey snatched the curtain from the window. 'We can leave this. They'll think it belonged to a tramp.' He gazed round the room. 'Anything else before I put out the lamp?'

Five minutes later they were making their cautious way through the woods and fields that bordered the rail track. As they entered a small village they heard the urgent scream of a siren. Hiding behind a stone wall, they watched two Kubelwagons packed with soldiers race into sight. As they tore past towards the distant wood, Arnaud spat and made an obscene gesture. 'Pity we couldn't get those bastards tonight. But let's hope they're the ones on duty on Sunday.'

Foix caught Levrey's eye. Shaking his head but making no comment, Levrey joined Arnaud on the road and the three men continued their walk to shelter and safety.

Moore smiled at the question. 'No, Davidson, it's not going to be another night-time job. It's true we'll be going out at low level again but this time we'll be able to see our target. Even better, we'll be able to see those who don't like us. So if those MEs get in our way again we'll be able to take care of them.'

'Amen to that,' someone muttered. As a laugh broke out, Young held up his hand. 'Does that mean we're not getting any cover, skipper?'

'I'm afraid it does, Teddy. Fighters are in short supply these days. They're all being used to strafe Jerry's transport systems. The powers-that-be think we can take care of ourselves and they're probably right. Harvey's lads will go in first and then they'll give you cover when you go down. We don't expect much interference because Jerry is having to keep his day fighters back to engage our deep penetration raids into Germany.'

It was Sunday morning and chilly in the operations room. The coke stoves had not been long lit and, in the way of coke stoves, more sulphurous fumes were being emitted than heat. Every now and then, half-suppressed coughs came from the crews and on the platform Henderson, whose own sinuses were under stress, was making a mental note to talk to Bertram, the station SWO. If Henderson knew his man, those lazy young bastards whose job it was to tend to the stoves would never fail in their duty again. Not with the risk of being skinned alive by Bertram.

The crews were occupying their usual benches, with Chalmont and Richards two benches behind the flight commanders. During the description of the mission Chalmont had been as attentive as the rest of the crews but Richards had sensed the pilot's unease as the briefing progressed. Wondering at the reason, Richards tried to put his mind back to the questions that were being asked. 'Did I hear you say the target is camouflaged, sir?' The question came from a member of Young's flight.

'Yes, Wall, it is. I know it's unusual for an industrial target but it does emphasize its importance to the enemy. From all I can gather it used to build parts for cars but Jerry's made it switch to parts for his aircraft. It also manufactures machine tools. I can't give you more details than that but you can see why it needs to be destroyed.'

The northern voice that followed surprised nobody. Harvey was always one to examine the weaker points of any plan. 'What about these partisans? Can we trust them to do their bit on time?'

Moore shrugged. 'We've no choice. We're told the camouflage is so good we might have problems pin-pointing the factory on our own. I don't think you need worry, Frank. SOE say they're trustworthy.'

Harvey was not finished yet. 'Why is it so important we attack at 17.30? Has it something to do with the Jerry defences?'

'No. It's when the night shift moves in. It's a pity the factory wasn't bombed before the Germans made the French work on Sundays but perhaps its importance wasn't known then. But as the shifts change over at 17.30, with luck we might save many lives.'

At this point Chalmont raised his hand. 'That was what I wanted to ask you, sir. Isn't this raid going to kill Frenchmen?'

As a murmur ran around the room, Moore gave a rueful nod. 'I'm afraid it is. That was why SOE had first to ask permission of General de Gaulle. He can't be happy about putting his fellow countrymen at risk but with the factory so important he had no choice.'

'But then he doesn't have to bomb it himself, sir, does he?'

A louder murmur broke out among the crews this time and faces turned to eye the speaker. One face belonged to Harvey and suggested the craggy flight commander did not believe what he was hearing. If Moore was surprised by the question, he took it in his usual urbane way. 'I take your point, Chalmont, but in modern wars generals and their kind aren't called upon to carry out their own orders. As the Yanks say, it's GI Joes like ourselves who have the dirty jobs to do.'

As Moore glanced away it was clear he considered the question answered but Chalmont was still on his feet. Richards tried to pull him down but the young pilot drew away. 'This is a dirty job, isn't it, sir? We shouldn't be killing Frenchmen. And certainly not innocent ones.'

This was too much for Harvey. With a growl he leapt to his feet and turned on the pale but persistent pilot. 'Sit down, Chalmont! Sit down and belt up! That's an order.'

If anything, Chalmont's face went even paler but he still resisted Richards's frantic efforts to make him obey. 'I'm sorry, sir, but I never thought I'd be asked to do a job like this.'

Harvey's face was thunder-black now but before he could reply Henderson rose from his chair at the side of the platform. 'You! What's your name?'

The young pilot swallowed. 'Chalmont, sir.'

'What are you going on about, lad? This bloody factory is turning out mechanical parts that are helping the enemy to kill our aircrews and our civilians. Do you want it to go on doing that just because Frenchmen are making the parts?'

'No, sir. But....'

'There are no bloody buts about it, lad. As things stand these Frenchmen are as much our enemies as the Jerries while they're working for them. Isn't that right?'

'But they're forced to do it. It's not their fault.'

Henderson made a grunt that might well have been a Gaelic swear word. 'We can't go into the bloody rights and wrongs of every order we get, Chalmont, or we'll all go up the wall. Damn it, we've picked a time when the workers are changing over, so there ought to be minimum casualties. If any Frenchmen are killed, blame Hitler for starting the war. Now belt up, sit down and let's get this briefing over.'

For a breathless moment it seemed Chalmont was going to continue the argument. Then, to Richards's enormous relief, he obeyed the order and sat down.

But the effect of his intervention was far from over. No crew member present had witnessed such a scene at a briefing before and the men were openly talking and arguing with one another. Realizing how Chalmont's mention of French casualties had disturbed the young crews, Moore, who had stood aside during Henderson's intervention, was quick to restore discipline and order. 'All right, you've all had your say. Now let's make sure we do a good job. The more accurate we are, the fewer French casualties there will be. So take careful note of your orders so we don't make any mistakes.'

Benches rumbled as crews rose to consult their specialist officers. Among these officers Adams was seated alongside Henderson. He had heard with misgivings the Scot's grunt of anger when he had flopped down in his chair after addressing Chalmont, now he was compelled to respond to Henderson's impatience. 'That young bastard has upset all the lads with his talk about killing Frenchmen. Who the hell is he, anyway? A pacifist?'

'He has a reason, sir,' Adams said.

Alerted now, Henderson turned towards him. 'You know him?'

'I know a little about his background, sir. It does explain his concern.'

The Scot's grunt was sarcastic. 'Why? Was he brought up in a monastery?'

Adams was about to mention Guernica when the first of the crews climbed the platform and stood waiting for his attention. Seeing him, Henderson made a gesture of impatience. 'Never mind. Come to my office when the briefing's over. Yes, and bring Moore and Harvey with you. I can't afford any rotten apples in my squadron.'

CHAPTER 15

CHALMONT THREW HIS cap on his bed and sank down after it. Following him into the billet, Richards closed the door before launching his question. 'What the hell came over you in there? Have you any idea the effect you had?'

Chalmont's voice was sullen. 'Have you any idea what we've been ordered to do?'

'Of course I have. We have to destroy a factory that is turning out aircraft parts for the Germans. I know it's French but as the CO said, it's no less a threat because of that.'

'I don't give a damn about the factory but I do care about killing Frenchmen. And so should you.'

'Who said I didn't care? We all care. But what can we do about it? The Germans are using foreign factories and slave labour all over occupied Europe. If we don't bomb those factories we'll lose the war and who'll be the loser then? Not just us but the occupied countries too.'

Chalmont eyed him with dislike. 'The Germans could have used that argument when they bombed Guernica. But I don't think it would have made Hilary feel any better, do you?'

The riposte, with its implications of Hilary's disapproval of his attitude, made Richards pause. 'Probably not. But she's not in the RAF, is she? She doesn't know about or understand the things we have to do.'

'She knows we fly fighter bombers. And she hates bomber crews. You saw and heard that the other week.'

Dismayed that Hilary was being brought into the argument, Richards felt the need to tone it down. 'We can't help being what we are, can we? You told her that yourself. She sees only the casualties of war. It gives her a different viewpoint from the one we have.'

For a moment Chalmont's glance made Richards fear the young pilot was going to use Hilary as a weapon to punish him. Instead his tone changed. 'This isn't the kind of job I expected when I asked to join this squadron.'

Richards showed sympathy now. 'I can understand that and probably half the boys feel the same way. But what can we do? Henderson is right. We can't let the enemy shield behind slave workers or he's bound to win.'

'So we kill the slaves. It's quite a choice, isn't it? What about the religious side of it? Doesn't that worry you?'

Richards was wondering why, until he had met Chalmont, he had not questioned the morality of the war and his role in it. Until then it had seemed a simple if violent equation. His country was forced into a war against a ruthless enemy bent on enslaving every nation that opposed it. To conquer such a tyrant had seemed the duty of every decent man and that duty had not seemed to clash with religious beliefs. In many ways the reverse had seemed the case.

Until he met Chalmont and his family. Hilary, Richards knew, had been the catalyst of his new self-assessment. Being no fool, Richards knew her looks and personality had played their part and in a sense their effect on his beliefs could be discarded. But her views as against her physical presence had probed at his conscience and created doubts and misgivings that had never troubled him before. Richards was in no way a convert to the maxim that all killing was sinful but for the first time since he had joined the RAF he was wondering if his religious instincts were in full accord with his role as a combat airman. His misgivings, immature as they still were, made his reply sharper than he had intended.

'Don't bring religion into it, for God's sake. I'm not to blame for the jobs Group gives us.'

Chalmont's reply suggested he was as anxious as Richards to fend off a quarrel. 'No one's suggesting you are. But I had to say what I thought back there. If we never questioned orders we'd be mere puppets obeying the orders of our masters. Like the German pilots were in Spain.'

His words brought Richards a vision of Harvey's expression at the briefing and lightened his mood. 'I like the sentiment but I wouldn't indulge it again. Arguing about orders isn't something the Armed Forces give out medals for.' When Chalmont made no reply, Richards threw him a cigarette. 'Don't get me wrong. I admired you for standing up and saying what you did. But it has made you a marked man. I'm surprised Harvey hasn't had you in his office already.'

Chalmont returned his smile ruefully. 'You're not the only one who's surprised. Perhaps he hasn't got over it yet.'

To both men's relief the subject was not mentioned again that morning. Yet it remained in each other's mind. Chalmont because of his history, Richards because of his awakened misgivings. Neither, however, had the slightest suspicion of the dramas and tragedies that would arise from the subject in the days ahead.

While the two crewmen were making their preparations, Moore, Harvey and Adams were entering Henderson's office. The Scot did not beat about the bush when the door was closed. His first words were directed at Harvey like bullets from a VGO. 'What's the matter with that kid of yours, Harvey? Why didn't you let me know he's a barbary young bastard?'

Harvey never took well to aggression. His expression turned as dark as storm clouds over his native fells. 'How could I tell you? He's only been here a couple of weeks. I'd no more idea he was going to act that way than you had.'

'But it's your job to know your men. You're their flight commander.'

Harvey was not having that. 'I only know whether they're good or bad in the air. Not whether they like Red Indians, Chinese or Frenchmen. That's not my job.'

Knowing Harvey was right, Henderson realized he had fired his volley too hastily. 'All right, what about his work? How do you find that?'

Harvey nodded down at a folder lying on Henderson's desk. 'Are those his documents?'

'Yes. The adjutant passed them over.'

'Then take a look at his training record, sir.'

'I have looked. And it's bloody good. But that's not the issue, is it? Has he caused you any trouble so far? Has he argued with you or disobeyed any orders?'

Adams held his breath as he waited for Harvey's reply. A bad liar, Harvey took a few seconds to answer. 'No, sir,' he said gruffly. 'So far he's been all right.'

Mentally congratulating Harvey, Adams switched his eyes to Moore and saw the young wing commander's lips twitch in amusement. Relieved Moore was not going to shop Harvey, Adams awaited his turn. It came a couple of seconds later. 'All right, Adams. It looks as if you're the only bugger who knows anything about the lad. So what were you going to tell me?'

Adams took a step forward. 'He's had a different background from most of the other crews, sir. I'm sure that accounts for what happened today.'

Henderson's brow furrowed. 'What sort of background? You mean he's served in some tin-pot air force where they allow kids to argue about their orders?'

Adams smiled. 'No, sir. He had a classical education and he spent some years in Spain during the Civil War. I think that accounts for what happened today.'

The Scot listened in silence while Adams told the rest of the story. When he finished, Henderson's expression was a mixture of interest and scepticism. He turned to Moore. 'What do you think, Ian? You're from a bloody classical background and you've always had a knack of getting into the minds of these kids. Could any of this account for his behaviour today?'

Moore laughed. 'I don't think his education has anything to do with it, sir, but I think his Guernica experience might. If he saw lots of civilians killed by aircraft when he was at his most impressionable age, it must have had a profound effect on him.'

Henderson's frown deepened. 'Then why did he volunteer for the air force.' He glanced at Harvey. 'He did volunteer, didn't he?'

Harvey nodded. Before he could speak, Adams broke in. 'An experience like that would make him want to get back at the Nazis, sir. But it would also make him want to protect civilians.'

Henderson grimaced. 'Trust me to get the odd sods.' His gaze travelled round the three officers. 'What's all this mean? That none of you think I should take the matter further?'

Adams and Moore nodded. Harvey only scowled. Henderson's eyes fixed on him. 'You don't think so, Harvey? Why?'

'I think he should be told not to question orders, sir. Certainly not in front of the other lads. It's bad for discipline and it's bad for morale.'

Henderson pursed his lips, then nodded. 'I'm inclined to agree with you. Do you want to do it?'

'Yes, sir. I had intended to anyway.'

Henderson gazed at the Yorkshireman's expression for a moment, then turned to Moore. 'On second thoughts, I think it's better you do it, Ian. He might take more notice of the officer who handles the briefings. It'll also help you to get inside of the kid and find out what makes him tick. All right?'

Moore shrugged. 'Yes, sir. Only I'd rather do it later if you don't mind. I want everyone on their toes for this operation.'

Henderson nodded. 'Yes, fair enough. Group want a good job doing. All right. That's all. Good luck this afternoon.'

Harvey threw up a salute and was gone almost before the words had left Henderson's mouth. Meeting Moore's eye, Adams had to suppress a smile when he caught the young wing commander's wink. Saluting in turn, both men left the office, leaving Henderson gazing down at Chalmont's documents.

CHAPTER 16

L ED BY MOORE, the sixteen Mosquitoes were skimming like flat
stones over the Channel. Tapping Moore's shoulder, Hopkinson
pointed to a dark grey object at two o'clock. Nodding, Moore
pointed at the flare chute. Ten seconds later a red flare shot out of A-
Apple and hissed into the swell below.

The message was not lost on the following crews. An enemy flak
ship was out there guarding the occupied coast. Venture too close and
a blizzard of fire could smash an aircraft out of the sky. Like a curling
whip, the Mosquitoes veered a few degrees to port. Although the
aircraft were now well out of range, a few venomous puffs of smoke
still broke behind them. As A-Apple settled back on course, Hopkinson
glanced at Moore. 'What do you think? Is there any point now in
keeping radio silence?'

The cockney was making the case that, having seen them, the flak
ship would already be in touch with German defences. Moore paused,
then shook his head. 'We'll keep on it a while, Hoppy. Maybe their
monitors won't be on good form today.' Then, as spray hissed in A-
Apple's propellers and spat on her windshield, he went on: 'But I think
we'll have to risk a little more altitude. It's getting rough down there.'

The sixteen Mosquitoes had flown in four tight echelons down to
the south coast, where they had topped up their tanks. When
Chalmont had puzzled over the formation, Richards had given the
explanation. 'It's because of Jerry's long-range radar. It seems it can
pick up our aircraft almost as soon as they take off. But if we fly in tight
echelon it merges on his screens. So hopefully it'll look to them as if
we're only four heavies. And when we vanish off their screens at
Manston they'll just think we've been having an air test.'

At that time a favourable Met report had suggested they could cross
the Channel at ultra low level and so surprise the Germans, as their
tactics had done during the supply-dropping operation. But now that
a strong westerly wind had arisen and was causing a heavy swell,

Moore had decided that if it was a choice of a watery grave or the threat of enemy radar, the latter was the lesser of the two evils. As the line of Mosquitoes followed Moore and rose to 150 feet, Richards nodded at the compromise. 'He's hoping we're still just under their radar.'

Chalmont made no comment. He had hardly spoken since they had left Sutton Craddock except to question their formation and Richards had thought it better to leave him alone. At least, he thought, Chalmont had made no further complaints during the squadron's preparations for the mission.

A second red flare shot from A-Apple. Enemy coast ahead and time to test guns. Wondering if Chalmont had noticed the signal, Richards was relieved when the pilot swung S-Suzy to starboard and thumbed his gun button. Whatever his private objections, Richards thought, at least he seemed prepared to carry out his orders.

Six minutes later, the Mosquitoes flashed over the French coast with its cliffs and shuttered holiday homes. Ahead Richards caught a glimpse of two gunners swinging a multi-barrelled pom-pom in his direction. A moment later a vicious fork of tracer shot out towards S-Suzy. For a moment Richards's spine cringed as he imagined the shells smashing through his unprotected seat and body. But S-Suzy did not shudder and in seconds the danger was passed.

With the treacherous sea left behind, Moore took his squadron down to ultra low level again. With Hoppy guiding him to a railway track, he flew along it with telegraph poles only yards below his wing tips. Acutely conscious that a single slip in concentration meant certain death, pilots had to focus their eyes at points half a mile ahead. Navigators had more freedom and although compelled to keep watch for enemy aircraft, they were also able to witness the effect their entry was causing, although images came and went at lightning speed. In a field alongside the rail track, two farm workers waved their arms frantically, reminding the crews they were flying over friendly territory. Startled cattle grazing on the next field took fright and bolted. Feeding starlings rose in a chattering cloud and were swept away. A road appeared alongside the rail track. A woman on a bicycle tried to wave but wobbled perilously instead. A bridge over a river appeared. Like horsemen taking a fence, the Mosquitoes rose over it and sank down. Hoppy glanced at his map then tapped Moore's arm. 'The main road coming up, skipper. You follow it to Soissons.'

The rail track sank into a cutting. Tall trees lined its banks, forcing the Mosquitoes to rise again. Their slipstreams flattened the budding leaves on their branches. A startled rook rose, struck Millburn's starboard wing, and was hurled away in a tangle of blood and feathers. Gabby gave a grimace. 'That's how I'm feeling. Shattered.'

Unable to turn his eyes for a second, Millburn gave an unsympathetic grunt. 'What do you expect after the booze you drank last night? If I'd shown any sense I'd have asked Moore for a sober navigator.'

Gabby gave him an indignant glare. '*You* should have asked? What about me? I'm out here with a drunken zombie. And he's the bloody pilot.'

Millburn, who had a headache, gave a growl. 'Keep quiet, you little fart. This job's tough enough without your bellyaching.'

Ahead Hoppy was pointing at a rail crossing. 'There's the road, skipper.'

Nodding, Moore waited a few seconds, then waggled A-Apple's wings. As he swung ninety degrees to starboard, the pilots behind him reacted as one man and followed him eastward along the wide road.

Here the atmosphere changed as the German occupation became visible. Two enemy transports, driving in the opposite direction, braked and soldiers were seen raising rifles before the Mosquitoes' speed carried them out of range. A high road bridge appeared ahead, guarded by a 37mm flak post. As the Mosquitoes roared towards it, gunners could be seen trying frantically to rip tarpaulins off their guns but there was no time before the line of aircraft had leapt the bridge. As A-Apple squatted down on the road again, Hoppy turned to Moore. 'Their Observer Corps must have some idea by this time where we're heading, skipper. Do you think they'll vector any fighters our way?'

Moore shrugged. 'Who can say, Hoppy? Let's just hope Group are right and the Yanks are keeping them too busy.'

Five minutes more and a crenulated line of buildings appeared on the skyline. Hoppy nodded at Moore's comment. 'That's it, skipper. Soissons.'

'What's the time?'

'17.20, skipper. Ten minutes to ETA.'

In years to come, men would not believe that aircraft could fly hundreds of miles over enemy territory and still be within minutes or even seconds of their estimated time of arrival. But it was done many times and 633 Squadron was a master at the skills. Moore waited another minute, then addressed his R/T. 'Swordfish Leader to Red and Blue Sections. Target coming up. Orbit when I tell you. Navigators keep close watch for bandits.'

With radio silence broken, crews knew the need for vigilance was greater than ever, although pilots were at least able to rub their strained eyes and relax their muscles as Moore led them to a higher altitude. Below, the suburbs of Soissons were sliding past while at the same time the town's defences were coming to life. Red-cored explosions began bursting around the climbing Mosquitoes and a hole the size of a football appeared in Blue Four's starboard wing. Andy Larkin, its New Zealand pilot, gave a startled look at his navigator. 'Why so much flak? They're guarding it the way they do their own cities.'

His navigator was showing equal surprise. 'It looks as if Group are right and they've put a high price on this factory.'

With the industrial part of the town sliding into view below, Moore ordered the squadron into a wide orbit. At his glance, Hoppy nodded. 'Only ninety seconds more, skipper.'

Although the afternoon light was still good, there was an industrial haze over the buildings and factories below. 'Can you pinpoint the factory?' Moore asked.

Ignoring the flak that was rocking A-Apple, Hopkinson studied a map of the town. After a few seconds he pointed down at a large complex of buildings on both sides of a railway line. Among them was a church and a large cemetery. 'It should be somewhere down there, skipper, but don't ask me where. You have to give it to the Jerries. They're brilliant at camouflage.'

Aware that fighters might already have been vectored towards them, Moore studied his own watch. When 17.30 came and went, he was considering his options if the partisans failed him when there was a sudden yell from Hopkinson. 'Down there, skipper! Target flares.'

Staring down, Moore saw brilliant green flares had burst into life to form the four corners of a large square. Inside the square was the church and cemetery. Hopkinson's excited yell changed in tone. 'The church! What the hell's going on?'

Moore gave a laugh. 'Don't you get it? That's the camouflage.'

Hopkinson swore. 'The clever bastards.'

Moore wasted no more time. 'Swordfish Leader. There's your target. Attack after me at twenty second intervals. Then give cover.'

As he gave the order Moore was already diving down. Levelling off at 500 feet, he headed for the centre of the illuminated square. A few seconds later A-Apple gave a jerk as her 500lb heavy case bombs plunged down. As she banked and climbed away, the ten second delays on the bombs exploded and debris and blazing shreds of netting were flung high into the air. As shouts of triumph came over the radio, Moore's voice quelled them. 'Carry on, Red Section. Twenty seconds apart.'

One after another the Mosquitoes of Harvey's flight went down. By the time it was S-Suzy's turn, the camouflage netting had been entirely burned or blown away and the huge factory beneath it was visible. With fire and smoke raging a hundred feet high, it was not possible to determine the extent of the damage or to see any of its personnel, but with the eastern part of the main building and a number of outhouses still intact, the raid had to continue.

Richards had expected some comment from Chalmont when their turn came to attack but there was none. Only the pilot's expression betrayed his feelings as he flew S-Suzy so low that the smoke from the devastated factory momentarily swept past her cockpit. Waiting until the eastern end of the building swept towards him, Richards dropped his full complement of bombs and then yelled for Chalmont to climb away. As S-Suzy swooped up towards the orbiting Mosquitoes, the heavy thumps that jolted her told Richards his bombs had exploded.

Although by this time the green flares had burned out, the factory compound needed no identification now. By the time Young's Blue Section had dropped all its bombs, the main factory, its outhouses and its transport yard were covered in a massive cloud of smoke through which lurid and devouring flames could be seen. If anything was certain in wartime it was that the French factory would never produce aircraft parts for Germany again.

Not that there was any jubilation among the Mosquito crews. Although all believed they had attacked the factory at the best time to keep French casualties down to the minimum, they were still aware that many men must have died and the radio waves were unusually quiet when Moore gave orders for the squadron to break from its orbit and formate behind him.

To this point the crews knew they had been lucky. Although by this time in the war it was true that the combined raids of British and American bombers, which had almost reached their peak, were forcing the Germans to deploy more and more fighters against them, there were still plenty of bases in France and the Netherlands where fighters were kept to discourage Allied mine laying and other excursions against the occupied countries. Fully aware of this and knowing their objective and their success would now be fully known to German controllers, crews were wondering if this was going to be one of those lucky missions when both crews and aircraft returned unscathed.

Their first intimation it might be otherwise came when they were breaking orbit to formate behind Moore. Below, the enemy gunners whose task was to defend Soissons's industrial complex were being urged on by their NCOs to gain some revenge out of the disaster. As their rate of fire increased and the deadly explosions of 37mm and 88mm shells made a net around the Mosquitoes, Moore glanced at the startled Hopkinson. 'I don't think they like what we've done, Hoppy.'

The cockney winced as an exploding shell rocked A-Apple like a rowing boat in a storm. 'I think you're right, skipper.'

The sixteen Mosquitoes had almost cleared the barrage when a shell exploded a few feet beneath F-Freddy, flown by the South African Van Breedenkamp. A calm voice notified Moore a few seconds later. 'Blue Three here, Swordfish Leader. Some of my hydraulics have gone and my port engine's losing revs.'

'Hello, Blue Three. Can you stay with us?'

'I doubt it, skipper. My undercarriage is down.'

'Hang on, Blue Three. We'll cover you as long as we can.'

Under Moore's orders, the Mosquitoes formed a phalanx around the stricken F-Freddy. In S-Suzy, Chalmont, who had barely spoken to Richards since the raid on the factory, now glanced at him. 'How much further to the coast?'

'About twenty minutes,' Richards told him. Guessing the reason behind Chalmont's question, he went on: 'At this speed we'll be lucky to make it without interception.'

Knowing their presence must be known to every enemy controller by this time, it had been Moore's intention to make height on their return, so giving them the dying sun if they were attacked. Now, with Van Breedenkamp unable to climb because of F-Freddy's damage, the squadron was caught at 5,000 feet, a height that was the worst of two worlds if enemy interception occurred.

Yet the squadron might have escaped but for a second stroke of bad luck. High to the north, two *staffels* of Fokker 190s had only recently broken off an attack on an armada of American B–17s. Ordered to intercept the bombers on their return from Regensberg in Germany, they had harried them until the B–17s had come within range of British-based Thunderbolts and Spitfires. Ordered to disengage, they were about to return to their base on the Pas de Calais when their controller had received news of 633 Squadron's invasion into France.

At first he had ignored the news, conscious his pilots were in need of rest. But someone higher up in the chain of command had overridden him and the order came that the two *staffels* must fly south and try to intercept the Mosquito raiders.

Because of the Mosquitoes' speed and tactics, this had proved impossible until the mission was accomplished and the factory destroyed. But now, high up among the late afternoon clouds, the 190s had caught sight of the phalanx of Mosquitoes and tired pilots felt new life enter their veins. Many Luftwaffe fighter pilots valued the destruction of a Mosquito more than a Lancaster or a B–17 because of the wooden fighter-bomber's astonishing performance.

Their jubilance was partly due to the aircraft they were flying, the latest 190 with 801 engines and Mauser 151s high-velocity cannon. While it was known the Mosquito had the edge in speed on both the 109 and the earlier 190s, which made pilots wary about engaging them, their latest 190 was a few miles an hour faster at sea level and the phalanx of Mosquitoes was within that definition. Moreover, their present speed and formation suggested they were handicapped by a crippled aircraft.

With conditions better than he could have hoped for, the *Kommodore* gave orders to attack. Seconds later the pack of 190s came down from the late afternoon sky like gannets diving for fish.

It was the eagle eyes of Hopkinson who saw them first 'Bandits, skipper! 190s. Six o'clock high.'

In normal circumstances and at operational height, Moore might have engaged them. The slight difference in speed between the aircraft could be compensated for by a pilot's skill and Moore had an abundance of such pilots. In addition, because of the many roles his special service squadron had to play, his Mosquitoes were specially equipped with short-barrelled Hispano cannon as well as bomb bays, something the German commander might not know.

But with a crippled aircraft to guard, it was no time for defiance. The coast was near and Moore knew that, if the 190s could be held off long enough, home-based fighters would be sent out to help. As the German pilots would know that also, the fight could not be prolonged. Accordingly, he gave the order to dive and fly at ultra low level again.

To Chalmont the order seemed suicidal. Ultra low level gave no room for manoeuvre or evasion of any kind. In the seconds left to him, Richards tried to explain. 'It'll be more difficult for them to dive on us. They could overshoot and hit a tree or a telegraph pole.'

Chalmont shook his head. 'But we'll be helpless. We can't twist or turn.'

'That doesn't matter. They won't be able to train their guns.'

'Why not? They can line up behind us.'

'Not necessarily. Many of their latest 190s have been modified so their guns are set up at two degrees. This forces them to fly below Lancs and Fortresses when they open fire. It's a safety factor to prevent pilots flying slap into a bomber's field of fire. Moore knows this. That's why he's brought us down.'

Chalmont was quick to grasp the tactic. 'So it depends whether these 190s have been modified or not?'

Richards twisted round in his seat, trying to spot the diving 190s. 'That's right. One thing is for sure. We'll soon find out.'

CHAPTER 17

THE NEXT FEW seconds were torment for the Mosquito crews. Although they knew it was more than likely the 190s had been adapted, the possibility existed their guns were still sighted and harmonized in the usual way, which almost certainly meant casualties among the rearmost Mosquitoes before the rest could rise and do battle.

The possible victims belonged to Harvey's flight. With F-Freddy one of Teddy Young's aircraft, Blue flight had the task of giving the crippled Mosquito cover. In the way of the squadron, Red Section provided a back-up protection which meant Harvey and his men formed the rearguard.

There was no possibility now of the squadron flying line abreast, not with the handicapped F-Freddy reducing the speed and the 190s almost in contact. The Mosquitoes were on both sides of F-Freddy and flying well apart from one another so as to present as difficult a target as possible. But as the 190s closed in, pilots were hugging the ground even closer than on their incursion into France. Every pilot knew that his life and the life of his navigator might depend on his ability to fly closer to the ground than the enemy behind him.

No one was better at this than Millburn. As T-Tommy leapfrogged a clump of trees, the aircraft shuddered as a wingtip caught a clump of twigs. Gabby gave a yell. 'What the hell are you doing, Millburn? This is a kite, not a bloody tank.'

Millburn, his forehead beaded with sweat, let out a curse. 'Stop moaning, you little fart. You rather those 190s get you up the arse?'

The pursuing 190s were close enough now for navigators to see their details, the menacing cowlings that contained their powerful engines, their long cupolas and short wings. The combined roar of their engines and the Mosquitoes' Merlins could be heard miles away. Men and women ran out of houses and farms to see what was happening. As they listened they heard the staccato drumming of cannon fire. The

190s were now down to ground level and picking targets for themselves, only to discover as gun buttons were pressed that their tracer shells lanced up and over the Mosquitoes.

Ironically, the first casualty came not from the Mosquitoes but from their pursuers. Determined to have a prized Mosquito on his list of kills, a young German pilot, frustrated by his inability to line his guns on Red Three, saw the Mosquito approaching a road bridge. With his eyes fixed on Red Three, the pilot waited a split second too long for the Mosquito to rise into his field of fire.

It was a fatal mistake. Intent on his prey, the German pilot suddenly saw the bridge looming into his windshield. Before his shout of alarm could leave his throat, his 190 smashed into the bridge like a high explosive bomb. Even at the speed they were travelling, some of Harvey's crews saw the vivid flash in their mirrors. Harvey was one and his satisfied comment was typical of the rugged flight commander. 'That's one of the buggers gone.'

It was also a warning to the *Kommodore* of the 190s, who transmitted a message to his pilots. They must be patient and wait. One of the Tommies must make a mistake sooner or later. Take no further chances until they do.

The first mistake came from Red Five. Leapfrogging over the small wood, he was slow to bring his aircraft down on the far side. His pursuer, an experienced pilot who had flown in both Italy and North Africa, was not slow to take his chance. His burst of fire first exploded into the wood, pulverizing and smashing off branches, but his second burst struck the rear fuselage of Red Five, causing her to swing violently before Baldwin, her pilot, got control of her again. A second Mosquito of Red Section had a cannon burst drill large holes in her port wing but again no mortal damage was done.

The Mosquitoes were nearing the coast now and the *Kommodore* knew time was running short. Home-based Spitfires would already have been alerted and might even be scrambled. More importantly his 190s would be getting low on fuel after their attacks on the B–17s. As the two formations of aircraft swept over the cliffs, with German NCOs yelling at gunners not to shoot because of the 190s, the *Kommodore* decided he had only minutes left to make a killing.

The cliffs fell away to a strip of beach and then the tossing sea. No opportunity now to fly at a safe height. Mosquitoes were forced to squat down so low their windshields kept misting from the windblown spray. Aggressive pilots like Millburn and Harvey were chafing at their role of the hunted but all crews knew that if they turned and did battle the crippled F-Freddy would never survive against the rapacious 190s. Their day for revenge would come later. As it was, they were fully engaged in keeping the hungry sea from devouring them.

A last glance at his own fuel gauge told the *Kommodore* he could stretch out the pursuit no longer. As it was, his two *staffels* would have to forget their Pas de Calais base and make for the one near La Hague. Reluctantly he sent out his call sign and ordered his pilots to break away.

What the *Kommodore* did not know was the deteriorating condition of F-Freddy. For long minutes Van Breedenkamp had been eyeing the temperature gauges of his two engines. The needle of the damaged one had been in the red sector almost since he had left Soissons and vaporized glycol had been streaming from it almost as long. Now the needle of the port engine was creeping towards the danger zone. Although in normal circumstances a Mosquito could fly on one engine, the need to fly at the highest speed possible with the impediment of a dangling undercarriage was proving a strain even for a legendary Merlin engine.

With F-Freddy's airspeed dropping further, Moore was growing anxious about the fuel situation in all his aircraft. Aircraft carried only enough fuel for the demands of their operation and no one had expected a return flight at low level, with the extra fuel such a trip demanded. Too much of a professional to risk his squadron for a single crippled aircraft, Moore nevertheless hated the thought of abandoning Van Breedenkamp when the English coast was just over the horizon and when Spitfires were almost certainly on the way to help. He had just decided to hang on a few minutes longer when there was a shout over the R/T from Harvey. 'Red Zero to Swordfish Leader. They're breaking off, Ian. They must be running out of fuel.'

Moore saw he was right. The 190s were turning to port and starboard and climbing away. Relieved, Moore contacted Van Breedenkamp. 'You should be OK now, Van, if I leave you a wingman. Make for Holmsley. Red Four. Do the honours, will you?'

Richards could not believe what he was hearing. Red Four was S-Suzy. As Chalmont gave him a surprised glance, Harvey's protest came over the R/T. 'Red Four's the new kid, Swordfish Leader. Let me or Millburn do the job.'

Moore's reply brooked no argument. 'Red Four is to give cover, Red Zero. At the double.'

Before the angry Harvey could reply, Moore switched off his R/T. Hopkinson was grinning. 'He'll poison your beer tonight, skipper. Better watch out.'

Moore laughed. 'I think you might be right, Hoppy.'

With the 190s sweeping away to the east, the Mosquitoes were freed from the tyranny of low-level flying. Climbing up from the sea, Millburn grinned at Gabby. 'That's put our tyke in his place. But why has Moore chosen the kid?'

Gabby shrugged. 'Maybe to test him out. But who cares? It's time someone else played the bloody policeman.'

With the squadron freed at last from their task, pilots were able to advance their throttles and soon F-Freddy and S-Suzy were the only two Mosquitoes visible against the tossing waves. The fact was noticed with intense interest by the pilot of a solitary 190 lurking in a cloud formation above. Hans Behr, the son of an ex-army brigadier who had won the Iron Cross 1st Class for conspicuous gallantry during World War I, was due for leave shortly and wanted nothing more than to boast an equivalent medal when visiting his proud and distinguished father. Young Hans had never received the same paternal treatment as his older brother Johann, now an officer in the Wehrmacht, and one more kill would win him the prize that so far had eluded Johann.

Behr was a member of the staffels detailed to engage the Americans but engine trouble had held him back and he had only joined them on their return from the German frontier. Consequently, to his frustration, he had missed an opportunity to shoot down one of the invading bombers. The advent of the Mosquitoes had seemed a gift from the gods but their tactics had proved yet another blow to his ambitions. Now, with his leave only days away, his frustration was intense, particularly when his *Kommodore* had ordered the 190s to abandon the chase.

Not by nature disobedient, Hans would have obeyed the order but for one thing. Whereas his comrades had nearly empty fuel tanks, his were still a third full because of his earlier abbreviated mission. The combination of frustration and adequacy of fuel had proved too much for the ambitious Hans. Switching off his radio so he could not pick up any adverse orders, he had detached himself from his comrades when they had reached the low evening clouds and under cover of them was now tracking the squadron of Mosquitoes.

Not being a fool, he had no intention of attacking the phalanx on his own. He knew the capability of the Mosquitoes and also knew the danger from home-based Spitfires. But he could also imagine the stress the Mosquito pilots would have been under in protecting their crippled member and guessed they might leave the slower F-Freddy when they felt the aircraft was safe from attack.

With his guess now proven right, with only one serviceable

Mosquito giving cover, Behr decided the gods had relented in his favour. For with the threat of the 190s removed, the pilot in F-Freddy had managed to coax his machine a few hundred feet above the dangerous swell, which meant both Mosquitoes could be within the range of his 190's guns. Thus Behr knew he had only to shoot down the covering Mosquito and the crippled one would be his also. Two kills and the Iron Cross would be firmly round his neck. Pushing his stick forward, Behr came down from the fading sky like a hungry falcon.

In S-Suzy, Chalmont was as curious as the rest of the squadron. 'Why did Moore choose us?'

By this time Richards had his suspicions but it seemed no time to vent them. 'We'll find out later. In the meantime, let's do a good job.'

Shrugging, Chalmont swung S-Suzy in closer behind F-Freddy. To the diving Behr they looked like two cormorants silhouetted against the tossing sea. As they grew larger in his windshield, his thumb moved to his gun button. If he were not seen, these could be the easiest kills of his career.

He would not have been seen but for Van Breedenkamp's navigator. Locked in the cockpit of F-Freddy, conscious of the struggle his pilot was having in keeping the Mosquito airborne, Thomas's vigilance was honed by his knowledge of their helplessness should an attack come. As he searched the dangerous sky above and behind for a hundredth time, he gave a violent start and then a yell into the R/T. 'Bandit, Red Four! Break to port! Break to port!'

Richards twisted round in his seat, only for sea and sky to swim dizzily around the cupola as Chalmont obeyed the frantic call. As centrifugal forces rammed him down in his seat, he saw a stream of deadly cannon tracer flash beneath S-Suzy's right wingtip. The G forces increased, straining his twisted body as Chalmont increased the Mosquito's banking turn. As Richards struggled to regain his posture, he caught a glimpse of Behr's 190 as the German tried to match the Mosquito's turning circle.

Unable to help, Richards suffered the helpless torment of all naviga-tors as he was flung against his seat straps one way and the other while the two aircraft fought for supremacy. Beside him he could hear Chalmont's heavy breathing as the young pilot struggled first to escape from the 190's gunsights and then tried in turn to fire at the twisting, swooping 190.

For a moment the mad vortex steadied down as Behr turned his attention on the less manoeuvrable F-Freddy but immediately Chalmont made it clear he would rather die than allow F-Freddy to perish. Flying like a madman, he flew straight at the 190, forcing Behr to break away to avoid collision. As the startled German climbed for height, a burst of cannon fire followed him and almost severed his stubby starboard wing.

Behr was a brave man but he knew he had met more than his match today in this madman. The crippled Mosquito he could probably destroy but he would almost certainly be killed in the process and an Iron Cross would give little satisfaction if it left him unable to hear his father's acclaim. Also his fuel tank would take little more of the action he had just encountered. Reluctantly, Behr continued his climb into the early evening sky, accepting that his Iron Cross would have to wait yet another day.

For a moment it seemed Chalmont would follow him. Then, drenched in sweat, he turned to Richards. 'That was close.'

Richards, equally drenched and breathless, managed a nod. 'Too close. Are we still alive?'

'I think so. Just about.'

The voice over the R/T carried a South African accent. 'That was a hell of a job, Red Four. The drinks are on me tonight.'

Richards was the first to get his breath back. 'We won't say no, F-Freddy. Where are you heading?'

'We think we can make Holmsley. What will you do?'

Chalmont answered for Richards. 'We'd better get back to Sutton Craddock. But we'll see you safe at Holmsley first.'

CHAPTER 18

OIX PAUSED IN the narrow street and listened. The marching booted footsteps were growing louder. Breaking into a run, he found a passageway and slipped into its entrance. Pausing there, he listened again. The footsteps had a metallic ring in the silent town. Four soldiers with an NCO, he estimated.

Controlling his breathing, he waited. The footsteps were loud now and menacing in their precision. Somewhere among the darkened houses a dog barked. Otherwise there was nothing but the footsteps. The curfew had been on for two hours and men and women who cared for their lives were long indoors.

Now the boots were reverberating across the narrow street, over which a sliver of new moon was poised. Foix shrank against a side wall, praying the darkness in the passageway gave him protection. As the patrol came level with him, the thin moonlight shone for a moment on metal helmets and slung rifles, an impression of brutal military efficiency. Then the patrol had passed and relief slowed down the heartbeat of the hiding man.

He waited a full three minutes before slipping out of the passageway. As alert as a prowling cat, he hurried down the street until he reached a house opposite an extinguished street lamp. Here he paused to listen. Then, reassured, he tapped on its door. He let five seconds pass, then tapped again. This time the door was opened and he slipped inside. The door was swiftly closed and a blackout curtain dragged over it before the light was switched on, revealing Pierre Levrey as the only occupant in the room. His voice was eager. 'Well? Did you get it?'

Foix nodded at a door at the far side of the room. 'Is Arnaud here?'

'Yes. He went to bed early. He said he had no sleep at all last night.'

Foix's voice was bitter. 'I don't wonder.'

Levrey raised an eyebrow. 'What does that mean?'

Foix spoke to him in low tones for the next couple of minutes. When he finished, Levrey looked pale and shocked. 'Are you sure of this?'

Foix nodded. 'Certain. I had it checked.'

Levrey glanced at the door across the room. 'But surely he can't have known.'

'The bastard knew all right. Otherwise why was he so insistent the attack came on time?'

Levrey was finding it hard to believe. 'But then why did de Gaulle give permission?'

'De Gaulle's in England. He can only work on the information he gets from here.'

Dismay was written all over Levrey's face. 'And we're the ones who gave it to him.'

Foix's laugh dripped with bitterness. 'You mean *I'm* the one who gave it.'

Levrey took a deep, steadying breath. 'What are we going to do now?'

'What can we do? Only explain what happened and hope London and de Gaulle still trust us in the future.'

'Do you think they will?'

'Who can say? But there's one thing I do know.' The glance Foix gave across the room was unusual for such a normally well-adjusted man. 'I want to kill that bastard in the room upstairs. I hope the day comes when I get the chance.'

Harvey's resentment was matched only by his curiosity. 'Why the hell did you do it, Ian? It was a job for an experienced man. Both Millburn and I would have been happy to do it for Van.'

Moore nodded. 'I know that, Frank.'

'Then why? Chalmont's a sprog pilot.'

'Yes, he is. But he's also a good one. You've only to ask Millburn or to look at his documents to see that.'

'Good pilot's one thing. Experience is something else. I don't get it, Ian. Why did you do it?'

Even-tempered though he was, Moore was not one to have his orders questioned. 'I had my reasons, Frank. Let's leave it there, shall we?'

With Harvey in his present mood, it was perhaps fortunate there was a tap on Moore's office door at that moment. A young Waaf appeared in the doorway. Seeing Harvey standing inside, she apologized. 'Sorry, sir, but Holmsley are on the phone. Do you want a word with the adjutant?'

Moore nodded. 'Yes. Put him through, Tess.' As the girl went back to her office, Moore glanced at Harvey as he picked up his phone. 'Now we can find out exactly what happened.'

Harvey's puzzled eyes watched Moore as the young wing commander took in details from the adjutant. 'So no one is injured? Good. You say Chalmont is flying back after refuelling? What about Flight Lieutenant Van Breedenkamp? You'll have him flown back tomorrow. Thank you, sir. Sorry for any trouble we've caused you.'

Replacing the phone, Moore turned to Harvey. 'Can you believe it? A 190 attacked them after we left.'

Harvey gave a start. 'But they all pissed off halfway across the Channel.'

'All but one. And it seems this sprog pilot of yours put up a good fight. He didn't shoot the 190 down but did enough to send it off with its tail between its legs. Van Breedenkamp saw it all and was impressed. And grateful, as you can imagine.'

Harvey showed surprise, then rallied. 'All the more reason why you should have sent me or Millburn to handle it. I said it wasn't a job for a new kid.'

Moore was not one to make excuses when proven wrong. 'As it happened, it would have been better. But, like you, I didn't know there was a lone 190 lurking about. The point is the kid did a good job and deserves credit for it.'

Harvey scowled. 'I suppose that means you're not going to give him the bollocking he deserves for his performance this morning.'

'I'll think about it, Frank. I agree he can't go off shouting his mouth like that at briefings but if what the adjutant says is true, he's the kind of man we want. Leave it for the moment while I—'

At that moment the telephone rang again. 'Yes, Tess. What is it this time?'

'It's the CO, sir. He says you and Mr Harvey have to go to his office right away.'

'Did he say what for?'

'No, sir. But it sounded very urgent.'

Henderson was standing looking out of his window when Moore and Harvey entered. As he turned, Moore noticed he was holding a slip of paper. Ignoring the salute the two men gave him, he held out the paper to Moore. Moore glanced at it then gave a violent start. 'Who told you this, sir?'

'Davies,' Henderson grunted. 'He was on the scrambler ten minutes ago. I wrote down the details.'

'Do you think it's true?'

Henderson lifted his wide shoulders. 'Davies believes it. And he was told it by Simms. If the SOE believe it, it must be true.'

'But then who sent over the details and the instructions in the first place?'

'How the hell do I know? But they can't have been more wrong, can they?'

'Can Harvey see this?' Moore asked, seeing the Yorkshireman's curiosity.

Henderson turned back to the window. 'That's why I called you both in.'

Harvey scanned the paper, then gave a whistle of shock. 'So many?'

'Davies says that's the minimum,' the Scot told him. 'There could be more.'

'What does de Gaulle say? Does he know about this?'

Henderson's eyes were on two Waafs laughing and joking as they crossed the path in front of the adminstration block but he was not seeing them. 'He must have heard, for Christ's sake. I shouldn't think he's the happiest Frenchman in the world at this moment, would you?'

Harvey was never one to cry in his beer about the feelings of politicians. He shrugged as he handed the slip back to Moore. 'That's his problem. He's lucky he didn't have to do the job himself. I wonder how he'd feel then.'

His comment brought a bitter laugh from Henderson. 'It's ironic, isn't it? I tore that new kid off a strip for complaining about the job but it looks as if he was right after all. We didn't just kill a few Frenchmen; we killed the entire bloody night shift. All because some sod gave us the wrong time.'

'Do you think it could have been deliberate?' Moore asked. 'Could someone over there have hated the factory staff so much for working for the Germans that he chose this way to punish them?'

Henderson scowled as he took back his piece of paper. 'It's possible, I suppose. But one thing is for sure. We'd better not let this new kid know about it or he'll be doing our briefings himself in the future.'

'Who else knows about it?' Moore asked.

'Adams. I had to tell him to keep his records straight.'

'If I know Frank he'd be shocked.'

Henderson frowned. 'He was.' The Scot paused and then went on: 'I want this keeping quiet. You never know what other jobs might come along and some of the lads might start feeling like Chalmont. So keep it to yourselves for the moment. All right, you can go now.'

The officers saluted and left the office. In the corridor outside, Harvey glanced at Moore. 'Do you think it was deliberate or just a cock-up?'

With no one else but Harvey to hear him, Moore made no attempt to hide his feelings. 'Who can say, Frank? Only that war's a filthy business and this one's getting filthier by the day.'

CHAPTER 19

S-SUZY ARRIVED BACK at Sutton Craddock after 2100 hours and needed the flare path lights to help her landing. A transport raced out for the crew and took them straight to Adams's confessional. With knowledge of the tragedy that lay behind the operation and perhaps understanding better than anyone on the station the depth of Chalmont's concern for the bombing of civilians, Adams trod carefully as he debriefed the two men.

'I've got from the other crews the details of the factory and its demolition, so we can move on to what happened over the Channel.' Adams's bespectacled eyes moved to Chalmont. 'The squadron commander told me he ordered you to give protection to Van Breedenkamp when the 190s gave up their attack. Is it correct that you were attacked by a single 190 only a few minutes after the main squadron had gone?'

Chalmont nodded. Like Richards alongside him, his appearance shared that of the many crews Adams had debriefed after combat: the slightly sunken eyes, the thinning of cheeks, the smell of sweat and oil, the after effects of fear and tension. 'Yes, sir.'

'Did you sight the 190 before it attacked you?'

'No, sir. The warning came from F-Freddy.'

Adams liked the honesty of the answer. 'Did he fire on you first or on Freddy?'

'Us, sir. We were astern of F-Freddy.'

'He didn't hit you, did he?'

'No. The warning came in time from F-Freddy. I turned to port and his first burst went by my starboard wing.'

'And then?'

'I don't remember much after that, sir. It all became a bit of a circus.'

'Did you get a shot at him?'

'I think I fired a couple of times, sir.'

'Did you hit him?'

'No, I don't think so.'

118

'Pity. Then we can't put down a damaged aircraft to your credit. Never mind. You did well.' Adams turned to Richards. 'How about you, Richards? Have you any comments to add?'

Richards lowered the cigarette he was smoking. 'Not really, sir. Only that Chalmont put up a hell of a fight. I think he put the fear of God into that Jerry pilot.'

Adams smiled at the compliment. 'It certainly looks that way. I'm certain Van Breedenkamp will endorse everything you say when he gets back tomorrow.'

Adams asked a few more questions before the debriefing was over, then allowed the two men to leave. Sue Spencer, who usually stayed on duty with Adams in case he needed assistance, gave him a smile when the two men left the hut. 'You like those two, don't you, Frank?'

Adams took off his glasses and wiped them, a habitual gesture when he was emotionally embarrassed. 'I suppose I do. I know Chalmont isn't everyone's cup of tea after the things he said this morning but I believe the lad is a bit special. I also like Richards. He's a thoughtful kid who seems to have a balanced view on everything we're doing here.'

Sue gave the affectionate laugh that Adams had always found attractive. 'You always think the best of people, don't you, Frank?'

Adams held his glasses up to the light, squinting to see if any dust or mist remained. 'I don't know about that. But I think I'm right about those two kids.'

Neither Richards nor Chalmont spent long in the mess that night. Both were feeling drained and exhausted after their experience and after a meal they found a couple of beers was all they wanted.

Another reason was the emptiness of the mess. After a successful operation it was almost a tradition for the squadron to congregate in The Black Swan and tonight was no exception. Apart from a few ground staff and non-flying specialist officers, the mess was empty and both men retired to their billet soon after 22.30.

It was there Richards found a letter and a note resting on his bed. The note was an apology from the guardroom at the letter's late delivery. The address on the envelope was in a handwriting Richards did not recognize. It was only when he tore open the envelope and pulled out the single sheet of notepaper that he gave a start. Noticing it, Chalmont displayed curiosity. 'Good news?'

For a moment Richards was too busy with the letter to answer. Then he gave an excited nod. 'It's from Hilary.'

Chalmont grimaced. 'You must have made an impression. I hadn't expected you'd hear from her for a month at least.'

Richards was devouring the letter. 'Listen to this. You remember that posting to York she was expecting? It came through. She moved up this week.'

Chalmont grinned. 'Only forty or so miles away? I suppose you'll be putting in for forty-eight hour passes now?'

Richards's eyes shone. 'Do you think she'll see me if I do?'

Chalmont's reply was full of the goodwill between siblings. 'She'd better or she'll get hell from me. But when do you think we're going to get forty-eight hour passes?'

Richards was not listening. Lonely man that he was, he was devouring the letter again, searching for some word or phrase that suggested the girl had some interest in him other than that he was her brother's friend and navigator. But he could find nothing that a woman would not write to any acquaintance of her family. Indeed, if he were truthful to himself, it was a letter that contained all the indifference she had shown at their meeting in Hereford.

It was only in bed that the thought struck him. Why had she bothered to tell him she had moved up to York? If she had no feelings for him, would she have mentioned that? She must know it would make him want to visit her. Why would she do that to a man who did not interest her?

The thought, thin though it was, represented hope and Richards accepted it gladly. Like so many sensitive men who flew combat missions, the night after an operation could summon many demons unless alcohol was there to anaesthetize the mind. With no drug potent enough to aid him this night, Richards used his thoughts of Hilary to keep his personal demons at bay.

The Waaf tapped on the door, then opened it. 'Pilot Officer Chalmont is here, sir.'

Moore lowered his pen to the desk. 'Send him in, Tess.'

Chalmont entered the office a moment later. As he came to attention and saluted, Moore waved him to a chair. 'Sit down, Chalmont. Smoke if you want to.' When Chalmont hesitated, Moore gave him a smile. 'I'm not going to bite you so please sit down. It'll be more comfortable for both of us.'

This time the young pilot obeyed. Offering him a cigarette only to have it refused, Moore rocked back in his chair. 'You know why I wanted to see you this morning, don't you?'

'Yes, I think so, sir. You didn't like the things I said at the briefing yesterday.'

Moore laughed. 'Why am I bothering to see you? You know it all already.' When Chalmont said nothing, Moore went on. 'No, there is something else first. You did a good job yesterday defending Van Breedenkamp and his navigator. Those 190s are good. In fact, they're the best kites the Germans have produced so far. So I want to congratulate you for scaring him off.'

Chalmont shifted uncomfortably in his chair. 'I don't know it was that, sir. He might have been short on fuel.'

'Maybe and maybe not. From what Van Breedenkamp says, you went at him like a mad bull. So I think we ought to give you the credit, don't you?'

Chalmont's comment was barely audible. 'Thank you, sir.'

Moore nodded. 'Now that's been said, let's take up my other reason for seeing you. Before I do, however, I should mention that Mr Adams has told me about your background in Spain. So I do understand your sentiments even if I can't approve of your questioning orders. Does that seem strange to you?'

'Not altogether, sir. I can see the difference.'

'I'm sure you can. You're an educated man. No one hates the killing of civilians more than I do. Nor do most of my men for that matter. But they're realists or have become realists since they were dragged into this war. They've learned what a dirty business war is, Chalmont. Something you learned in Spain even before they did.'

'Yes, sir. But then why didn't more of them complain about killing innocent workers? I didn't hear a single man back me up.'

If Moore had not guessed it before, he knew now this young man had the strength of will to defend his case against anyone, no matter what their rank. 'What are innocent workers, Chalmont? Isn't the man or woman who makes explosives and shells just as guilty as the soldier who uses them? You have science to blame for that. Once armies could create their own weapons although even then they needed armourers to help them. Today science has made everyone involved. So how do you fight a war without now and then attacking Mr and Mrs Everybody?'

Chalmont shook his head. 'I still think it's wrong, sir. I call it murder.'

Moore let his chair rock forward. 'Shall I tell you something, Chalmont? I call it murder too.'

His comment clearly rocked the young pilot. 'You, sir?

'Yes. Why not?'

'But you're a professional airman.'

'No, I'm not. I'm a volunteer like you. I've just been longer in the service than you have, that's all. So I've had more time to find out what a murderous business war is.'

Seeing how his words had surprised Chalmont, Moore went on: 'I know. I lead one of the most efficient killing machines in the country. But that doesn't mean I enjoy the work we do. This war did a cruel thing to our age group, Chalmont. It made us choose between the lesser of two evils. If we refused to fight we abandoned millions of innocent people to slavery or worse. If we chose to fight it meant we had to kill many people with whom we had no quarrel. A hell of a choice. Didn't you think that before you joined up? After all, you're a volunteer too.'

'Of course I gave it thought, sir. It was the reason I asked to join this squadron. I thought it was only used against military objectives.'

'Most of the time it is. But your common sense should have told you its operations couldn't always be that clear cut. Like that job we did yesterday. The CO was right in what he said. Allies or not, those French workers were just as big a threat to us as the enemy aircraft they were helping to build.'

'But those workers are forced by the Germans to do that work. It was like punishing slaves because of their enslavement. No one can tell me that's right or just.'

Moore wondered what this young man would say if he knew the full facts of the operation. 'I totally agree. War often turns right and justice upside-down. In fact, by and large war is a disgusting business and we who have volunteered to take part in it have to accept its filth and its slime. Perhaps that's our punishment for the human species being the most aggressive creature on earth. Perhaps when all is said and done we deserve it. Have you ever thought that?'

Chalmont was eyeing the wing commander with new respect. 'No, sir. But I can see your point.'

Moore rose to his feet. 'That's all, Chalmont. My lecture's over so now I'll let you go. Perhaps one of these days you and I and Mr Adams will have a long talk about the morality of war. You'll find he shares most of your views, if not all of them.'

Chalmont did not remember leaving the office. His only thought as he acknowledged Tess, who smiled at him through her open door, and made his way down the corridor, was that not once had Moore reprimanded him for his transgressions.

He found Richards waiting for him at the bar of the mess. Nodding at the waiter, Richards gave him a rueful grin. 'Well? How bad was it?'

'It wasn't bad at all,' Chalmont confessed. 'If he reprimanded me it was so painless I didn't feel it. All he talked about was war and how disgusting he found it.'

'Moore said that?'

'He said more than that. He agreed that killing civilians wasn't right or just. More or less what I said at the briefing.'

'Then what did he call you in for?'

Chalmont took the beer Richards had ordered for him. 'I don't honestly know. I suppose he wanted to show me that I wasn't the only man on the station who disliked yesterday's job.'

'You weren't,' Richards told him. 'I was one of them.'

'Yes, but none of you complained, did you? Moore said that was because you all felt it was necessary but I couldn't go with that.'

'Why not? Those workers were helping the German war effort.'

'So is every woman who nurses a German soldier's wounds but you don't want to murder them too, do you?'

Richards wondered if it was his newly awakened religious feelings or delayed shock that made his reply so aggressive. 'That's a stupid comparison. You're carrying this thing too far, Jeremy. It's become an obsession with you.'

Chalmont took a sip of beer. 'Moore might share your ideas on war but he doesn't share them on religion.'

Richards frowned. 'What does that mean?'

'He thinks we're the most aggressive animal on earth. That hardly fits in with your Christian belief that we're created in the image of God, does it? Unless God hasn't any objection to killing the odd innocent civilian himself.'

Richards flushed. 'Keep God and religion out of it, please. It's not my fault if the Nazis force these filthy jobs on us.'

Chalmont lowered his face to his glass, hiding his expression from the upset Richards. 'Put it any way you like, Mark, but to me it's still murder. And murder it always will be.'

CHAPTER 20

THERE WAS NO rest for the squadron crews during the next ten days. With the Allied offensive against the enemy communications now in full swing, barely a day passed when the squadron was not attacking marshalling yards, railheads, radar stations or the strange metal ramps that were beginning to appear along the French and Dutch coasts.

With men barely having time to breathe between briefings, combat activity, subsequent debriefings and the necessary intake of alcohol to dull the stress of the days, there was little time left to speculate on the peculiarities of the various crew members. Moreover, there was personal danger to occupy overtaxed minds. Ground attacks on relatively small targets meant facing LMG fire and during the ten days of action Harvey's Flight lost one crew and Teddy Young's lost two.

It was true that men had wondered about Chalmont after his behaviour during the factory briefing but his courageous defence of Van Breedenkamp and his subsequent conduct in the days that followed completed his restoration. Obeying orders meticulously and showing courage and dedication, Chalmont had quickly proved himself an excellent addition to the squadron. In fact, when Adams asked Harvey how the young pilot was faring he received a gruff grunt and a muttered 'all right'. To those who knew Harvey, it was the equivalent of bestowing the pilot with the Distinguished Flying Cross.

It was all a huge relief to Richards. Although it was known that the Atlantic Wall, as Hitler had named his western defences, was chock-ablock with German troops in readiness for the Allied invasion, Richards felt there must be many French workers helping to keep the rail and telephone communications open and he had feared Chalmont would make this point sooner or later. The fact he had not mentioned it could only mean one of two things. He had either decided the few French involved could not allow the essential raids to be discontinued or he had been convinced by Moore and Henderson that his larger objection had been misguided.

Ironically, Richards felt he would be disappointed if the latter were the cause. From the onset, the religious side of him had found sympathy with Chalmont's repugnance at bombing civilians, even although he had accepted the inevitability of the raid itself. Now, sharing Chalmont's company on and off duty, he was finding himself leaning more and more towards his friend's philosophy. Not entirely – Richards was still a first-class military navigator – but deep in his heart he hoped the squadron would be given no more operations like the annihilation of the French factory.

The end of the ten days brought joy and relief to most of the crews and to no one more than Richards. Aircrews could have a weekend pass from Friday night until 2400 hours on Sunday. While few of the men tried to look the gift horse in the mouth, a few of the older sweats did their best to prize it open and see what lay inside. Harvey, sharing a beer with Young in the mess, was one of them. 'I never like it when they rest us this way. It usually means that little bugger Davies gives us a big job afterwards.'

Young grinned. The love-hate relationship between Harvey and the irascible Davies was legendary on the squadron. 'You think so?'

'No question about it. He hates us to be idle. He's probably already cooking up something like Black Fjord or Valkyrie.'

Young's grin spread. 'You know what everyone loves about you, mate? It's that optimism of yours. A couple of minutes with you and a man can't wait to cut his throat.'

Harvey scowled, drained his glass, and clapped it down on the bar. 'You know what you can do, you Aussie Aborigine? You can either buy me another beer or go off and piss yourself.'

While this enlightened conversation was taking place, Richards and Chalmont were arguing outside the station's only public phone box. With a chance of seeing Hilary suddenly dropped in his lap, Richards wanted Chalmont to ring her to arrange a meeting. 'If you say you'd like to see her she's bound to agree. Then she'll have to accept me if I'm with you.'

'But I don't want to see her,' Chalmont told him. 'I'm going home to see my folks. Mother said Father wasn't too well in her last letter. She'll be upset if I see Hilary instead.'

'Then won't you ring her for me?' Richards begged. 'She might be on duty and the hospital might not pass on a message from me. But if you say you're her brother they're sure to tell her.'

Chalmont looked both amused and scornful. 'You're scared of her, aren't you? Why the hell do you want to waste the weekend with a cold woman like that?'

Richards held out a slip of paper. 'I've looked up the number of the hospital. Phone for me, Jeremy, and ask if she'll see me. Please.'

Chalmont eyed him impatiently, then snatched the paper. 'Oh, all right. Only don't blame me if she isn't interested.'

Listening outside the phone box, Richards heard Chalmont giving the operator the York number and address. Then, hearing coins drop, he found himself unable to listen to the conversation that followed. With his heart beating painfully, he moved out of earshot. When a minute passed without Chalmont calling him, he felt certain Hilary had refused. Then he saw the phone box door open and heard Chalmont's shout. 'Mark. She wants to speak to you. Hurry up.'

No sprinter off his blocks ever moved faster than Richards. He snatched the receiver from Chalmont. 'Hilary?'

'Hello. Is that Mark? What is it you want?'

Richards felt his tongue was too dry to serve its purpose. 'I got your letter saying you had moved to York. We've just been given a forty-eight hour pass. So I wondered if I could come and see you tomorrow or Sunday.'

'See me? Why?'

No question could have made Richards more tongue-tied. 'I'd just like to, that's all. I've nowhere else to go and thought perhaps I could take you for a meal or something.'

The cool, clear voice sounded amused. 'Of course. Your family's in Canada, aren't they? Why don't you go to Hereford with Jeremy? I'm sure Mother and Father would be glad to see you.'

Desperate, Richards summoned up all his courage. 'Yes, I know they would but I'd rather see you. I won't keep you long but I would love to see you again.'

Richards died a thousand deaths in the pause that followed. As the line crackled, he believed it had gone dead. Instead her voice returned. 'I suppose I could manage half an hour tomorrow morning. Not longer because we're very busy here.'

Richards felt his blood had broken free from its stoppage and was circulating again. 'That's wonderful. Where can I see you?'

'Do you know where the hospital is?'

'Yes. I've located it on a map.'

'There's a little café just opposite the front entrance. I'll be in there around 10.30. Can you be there at that time?'

Richards knew he would be there if it meant stealing S-Suzy and flying it to York himself. 'Yes, that'll be fine. The café opposite the hospital. Thanks, Hilary. I'll look forward to—'

The operator broke in at that moment to ask if he wanted more time. Richards fumbled in his pocket for cash, then changed his mind. Better leave well alone. She might change her mind if he pestered her again. Chalmont, waiting outside, grinned as he left the phone box. 'Well, what happened?'

Richards had the sudden desire to sing and dance. 'She's seeing me at 10.30 tomorrow. I can't believe it but she is.'

Chalmont's shrug expressed little sympathy for his sister's predilections. 'So she bloody well should. Are you taking her out afterwards?'

'I don't think so. She says she hasn't the time.'

'If you do, make her pay her way,' Chalmont told him. 'Her grandfather left her some money before he died. So don't let her sponge off you.'

Richards was not listening. His mind was already fifty miles away in a town he had never visited and in a café he had never seen.

Hilary Chalmont entered the café one minute before 10.30. Richards, who had been there over thirty minutes, spotted her the moment she appeared in the doorway although she was wearing the full regalia of a staff nurse. There was no friendship in the glance she gave him as he jumped to his feet. If anything it had a trace of hostility, as when they had first met at her parents' house in Hereford. Yet her composed face, the jet black hair that her nurse's cap could not hide, and the proud way she carried herself, excited Richards in ways he could not define. He saw her smile at two other nurses who were chatting at a table near the window, then she made towards him. 'Hello. So you found your way here all right?'

Richards drew out a chair for her. He could feel his heart pounding. 'Yes, thank you.'

'Have you been here long?'

'Only a few minutes,' Richards lied. He caught the eye of a waitress, who moved towards him. 'What can I get for you?'

She shrugged. 'Just a cup of tea. I can't stay long.'

Disappointed already, Richards gave the order, then turned back to her. 'Are you on duty today?'

'Yes. This is my morning break.' Her question came without any warning. 'Mark, why did you want to see me? Has it something to do with Jeremy?'

Caught by surprise, Richards floundered. 'Jerry? No. He's fine. He's gone down to see your parents. Didn't he tell you?'

'Yes, he said he might go. But I wondered if something was wrong when you were so anxious to see me.'

'No, it wasn't that. Jerry's doing well in the squadron.'

She gave a half laugh. 'You mean he's dropping his bombs nice and accurately?'

Richards winced. 'It's not like that, Hilary. It really isn't.'

She ignored his protest. 'Then why did you want to see me? From the way Jerry went on, it was urgent.'

At that moment, the waitress arrived with a tray. Grateful for the interruption, Richards helped the waitress to set down its contents. 'Are you sure you won't have a scone or anything?' he asked. As Hilary shook her head, he fished in his tunic pocket. 'Then will you have a cigarette?'

'No, thank you. I don't smoke. But you have one if you feel like it.'

Believing he had side-stepped the question that had left him hopelessly embarrassed, Richards was returning his pack of cigarettes to his tunic when her gaze fixed on him again. 'You still haven't said why you wanted to see me so urgently, Mark.'

Although the tone of her question seemed innocent enough, Richards could not help wondering if she was mocking him. 'It wasn't exactly urgent. I just wanted to see you, that's all.'

'Why? Because you had no one to talk to after Jeremy left for Hereford?'

Richards had never known a girl so forthright with her questions. 'No, not really. I've got friends in the squadron.' He took a deep breath. 'It was just that I like you and thought this was a chance to see you again.'

There was a trace of amusement in her dark eyes now. 'You mean you like me as a woman?'

Richards took a second deep breath. 'Yes. Yes, I do. Very much.'

She gave an amused shrug. 'I'm surprised. Most young men find me cold. I know Jeremy thinks I am.'

Richards found his words coming in a rush now. 'Jerry's wrong. You just take things more seriously than most people, that's all.'

'You mean I say what I think and believe? Jeremy thinks it's awful of me. What about you?'

'I like it,' Richards said. When the girl smiled, he went on: 'I do, truly.'

She stirred her tea, then lifted the cup to her lips. 'Do *you* always say what you think, Mark?'

'I like to think so. Most of the time, anyway. I don't like liars.'

'Why, Mark? Are you religious?'

He was surprised at the perception of her question and found difficulty in answering it. 'My parents brought me up that way so I suppose I am. But I haven't thought about it that much. Not until recently, that is.'

She lowered her cup. 'Why recently?'

He felt he should not tell her but the desire to talk about his recent thoughts proved too much. 'I think it's since I met you and Jerry. Until then the war had seemed simple in some ways. It was them or us. Now you've made it more complicated.'

There was a trace of sympathy in her voice now. 'Because of my talk about the bombing of innocent people?'

'Yours and Jerry's, yes. I hadn't given it much thought before.'

She took another sip of tea before speaking. 'Poor Mark. You must wish you'd never met us.' Before he could protest she went on: 'Tell me more about Jeremy. Is he happy in your squadron?'

'Yes. I think so. Not initially but he's settled down well since.'

'What happened initially?'

He wanted to tell her and talk about it but knew he must not. 'Nothing really. He's fine now. Even our tough Yorkshire flight commander likes his work. And that's quite a compliment.'

To his relief she changed the subject. 'You must miss your parents. When did they leave for Canada?'

'Before the war. My father was offered a good job over there. He didn't think at the time there would be a war.'

'Why didn't you go with them?'

'My father wasn't certain if the job would last and thought I'd better stay at my school until he found out. So I stayed with my aunt. Then the war started and it was too late for them to come back.'

'Had you left school by this time?'

'Yes. I got a job for a few months and then I volunteered for the RAF.'

'You volunteered?'

'Yes. I'd always wanted to fly so the air force seemed the right choice.'

She was toying with her teaspoon in her saucer. 'How do you feel about that choice now?'

Knowing what might be at stake, Richards had to steel himself to give his answer. 'I believe it was the right one. The Nazis had to be beaten and with our army back in England we were the only unit that could hurt them. If we hadn't beaten them in the Battle of Britain the war might have been lost by this time.'

He felt hot and cold as he sat back in his chair. Expecting her contempt, he was surprised to hear a new warmth in her voice. 'You do say what you believe, don't you? I like honest people even if I don't always agree with them.' Her tone changed. 'So you and Jeremy have become friends?'

'Yes. I like to think we have. We certainly get on well together.'

'In the air or on the ground?'

'Both, I think. He's a very good pilot.'

'What about you? Are you a good navigator?'

He was feeling more relaxed now. 'I don't think I'm a bad one. Anyway, Jerry seems satisfied.'

She glanced at her watch. 'I'll have to go in a few minutes. I'm sorry it's been such a short meeting. What will you do now? Go back to the station? Or will you go and see your aunt?'

'I can't stay with her. She's in a nursing home now.' Richards, who had made no plans beyond seeing the girl, was thinking how empty the café would seem once she had gone. 'I might stay in York overnight. But it doesn't matter. I'll sort all that out later.'

Her calm, composed face was looking at him, making him wish he could read her thoughts. She sat very still for a moment, then seemed to come to a decision. 'Listen. I have tomorrow afternoon off. If you are staying in York, I could see you then. Would you like that?'

Richards was trying to believe what he was hearing. 'Do you mean it?'

A look of irritation flickered across her face for a moment. 'Of course I mean it. You could meet me in this café at two o'clock. Then we could look around York. Do you know York?'

Richards shook his head. 'No. It's my first visit here.'

'Then we can explore it together. I haven't had time to look around it myself yet.' She paused. 'Where will you stay tonight?'

To the stunned Richards, who had just been offered a golden present, matters of accommodation were pure trivia. 'I don't know. But I'll find somewhere. That's no problem.'

She nodded and rose to her feet. 'Then I'll see you here tomorrow at two o'clock. Enjoy yourself for the rest of the day. Goodbye.'

Richards remembered nothing of those few seconds of farewell. When a world suddenly turns from bleak desolation to a scene of shining promise, the mind finds difficulty in coming to terms with the change. When Richards left the café five minutes later, he felt a warmth for every man and woman he passed on the pavement. Richards was very much in love with the world at that moment.

CHAPTER 21

ARVEY'S PESSIMISM REGARDING the squadron's short leave was justified although for once the fault did not lie with Davies. During the off-duty weekend, Davies and Henderson had been unexpectedly called to High Elms, the huge house near Sutton Craddock from which the highly secret Special Operations Executive operated. It had been a sunlit morning after the dubious skies of the previous week and the resident rooks had been in full cry when the two men had stepped out of the staff car. A buzzard had soared over the elms that surrounded the sunken garden and was being told in no uncertain terms that he was not welcome. As Henderson followed Davies towards a flight of stone steps that led from the courtyard to the main building, the commodore jabbed a finger at a military policeman who was leading a German shepherd towards a second flight of steps nearby. 'Nothing changes here, does it, Jock? They keep it tighter here than a bull's arse in fly time.'

Henderson, who had grown used to Davies's favourite expression, reminded himself that now spring was here in earnest he must keep an eye on the next bull he encountered to see if the axiom was true. Feeling he was expected to say something, he disappointed himself with a banality. 'I suppose they must, sir, considering what goes on here.'

Davies's grunt gave the Scot no indication whether his reply had been a disappointment or whether he found the tight security an irritation. His staff car had been stopped at the gate by a somewhat imperious MP, then stopped again halfway down the drive by a second MP and now a young lieutenant in the Provost Corps was marching towards them. Although he halted before Davies and snapped up a salute as precise as a karate stroke, his expression made it clear he was the one in control of the situation. 'Good afternoon, sir. May I see your papers, please?'

Davies's bark made the distant German shepherd jerk round its ears. 'Good God, man, how many more times? I've shown them twice already.'

The young lieutenant, spic and span from cap to toe, did not even blink. 'I'm sorry, sir, but these are my orders. Your papers, please.'

With something approaching a snarl, Davies jerked out a card from his tunic and thrust it at the erect lieutenant. It was calmly scanned and then held out to him. 'Air Commodore Davies. Thank you, sir. Please follow me.'

Davies glowered at the order. Beside him Henderson was having problems in keeping his face straight. Entering the large house, they followed the lieutenant down an oak-panelled corridor where another MP was positioned outside a closed door. Saluting the party, he stood aside while the lieutenant tapped on the door and opened it. 'Air Commodore Davies is here, sir.'

The room they entered was not unfamiliar to Henderson, who had visited it in the prelude to Operation Valkyrie. Oak-panelled, lined with hide-bound books, sparsely populated with dark mahogany furniture, and with a long table that almost reached the large French windows at its far end, it had once been High Elms library. Now it was the conference room of Brigadier Simms of the Special Operation Executive. A slimly built, elderly man with a sensitive face and a trimmed military moustache, he had worked on and off with Davies and his squadron since the Black Fjord operation of the previous year. With Simms a quiet, reserved man who accepted triumph and disaster as twin imposters and with Davies volatile, quick-tempered and a man who detested failure, it had seemed at first unlikely that such characters could ever become bedfellows. Instead, to each man's secret surprise, their views had turned out to be complementary instead of conflicting, and today they had mutual respect for the other's judgements.

The brigadier approached Davies with outstretched hand. 'Good afternoon, Davies. Thank you for coming so promptly. And you, Group Captain Henderson. It's a pleasure to see you again.'

Henderson saluted before shaking the brigadier's hand. 'It's good to see you, sir. Unless you've got some hairy job for us, that is.'

A man with a sense of dry humour, Simms smiled. The look Davies gave the comment contained less humour than unease. Smarting from the possibility his beloved squadron might be taken away from his command until the invasion, he feared this call to SOE might signify the first move in the process. His impatience to know the truth was not helped by the hospitality Simms always displayed to his guests. 'You will have coffee, gentlemen? Or would you prefer something a little stronger? It is a chilly morning for the time in the year.'

Davies frowned. 'Just coffee for me, thank you, sir.'

The brigadier turned to Henderson. 'And you, Henderson?'

The Scot in Henderson made the choice no contest but Davies's disapproval of morning drinking was too well known. Henderson suppressed a sigh. 'Coffee, please, sir.'

Simms indicated the chairs that lined the long table. 'Do be seated. Coffee will only be a moment.'

As the two airmen moved towards the table, Davies's glance at Henderson said it all. Simms's courtesy was a byword among those who knew him but there were certain times when it could be an irritation. As the brigadier gave his order to a smartly uniformed girl who appeared, Davies slipped a whisper at Henderson from the side of his mouth. 'What the hell's going on, Jock? What's he want us for?'

Aware what was in Davies's mind, Henderson was as anxious to know himself. Before he could think of a reply, Simms turned towards them, his comment suggesting he had overheard Davies's question. 'You gentlemen must be wondering why I asked to see you today? No doubt you think it has something to do with interdiction raids you are carrying out for us so successfully. By the by, I must congratulate you on those raids. That attack on the French factory was a massive success. Our agents say the factory is a total write-off.'

Henderson could not withhold his comment. 'Maybe so, sir, but the intelligence we were given about that operation wasn't very accurate.'

Davies frowned at the implied criticism of the brigadier's part in the action but the man's sensitive face showed only regret. 'I couldn't agree with you more, Henderson. We received the information in good faith and so had no reason not to act on it. But we were shocked on learning how we had been misled.'

Now the subject was opened, Davies wanted to hear more. 'Who was to blame? Do you know?'

'Yes, I think we do. As you can imagine, Resistance groups are made up of all kinds of men, mostly patriots, but with some adventurers among them and a few misfits or psychopaths. We believe our misinformer was one of the latter. The raid and his role in it gave him a perfect opportunity to indulge his particular dislikes and hatreds.'

Henderson was never a man to mince his words if the occasion demanded it. 'I hope you don't use him again, sir. If the news got out among my boys what they'd done they wouldn't be keen on carrying out a similar operation.'

Neither man noticed the brigadier's slight hesitation. 'He certainly won't be used by me again, Henderson. But from our position here it is not always possible to judge the calibre of the men we are dealing with.'

With the matter closed, Davies's impatience returned. 'You asked to see us today, sir. From what you say I gathered it has nothing to do with these interdiction raids. So has something else cropped up?'

Simms nodded. Eyeing him curiously, Henderson was not encouraged by the gravity of his expression. 'You're quite right, Davies. It is something quite different. I take it you are both fully acquainted with the situation of our armies in Italy?' As both men nodded, he went on. 'Then you both know the Germans see that campaign as a shield against the forthcoming invasion. By holding up our armies there they are reducing the troops we can send over into Western Europe. This is why their defence lines have proved so difficult to break.'

Davies was looking puzzled. 'Yes, but it hasn't prevented our build-up, has it? We've still got enough troops down south to make an invasion possible, haven't we?'

'We believe so, Davies. But what if the Germans were to break out of their defence lines and throw our armies back? What effect would that have?'

Davies looked startled. 'But how can they do that? With the Russians driving at them in the East, they haven't the men or the fire-power to go on the offensive.'

'Not yet, Davies. But what if they were to find a way to augment that firepower?'

'How can they do that?'

'Let me explain.' Simms spoke for over five minutes. When he finished the room was so quiet the cawing of the rooks outside sounded loud and shocked.

It was Henderson who broke the silence. 'Surely they won't do it.'

'They might not, Henderson. It might only be a precaution in case we do it ourselves. But with so much at stake dare we wait to find out? That's why we need your help.'

Henderson was looking horrified. 'But it's inhuman, sir. Horrible.'

Simms sighed. 'I agree. But what is the alternative? If we ignore the possibility we not only risk our men being slaughtered but risk the success of the invasion itself with all the disasters that might cause. I feel like you do, Henderson, but what choice do we have?'

Although Davies had shown his own degree of shock, he was the first to assess the logistics and problems of the mission. 'It's a hell of a long trip, sir. How could we get there without unacceptable losses?'

'The Americans will help you as they did during Rhine Maiden. They've got Mark Clark and his army down in Italy too so they're just as anxious as we are to knock out the threat. I've already spoken to Staines and he offered help immediately.'

Henderson's interruption betrayed the Scot's hopes and fears. 'But you said it's not confirmed yet, sir. Couldn't it just be a rumour?'

'We don't think so, Henderson, but that's what our agents are trying to find out. They'll be in touch the moment they have something definite.'

The room went silent again. This time it was Davies who broke it. 'So we have a few days yet?'

'I hope you have longer, Davies. I hope I never have to ask your men to do it. But I'm afraid the war situation leads one to think it is the enemy's next logical move. After all, if we were in his situation we might consider doing the same ourselves.'

The Scot shook his head. 'I hope not. My God, I hope not.'

'I hope not too, Henderson. But history teaches us that war gives no laurel leaves to the righteous. It is only the victors that gain its favour.'

Henderson remembered little of the conversation that followed. It was only when he and Davies were back in their staff car and driving through the gates of High Elms that he felt able to put his question to the silent Davies. 'How do you feel about this, sir?'

Davies's reply was short and to the point. 'That's a damn fool question, Jock.'

'Sorry, sir, but surely it could be done in another way if it has to be done at all.'

Davies frowned. 'If there was another way, Simms would have found it. In spite of his work, Simms is a humanitarian. You saw that during the Rhine Maiden job.'

'I know that, sir. But if this comes off won't it be asking too much of the lads?'

Shocked or not, Davies was not having that. 'We're an elite squadron, Jock. That means we do our duty no matter what it costs us. So keep thoughts like that to yourself. Now and always.'

A reply was on the tip of Henderson's tongue but he bit it back.

There was still a chance the unthinkable might not happen, he consoled himself. Perhaps the same thought was in Davies's mind because hardly another word passed between the two men on their way back to the airfield.

CHAPTER 22

WITH THE BLACKOUT faithfully kept in York, the staff entrance to the hospital was lit only by the sliver of moon. Pausing at the foot of the steps, Hilary turned to Richards. 'You shouldn't have come back with me. How are you going to get to the station?'

'Walk,' Richards told her. 'It's no more than a mile or two.'

'But what if you miss your train?'

'I won't miss it. I've still got forty minutes.'

'All the same, you'd better go. You've still to get from the other station to your airfield.'

He ignored her words. 'Have you enjoyed today?'

'Yes. Yes, I have. I thought those daffodils round the old walls were beautiful. I think I'm going to enjoy living in York.'

'I enjoyed it too,' he said. 'I think it's been the happiest day of my life.'

She laughed. 'Now you're exaggerating.'

'I'm not. I can't remember being so happy.'

She laughed again. 'Poor boy. What a dreary life you must have led.' As a distant clock bell struck the time, she moved towards the entrance door. 'I'll have to go, Mark, or I'll get into trouble.'

She had moved out of the shadows into the moonlight, which gave a sheen to her black hair and dark eyes. Gazing at her, Richards felt something catch in his throat. Fumbling in his greatcoat pocket, he brought out a small parcel. 'May I give you something?'

She looked puzzled. 'Why? What have you got?'

He offered her the parcel. He stammered an apology as she drew out a small bracelet. 'I know it's only a cheap one. But I saw it yesterday afternoon and I did want to give you something.'

Her eyes moved to his embarrassed face. 'Why did you want to do that, Mark?'

'I don't know. I suppose I wanted to thank you for coming out with me. I never thought that you would.'

For an instant she did not move. Then, with a hand on his sleeve, she suddenly leaned forward and kissed his cheek, an impulse that surprised her as much as it surprised him. 'That was very sweet of you, Mark. You mustn't waste your money on me but of course I'll accept it. I shall value it very much.'

His reaction to her kiss astonished her. With her hand still on his arm, she could feel him trembling. She tried to lighten the moment. 'You must have thought me a real dragon. Had Jeremy been telling you stories about me?'

He tried to laugh. 'No. Of course he hasn't.' In the pause that followed, she could feel the effort it took to ask his question. 'Would you come out with me again sometime? I won't be a nuisance. In any case we don't get that much time off duty. But I'd love it if you would.'

She hesitated, then gave his arm a squeeze. 'Of course I will. I'll find out when my next free days are and drop you a line.' She glanced down at her watch. 'Now I must go and you must catch your train. Thank you again for a lovely day. And take care of yourself.'

Aware he would never go while she stood there, she gave him a wave, ran up the steps, and closed the door behind her. She waited a few seconds, then opened it to glance out. In the faint light he looked as if he were skipping as he ran down the street. Smiling, she closed the door and walked slowly to her room. Until that day Hilary Chalmont had tended to see men as either insensitive, aggressive creatures who needed women to soften their activities or supine creatures hardly worthy of contempt. To find a man who could play an active role in a brutal war and yet show such gentleness in his private life was an experience she found both novel and moving.

When Richards finally reached Sutton Craddock he was only fifteen minutes from incurring Bert the Bastard's disapproval. Clocking into the guardroom, he found his billet in darkness and Chalmont in bed when he entered. Not wanting to wake him, he tiptoed to his bed and was about to undress when Chalmont's voice broke the silence. 'It's OK. I'm not asleep. You can put the light on.'

Clicking on the switch, Richards saw the pyjama-clad Chalmont propping himself up in bed. 'Sorry. I tried to come in as quietly as I could. How did your weekend go?'

Chalmont yawned. 'Fine. Father had a bit of a cold but Mother was in great shape. They both sent their best wishes, by the by. They were sorry you hadn't come with me.'

Richards slipped off his tunic. 'Did you tell them I was seeing Hilary?'

'Yes, I did. They looked quite surprised.' Chalmont's tone changed. 'How was it? Did she turn up as she promised?'

Richards nodded. 'She could only stay a few minutes on Saturday because it was her morning break. But I saw her again on Sunday afternoon.'

Chalmont showed surprise. 'She saw you again?'

'Yes. We went round York together and then went to an early cinema.'

Chalmont was eyeing Richards with new respect. 'She didn't freeze you or make you swear to be a pacifist?'

Richards laughed. 'No. She just seemed to enjoy herself.'

'Then I take my hat off to you, old boy. You've done something I didn't believe any man could do. You seem to have made a real woman out of a block of ice.'

Richards hung his pants over a chair and pulled off his shirt. 'She isn't a bit like that, Jerry. She just thinks more deeply than other girls, that's all. I think she's terrific.'

Chalmont was clearly fascinated by this new vision of his sister. 'Did she let you kiss her?'

'I never tried,' Richards confessed. He felt he should not make the admission but the richness of the memory proved too much. 'But before we said goodnight she did give me a kiss.'

'Hilary did? On her own? My God, where had you taken her to? Buckingham Palace?'

Richards switched off the light and slid into bed. 'You're wrong about Hilary, Jerry. She just hates cruelty, that's all.'

This time there was no answer and Chalmont's heavier breathing explained the reason. Richards was not disappointed. Tucked up in bed, with military matters and the activity of the world momentarily at bay, he was able for the first time since their parting to give his full thoughts to Hilary. Incredibly she had kissed him. Incredibly she had agreed to see him again. From his doubts on Friday that he would ever make any headway with her, he was now in a new world where anything was possible. With any luck at all, he and she might be engaged in a few months' time. The very thought made Richards hug himself.

The irony of his optimism was totally lost on the young navigator. He was a member of a military unit whose loss rate was seldom less than ten per cent per month. In a few days' time, perhaps even on the morrow, the operations that took him and his colleagues into peril from screaming shells, probing cannon fire and consuming flames would begin again. Yet that night, with the confidence of the young in their immortality, Mark Richards dreamt of a future full of rich and glorious promise.

CHAPTER 23

NTERDICTION OPERATIONS FOR 633 Squadron began again the following Tuesday. Once again they were sent out to attack the enemy's rail and road systems from the Pas de Calais down to Normandy. Their first two operations went without loss but on both the third and fifth day Teddy Young lost crews from ground fire.

The enemy, fully aware that the interdiction raids were a prelude to the invasion and with the urgent need to protect their transport and communications systems when that invasion came, was packing every vital artery in the system with anti-aircraft guns. A high percentage of these were heavy and light machine guns, not effective over 4,000 feet, but highly dangerous at low level.

As accurate bombing was necessary to take out relatively small targets such as train signal boxes and their like, crews often found themselves flying through a blizzard of fire when they made their attacks. Although there was little opposition from enemy fighters – they being kept occupied by the Allied heavy bombers that were pounding the German hinterland – most Mosquito crews would have preferred to face fighters than the sheets of deadly tracer that reached towards them every time they dived on a target. Their Mosquitoes were more than a match for enemy aircraft but no crewman, however seasoned or skilful, could insure his life against automatic ground fire. Luck was the only arbiter here and one's luck had a way of running out, a fact that was not lost on the longer-serving members of the squadron.

The most hated targets were rail and road bridges. From high to medium height they looked no wider than matchsticks and were as difficult to hit. At the same time the larger ones were so strongly built they needed both heavy bombs and the high terminal velocity that height gives bombs to effect any serious damage. This meant only heavy bombers carrying 12,000lb 'block busters' were effective against them and even then results were often disappointing.

It was the lesser bridges that came into 633 Squadron's brief, structures that spanned narrow gullies, rail tracks or minor rivers. Less massive in their construction than the major bridges, they were nevertheless every bit as vital a target to prevent the enemy rushing up troops, trains and ammunition wagons towards any forthcoming Allied beachhead.

It was one of these rail bridges that became the squadron's target the following Monday. It was a link in the French rail system that ran towards the massive bridge at Antheor and onwards towards Italy. If it could be severed it would greatly hinder the Germans should they try to rush up troops from their Italian Front to reinforce their Atlantic defences.

But small bridges were no easy targets either. Not only did they present an even smaller target from high to medium level, they were still solid enough structures to need a sequence of hits to sustain appreciable damage. Worst of all, they bristled with every gun from 37mm down to the vicious LMG fire that could rip an aircraft open from nose to tail.

Few men, if any, that attended the briefing on Monday morning were unaware of this and the silence in the large Nissen hut was more thoughtful than usual as Moore gave the tactical and combat details. All aircraft would be carrying 500lb heavy case bombs; B Flight would launch the first attack from medium height while A Flight gave overhead cover. If the damage inflicted was not serious enough to put the bridge out of action, the two flights would switch roles but this time A Flight would attack at low level to guarantee precision.

At this point, not unexpectedly, Harvey put up a hand. 'I don't understand this, skipper. Why aren't our heavies or the Yank heavies doing this job? Our Lancs could carry 12,000 pounders.'

'I can't answer that, Harvey. I suppose they've just got too many targets in their books at the moment.'

'All right, but I can't see 500lb heavy case bombs doing the job. Not if we have to drop 'em from low level. They won't have enough terminal velocity to penetrate. They just slide off into the river or whatever's below.'

Teddy Young joined in the argument. 'I agree with that, skipper. How are we going to get penetration if we have to go in at low level?'

Moore's thoughts were rueful. He had used the same argument with Davies the previous morning when the orders had been passed on to him, only for Davies to explode. 'Do you think I haven't thought of this, Ian? I've played hell about the order but it's got me nowhere. I think this bastard McBride is behind it. Somehow he's got permission to use us and because we're designed as a special service unit he thinks we can work miracles.'

'But surely this hasn't anything to do with his resistance groups, has it, sir?'

'Not that I can see. But whoever is behind it, Group have given us the job which means we have to do it. So I've asked for a Spitfire from Benson to go over and photograph the bloody thing. We should get the photos later today and then maybe we can make some sense out of the order.'

The aerial photographs had arrived at Sutton Craddock that afternoon and Davies, Moore, Adams and a constructional engineer brought in by Davies had spent two hours examining it and trying to work out a method of attack. Expecting Harvey's question, Moore explained it now. 'I agree about the penetration problem. So we've had to devise ways of getting the maximum effect from our stores.' At this point Moore nodded at a projectionist at the rear of the assembly and an enlarged photograph of the bridge appeared on a screen behind him. Picking up a cane, Moore pointed at the two ends of the bridge that spanned a narrow valley. 'In fact we're in luck. As you see, it's a suspension bridge with its two supporting columns rooted on both sides of the valley. Our engineering experts reckon that if we can drop enough 500 pounders at the base of one or the other, the bridge's own weight should ensure its collapse. So the eastern end will be the target for both our flights. Not the bridge itself, but its eastern pylon. Aim at that and with any luck down should go Jack, Jill, pail and all.'

'What about flak posts, skipper?' It was Harvey again, asking the question in everyone's mind.

Moore was never one to duck the unpleasant facts. 'Like all Jerry's bridges it's well defended. Mr Adams has tried to pinpoint all the posts both from the photographs and from the Spitfire pilot's reports and they will be marked on the photograph copies you will be given. But of course we can't guarantee they have all been spotted or that other guns haven't been rushed up since yesterday. So, A Flight, keep your eyes well open if you have to go in at low level.'

'I take it A Flight's bombs will be time fused, skipper?' The question this time came from Van Breedenkamp.

Moore nodded. 'Yes, Van. Twenty second delays. Any more questions?'

The briefing terminated forty minutes later. Filing out from the large Nissen hut, Gabby gave a grunt of disgust. 'Bloody railways and now railway bridges. Haven't they got anything else on their minds these days?'

Millburn winked at Chalmont and Richards, who were right behind them. 'You should count yourself lucky, boyo. They could send you out to help the Russians. They tell me gremlins hate the snow. It makes their bits and pieces fall off.'

Gabby scowled. 'Funny, funny, Millburn. What makes you Yanks think you're comedians? I've had more laughs watching Harvey's dog scratch himself.'

Millburn grinned. 'That's because gremlins have no sense of humour. Come to think of it, they couldn't have, could they? Or they'd kill themselves laughing every time they heard themselves talk.'

There were chuckles from the men behind them. Seasoned men nodded to one another. Whenever a dangerous operation was forthcoming, Gabby and Millburn could always be relied on to lighten the general mood.

The crews air-tested their aircraft that morning, had an early lunch, and were airborne at 1400 hours. They topped up their tanks down south and, to keep out of sight of enemy flak ships, headed along the English coast until they reached Torquay. Here Moore swung due east and headed straight for the enemy coast.

Until now it had been little more than a pleasant exercise. The spring had relented at last and the sky was a deep blue with fluffy white clouds. At 10,000 feet the English countryside had looked at its loveliest, its neat patterned fields showing every shade from rich brown to verdant green. With the warm sun shining through S-Suzy's canopy, Richards was finding himself pondering once again on the paradox of a world where war and beauty could live in such proximity.

With the English Channel wider here, it was twenty minutes before the order came to test guns. As cannons chattered and Mosquitoes shuddered under their recoil, the message reached every man that soon his manhood was to be tested once again.

The enemy coastal guns provided the first trial. Although this time the Mosquitoes were flying at 10,000 feet, the sky around them was soon festooned by ugly black bursts that hurled out murderous shards of steel in all directions. Although no aircraft was destroyed, more than one pilot and navigator winced as steel ripped through wings or fuselage.

Leaving the pock-marked sky behind them, the sixteen Mosquitoes latched on to the rail track that led them south. With navigators keeping a keen eye on the fluffy clouds above and around them, they droned on for forty minutes before a green flare shot out of Moore's A-Apple. Richards tapped Chalmont's arm. 'That must be the bridge. At eleven o'clock.'

Chalmont saw the photographs were correct. Suspended across a narrow wooded valley, the bridge had no piers but was suspended between the two pylons rising from the surrounding hills, which were rock strewn and thick with trees. Although from the height the Mosquitoes were flying the bridge looked toylike in size, when the two men viewed it through their binoculars they could see it was substantial enough to carry two rail tracks across the valley. In other words it was a substantial target and from the frantic preparations taking place among the gun posts on either side of the bridge, the enemy knew its importance. Already some flak was bursting around the Mosquitoes. The larger explosions that joined them a few seconds later betrayed the presence of the enemy's feared 88mm guns.

With radio silence serving no further purpose, Moore switched on his R/T. 'Barracuda Leader to Blue Section. Begin your attack. Red Section give cover.'

With Harvey's flight keeping its altitude, Young took his men down a thousand feet where they went into orbit. Then, in line astern, with Young leading the way, they began tracking over the bridge in a bombing run. Watching through his binoculars, Richards saw bomb after bomb falling towards the base of the eastern pylon. Explosions erupted all around the pylon, hurling trees into the air like matchsticks and now and then hitting and severing the rail tracks that ran towards the bridge. Within minutes the trees around the pylon were ablaze but there was no sign of the bridge itself giving way under the onslaught.

The sight was no comfort to the members of Harvey's flight. In his heart every man had hoped the first attack would suffice and there would be no need for a second assault. The shells that were bursting around each attacking Mosquito gave grim evidence of the firepower they would have to face if they went in at low level.

Their hopes died when the last Mosquito of Young's flight came circling back into orbit with the pylon still erect. Moore's voice, as calm as always, heralded the second onslaught. 'Barracuda Leader to Red Zero. I'm going in now. Follow me at twenty second intervals.'

Richards gave Chalmont a glance as on Harvey's instructions S-Suzy went into a lower orbit with the rest of the flight. 'Always the first. Moore's a hell of a leader.'

Chalmont nodded his agreement as A-Apple dived and circled

round to make its attack. Fifteen seconds later, hugging the ground, it headed straight for the pylon. Although the Mosquito's camouflage made it difficult to see, its passage could be read by the forks and whiplashes of tracer attempting to destroy it. For a few seconds it vanished in the smoke of the burning trees and men felt their breathing cease and their muscles tighten. Then it appeared again, as small as a fluttering moth, and men sighed with relief.

But then it was their turn. Down towards the dark trees and pitiless boulders from which tracer was squirting. The stomach-wrenching breathlessness as they pulled out of their dive only feet above the trees. The relative speed that turned the hillside below into a menacing blur beneath their wings. The fear that burned the heart as ahead the first spears of tracer came lancing out from the hidden gun posts.

Red Two did not survive. Just before it entered the cloud of black smoke it faltered as a fork of tracer ripped it from end to end. A moment later it burst into flames and like a crazy catherine wheel went spinning along the hillside until a huge explosion marked its end.

Red Three made it safely and its time-delayed bombs exploded at the base of the pylon. Then it was S-Suzy's turn. Chalmont glanced at Richards and eased the column forward. Feeling his throat go as dry as parched sandpaper, Richards attempted a smile, grabbed hold of his harness straps and waited.

Time went off the clock for both men in the moments that followed. Seconds expanded into minutes and then shrank into milliseconds as S-Suzy completed her dive and headed for the hell that lay ahead. Inside his flying boots Richards could feel his very toes cramping and contracting. As always, Richards feared white-hot tracer ripping up through his unprotected seat and his spine cringed in anticipation. As the billowing black cloud raced towards him and the guns began their murderous chatter, he could hear himself praying although he knew nothing of the substance of his prayer. A few seconds more and then the canopy darkened and the acrid smell of smoke filled the cockpit. Peering through it, he caught sight of the tall grey pylon looming ahead and as Chalmont gave a yell he released his clutch of bombs. A second later S-Suzy banked violently to starboard, her engines screaming as Chalmont fought for height.

It was then it happened. A twin line of tracer that ripped up through the smoke and struck S-Suzy as she banked away. Both men felt her shuddering under the impact and as Chalmont fought to hold her steady there was a huge thump beneath her and for a moment she faltered. Then she recovered, enabling Chalmont to continue her climb to the orbit above. White-faced, he glanced at Richards as the smoke and tracer below fell away. 'You all right?'

Richards managed a nod. 'Where did they hit us?'

Before Chalmont could answer, the R/T gave a harsh rasp. 'Red Four. How bad is it?'

Knowing it was Harvey, Chalmont tried to calm his voice. 'I don't know, skipper. We were hit below but she seems to be flying all right.'

'Keep her steady. I'll come below you and take a look.'

Down below, S-Suzy's bombs had exploded and Red Five was making its run. As they waited for Harvey's D-Danny to fly beneath them, the two men watched Red Five launch its attack. Looking like a moth being pierced by a dozen needles, it seemed impossible it could survive and it did not. Before it could release its bombs, it exploded in a ball of flame that sank into the unforgiving trees. An unprintable oath came over the R/T. Harvey was suffering badly from the loss of his crews. 'All right, Red Six. See if you can punish the bastards.'

A few seconds later, D-Danny appeared beneath S-Suzy and in the sunlight Richards could see Harvey gazing upwards. 'You've got damage to your starboard wheel nacelle, Chalmont. Does she handle OK?'

'She's a bit stiff on the controls, skipper, but otherwise she seems all right.'

'Then you think you can get back to base?'

'I think so, skipper.'

At that there was a series of yells in the R/T. 'It's going, skipper. The bastard's going.'

Staring down, Richards saw the huge pylon was starting to topple towards the ravine. As it moved, the bridge it supported was cracking in the centre under its own weight. Seconds later, the crack opened into a gap as the two ends of the bridge began to fall, dragging lines of rail track after it. A huge cloud of grey dust rose up as hundreds of tons of concrete smashed into the rocks and trees below and exploded under the impact. Harvey's voice came over the R/T, hoarse with relief. 'That's it. All right, Red Seven. You're the lucky one. Join us in orbit.'

Moore's voice followed a few seconds later. 'Well done, men. Formate behind me and let's get back home.'

For a few moments the bursting shells round the orbiting Mosquitoes had eased as if the gun crews below had either been shocked at the destruction of their charge or had shared in its destruction. Now the red-cored explosions began again in an effort to extract vengeance from their attackers.

But their efforts were now in vain. Anxious to avoid further losses, Moore led his surviving Mosquitoes into a cloud bank that had appeared to the east. In a minute they were out of sight and the only evidence of their passage were the fires burning in the woods and the grey cloud that hung over the valley.

CHAPTER 24

WITH EARLIER PLANNING allowing the Mosquitoes sufficient fuel for the exercise, Moore was able to avoid a refuelling stop on their return and the squadron reached Sutton Craddock well before the advent of evening. With the wind blowing from Bishops Wood at the southern end of the airfield and billowing out the wind socks in her direction, Maisie knew the returning Mosquitoes would pass over The Black Swan when landing and made sure she was at the gate when their distant drone was heard. As always she was planning to count the number of survivors when a red Very light shooting up from the control tower told her that at least one aircraft was receiving landing priority. As she gazed up anxiously at the late afternoon sky, she heard the wail of fire trucks and ambulances as Sutton Craddock made preparations to receive its damaged Mosquito.

S-Suzy was that aircraft. On releasing his undercarriage, Chalmont had been told by Harvey that one wheel had been shattered by cannon fire, leaving him with the choice of landing on one wheel or pancaking with a totally retracted undercarriage. Knowing there were risks either way, Harvey had allowed Chalmont to make up his own mind after giving him advice on both methods of landing. Chalmont had chosen the former and now, with one wheel fully down and the other dangling half down like a broken claw, he was gingerly lowering S-Suzy down to her landing approach.

It was when the slate-covered roof of The Black Swan was sliding beneath him that he saw Maisie at the gate anxiously waving a scarf. Somehow he managed to rock S-Suzy's wings a couple of times, then the airfield with its waiting emergency vehicles was reaching up towards him. In his ears Harvey was giving advice. 'Keep her starboard wing up, lad. Hold it up as hard as you can. Now give her a bit more engine. Hold it there.... Hold it....' Then, as S-Suzy bumped along without cartwheeling, there was a shout from the Yorkshireman. 'Well done, lad. Bloody well done.'

As S-Suzy's speed dropped, it was impossible for Chalmont to hold up the damaged wheel struts any longer but by this time her momentum was such that the ground loop she made did no damage to her starboard wing. Richards, helpless throughout the exercise, recovered his breath and clapped Chalmont's shoulder. 'That was terrific. When did you learn to do that?'

Chalmont, out of breath himself, switched off the ignitions then managed a rueful grin as a fire truck pulled up alongside. 'I thought I'd made the wrong decision when that broken wheel dug in. I think I need a drink.'

Alongside them the fire truck crew were shouting at them and uncoiling hose. On the port side a breakdown truck was already preparing to drag S-Suzy to the fringe of the field. Unfastening their straps, the two men dropped out of the aircraft, their legs feeling like jelly as they hit the ground. In the distance a crew transport was speeding towards them. As they waited for it, one after another of the Mosquitoes, many with battle scars, came in to land.

Henderson turned from the control tower window, his expression a mixture of disgust and dismay. 'Another two of my best crews gone, sir. I never liked this operation from the start.'

Davies, who had arrived at the station half an hour earlier, showed a modicum of sympathy. 'Don't blame me, Jock. I didn't think it up. All the same, it's another feather in your cap, isn't it? The lads have done a fine job.'

A feather in whose cap, the big Scot was thinking. 'An expensive job, sir. One we should never have been given. I hope this is the end of them.'

Never one to appreciate criticism, even if obliquely directed, Davies frowned. 'I can't promise that and you know why. But anyway you'll be able to take a rest for a few days while your kites are repaired. I suggest you give your boys twenty-four-hour passes in the meantime. Let 'em relax and enjoy themselves.'

Henderson glanced back at the scene below where aircraft were being towed to their hardstandings or to the hangars for more serious repairs. It took an effort to ask his question. 'I take it you've heard no more news from Simms, sir?'

'No. Only that he's got his agents watching the Jerries day and night. He says we'll get plenty of warning.'

Henderson made a confession he had never imagined he would make. 'I get nightmares thinking about it. Surely there's a chance the Jerries will change their minds.'

Davies shrugged. 'It's possible, I suppose, although won't they be thinking the same about us? Can they take the risk? That's the problem with war. Without communications neither side can afford to take chances.'

Henderson managed to suppress a shudder. 'Let's hope it's a false alarm, sir. We've had some hairy jobs to do but at least they were within the parameters of war. To me this one is different.'

Davies clapped his arm, an unusual gesture for the air commodore to make. 'Don't get soft on me, Jock. If we have to do it, it'll be in a good cause. What about the briefing? Are you going to it?'

Henderson moved away from the window. 'No, I'll see Adams later. Do you want to go?'

Davies shook his head. 'No. I must get back to Group.' He moved towards the staircase. 'I'll keep in touch, Jock. And stop worrying about that job or you'll get old before your time.'

When no response came from Henderson, Davies bustled down the control tower towards his parked car. As he took the path that led past the administration block, a young pilot emerged from the building ahead of him. Catching sight of the air commodore, he stiffened to attention and saluted.

Approaching him, Davies returned the salute, then halted. 'What's your name, lad?'

'Chalmont, sir.'

'You're the lad that just brought in that damaged kite, aren't you?'

'Yes, sir.'

'You did a good job, Chalmont. Are you all right?'

'Yes, thank you, sir. I was told to see the MO but there's nothing wrong with me.'

Davies was noticing and impressed by the young man's upper-class accent. 'Wait a minute. You're the man who gave cover to Van Breedenkamp after that French job, aren't you?'

'Yes, sir.'

'I remember it now. Didn't you drive off a 190?'

'I like to think so, sir. But he might have been getting low on fuel.'

It was not Davies's way to spend long chatting to a pilot officer but he was impressed by the young pilot's modesty, self-assurance and, let it be admitted, by his accent. 'Are you happy with your posting, Chalmont?'

'Yes, sir. Although I did request it.'

Davies looked amused. 'Why? Because of the squadron's reputation?'

'Partly that, sir. And partly because it is used against military instead of civilian targets.'

Davies lifted an eyebrow. 'What does that mean?'

'It doesn't often bomb targets like that French factory. That was why I was glad to be accepted.'

Davies thought he understood. 'Yes, that was a pity although it couldn't be helped. No one was to know the timing was wrong.'

Chalmont gave a start. 'The timing, sir?'

'Yes. The night shift came on earlier than we thought. But that's war, Chalmont. Something you get used to.' Deciding he had spent too long talking to a junior officer, Davies started towards his waiting car. 'Keep up the good work, Chalmont, and you've got a future with this squadron.'

In his haste to leave, Davies did not notice Chalmont's omission to salute. Instead the young pilot was standing pale and motionless as if turned into stone.

The thump on the billet door made Richards glance up from the letter he was writing to Hilary. A moment later, Chalmont appeared in the doorway. His appearance made Richards start. 'What's the matter? What's happened?'

The young pilot's eyes, heavy with drink, stared at him. 'The bastards. The lying, cheating bastards.'

Richards rose to his feet. 'What are you talking about? Why weren't you at dinner tonight?'

Chalmont steered himself to his bed and dropped on it. 'Dinner? You think I could eat dinner after what I heard this afternoon?'

'What did you hear?'

'That air commodore – what's his name?'

'Davies?'

'That's him. He stopped me when I was coming out of the MO's surgery.' Chalmont's bloodshot eyes stared accusingly at Richards. 'You know what he told me?' Richards shook his head. 'He told me the French raid had been a mistake. That we'd bombed it at the wrong time.'

Richards looked puzzled. 'I don't follow. We bombed it when the flares were lit. Almost exactly at 17.30.'

'That's right.' Chalmont's voice was thick with drink and distress. 'But by that time the shift had already changed over.'

Richards felt as if his face had been slapped. 'You're saying we bombed it when a full shift was on duty?'

153

'That's right. We must have killed dozens if not hundreds of Frenchmen. I was right at the briefing, wasn't I, Mark? Wasn't I?'

Richards was struggling to understand. 'But someone must have got the times wrong. Otherwise what would be the point of bombing at exactly 17.30?'

Chalmont had all the dogged persistence of the half drunk. 'We should never have done it in the first place. I told them that and what happened?' The young pilot swung round to face Richards. 'You know something, Mark? I'll never trust the bastards again. Not Henderson, Moore or even Harvey. Not one of them again.'

Richards was feeling distress himself now. 'It must have been a mistake. Didn't Davies say so?'

'All that little bastard said was that it was a pity. Something you get used to in wartime.' To Richards's dismay, a sob burst out from the young pilot. 'And we were the ones who did the most damage. Do you remember how we blew up that eastern end of the factory?'

As memory brought back the devastation his bombs had inflicted, Richards knew the young pilot was right. He made an effort to conquer his distress. 'You mustn't take it so much to heart, Jeremy. It's this damned war that causes these things to happen.'

He could have been talking to himself. Chalmont was lying on the bed with his face buried in his arm, racked with shame and guilt and suffering from a childhood memory that nothing could erase.

CHAPTER 25

WITH CHALMONT BARELY exchanging a word that evening and with Richards needing alcohol to sedate his nerves, the navigator went across to The Black Swan that evening. When he approached the bar to order a drink, Maisie, looking voluptuous in a low-cut black frock, drew him to one side, leaving Joe Kearns to attend to the other customers. 'That friend of yours, Mr Chalmont. What's wrong with him?'

Aware he must be careful what he gave away, Richards pretended innocence. 'Sorry. I don't know what you mean. Has he been over here?'

'Yes. He came just after we opened. I asked him why he was missing dinner and he hardly said a word to me. Yet he seemed such a polite person when Frank Adams brought him over the other day. He hasn't had a row with somebody, has he?'

Remembering Maisie had seen their damaged Mosquito coming in to land and knowing she was to be trusted on most military matters, Richards decided he had a safe excuse. 'We had a spot of trouble this afternoon and sustained some damage. It meant we had to make a hairy landing. Perhaps that's the reason.'

Maisie's eyes opened wide. 'Was that you who came in first? With the broken wheel?' When Richards nodded, Maisie became all motherly. 'I never knew that. If I'd have known I'd have found a drop of whisky for him. What happened when you landed? Was either of you hurt?'

'No. Thanks to Chalmont we were OK. But as the pilot he probably had a bit of a reaction afterwards.'

'The poor lad. I'm sure he did. What about you, Mark? Would you like a drop of Scotch? We got a couple of bottles in yesterday.'

Richards shook his head. 'No, I'll stick with beer, thanks.'

Maisie, who loved her pilots and navigators, would have stayed chatting to him longer had not a clutter of airmen just walked in, bringing a request for help from Joe Kearns. Seeing a number of Harvey's flight among the entrants, Richards stayed chatting to them until closing time. Although the mess was still open when he returned to the airfield, he decided he had drunk enough and made for his billet. Half expecting Chalmont to be there, he found the cubicle empty. Thinking he must be in the mess, Richards undressed and slipped into bed.

As always after a dangerous operation, he found it difficult to sleep. Every time he closed his eyes he could see tracer stabbing towards him and feel his body cringing in anticipation. Damning his imagination, he wished he had dulled it with more alcohol. When at last he did fall asleep he was awakened by voices and shouts outside that made him believe Chalmont was back. But when the billet door remained closed and the voices died away, he lay awake wondering where the pilot had gone.

He found out the following morning. When Chalmont was not present at breakfast he made enquiries from the guardroom and discovered the pilot had obtained a twenty-four-hour pass and had left camp just before 21.00 the previous evening. Discovering there was a train from Highgate at 22.15, Richards wondered if Chalmont had gone home again, although why he should and why he had not made his intentions known to Richards worried the young navigator.

He phoned Hilary just before lunch. 'Hilary, it's Mark here. Do you know where Jerry is? He got a twenty-four-hour pass and left camp yesterday evening without telling me where he was going and I haven't heard a word from him since.'

Hilary sounded in a great hurry. 'Perhaps he's gone home. I certainly haven't seen him.'

'Should I phone your family?'

'Why should you do that? If he hasn't gone you'll only worry them. In any case, why are you so concerned? Perhaps he's seeing a girl somewhere.'

Richards realized she could be right. Before he could say more, Hilary broke in again. 'I can't talk now, Mark. We've just got some aircrew casualties in. When can I see you?'

Richards had not dared to hope for this. 'I can get a twenty-four-hour pass any time this week.'

'Then can you make tomorrow? I've got the afternoon off. Can you meet me in the café at 12.30?'

Richards felt his heart leap. 'Tomorrow? For the rest of the day? Yes. I'll be there.'

'Good. Now I must go. Goodbye.'

Hardly believing in his good luck, Richards made an immediate application for a pass. In the anticipation of seeing Hilary again, his concern about Chalmont and his own distress at the news of the French factory began to take second place in his mind. It was a tragedy but only one of the many tragedies that war caused. Once the initial shock of the news was over, Chalmont would also see it that way. In the meantime he was to see Hilary again for a full afternoon and evening. Richards could not wait for the rest of that day to end.

She was already having tea in the café when Richards arrived. This time she was wearing civilian dress, a green frock under a light summer coat. With her black hair uncovered and shining in the sun that slanted through an open window, Richards knew again she was the most beautiful woman he had ever seen.

She stirred on seeing him and for a moment Richards thought there was welcome in her glance. But the look she gave him as he reached her table was almost hostile. With his enthusiasm suddenly chilled, Richards felt apprehension. 'I'm sorry if I'm a few minutes late. It was the train. And I had trouble getting a taxi.'

She shook her head. 'It doesn't matter. Mark, have you had any contact with Jeremy yet?'

Richards sank into a chair. 'No. I haven't seen him since I phoned you. Didn't he go home?'

'I don't know. He might have done. But only after I saw him this morning.'

Richards gave a start. 'You saw him this morning? Where?'

'At the hospital. At 8 a.m. He demanded to see me. He looked terrible. God knows where he'd been all night.'

Richards was beginning to understand. 'What did he tell you?'

'Everything. How you'd been tricked to bomb a factory full of French workers. How ashamed and disgusted he was. I know he shouldn't have told me about a military operation but he was too upset to care about that.'

Richards took a deep breath. 'Hilary, our people didn't trick us. It was a horrible mistake. Jerry doesn't need to feel that way.'

Her dark eyes were very hostile now. 'A mistake? After all that planning and preparation? Don't you realize there would be fathers with children in that factory? You and Jeremy made those children orphans with your damn bombs. Don't you even feel sorry about it?'

After his earlier excitement at meeting her again, Richards's dismay was the more profound. 'Of course I feel sorry about it. I was as shocked as Jerry when he told me. But what can either of us do? We're just pawns who have to do as we're told.'

Her contempt burned him. 'Of course you're not pawns. You're fully grown men. What do you do? You refuse. You tell them you won't be a party to mass slaughter.'

Richards was suddenly feeling he was in an Alice in Wonderland world where one valid rule contradicted another. 'Hilary, if we did that we would be court-martialled and branded as cowards. Do you want that to happen to Jerry?'

Her reply was as fierce as a lit blowtorch. 'Yes. I'd love it to happen to Jeremy. He wouldn't be a coward to me. He'd be a hero. And so would you if you stood by him.'

Believing he was losing the girl, Richards was near to panic. 'Do you think I don't care either? I'm not a killer by nature, Hilary. The truth is I hate killing anything. Flies, beetles, rats – to me they're all part of the same world. Ask my parents. They would tell you. But we're at war and Jerry and I have been dragged into it. How can we pick and choose what we do? God knows if only we could, how different it would be.'

His distress and impassioned words had made her eyes search his face. When his voice choked away, her expression had changed. 'It has affected you too, hasn't it? I'm sorry, Mark. I shouldn't have attacked you like that.'

His voice was almost inaudible now. 'I know how you feel and I don't blame you. But what can we do? Oh God, how I hate this war.'

She saw now that he was trembling. Her hand reached out and touched his arm. 'Leave it now, Mark. Did you have breakfast this morning?'

Her question seemed to bewilder him. 'No. I caught an early train. Why?'

'Then you must have something now,' she told him. 'I'll see to it.'

He made a gesture of denial. 'No, I'm not hungry. Where do you think Jerry is now? If he hasn't gone back to camp he's AWOL.'

Her face clouded. 'I don't know. Perhaps he has gone on to Hereford. I'll phone Mother later to find out.' Then her tone changed. 'If you won't eat can I get you coffee?' When he again refused, she waved the waitress towards her, laying a hand on Richards's arm when he fumbled for money. 'No. I'll see to this.' She paid the waitress then turned back to him. 'As it's such a fine day do you know what I'd like to do this afternoon?'

Still distressed and bewildered by her change of mood, Richards shook his head.

'I'd like to go to the seaside. Scarborough perhaps. We could walk along the cliffs, go round the shops, and perhaps go to a show in the evening. We can take a bus there. What do you say?'

Still trying to relate this girl with the one seen a few moments ago, Richards would have agreed with any suggestion at that moment. His one wish was to restore a relationship that meant the world to him. 'Yes. Yes, I'd like that too.'

Smiling, she rose and took his arm. 'Then let's go and do it.'

'But are you sure you want to go that far from the hospital? What if Jeremy tries to contact you again?'

'He can leave a message. It's not fair on you to waste your few hours off duty. Come on. Let's catch a bus and get some sea air. It'll do us both good.'

CHAPTER 26

THE AFTERNOON THAT followed was magic for Richards. On Hilary's insistence they had lunch on arrival at the picturesque seaside resort and then spent the early afternoon wandering through the narrow streets of the old town, walking the promenade, and exploring its harbour. Afterwards they took a bus to its famous park where, like two children, they fed scraps of bread to the ducks and swans on its huge lake. Before leaving the park they had tea and sandwiches and, with Hilary more talkative than Richards had known her, the sun was dipping over the distant moors before they emerged from the café. 'What would you like to do now?' he asked her. 'Go to a cinema?'

She pulled a face. 'No. It's too nice an evening. Let's go back to the sea again.'

Happy to do anything she wanted, he followed her through the northern suburbs to the coast again. Here the high, shelving cliffs gave a panoramic view of the bay and the incoming waves. As they made their way down a path that led to a promenade below, she paused by a seat. 'We must have walked miles today. Do you mind if we have a rest?'

He was only too glad to sit beside her. The evening was still and the sound of the waves below was little more than a murmur. On the far horizon the sea was tinted pink by the setting sun. A clatter of wings drew their eyes as a flight of homing birds passed overhead. Her sigh broke the silence that followed. 'You'd never think there was war on, would you?'

He was longing to hold and kiss her. 'No,' he said. 'You wouldn't.'

It was then they heard a low whimper from the path above them. At first they thought it came from some injured rabbit or weasel. As Richards was about to rise, she caught his arm. 'No. Wait. It's coming closer.'

He saw she was right a few seconds later when a small mongrel dog appeared on the winding path. From its painful progress it was clear that one of its front legs was injured. As Richards jumped up and approached it, it tried to run away but stumbled instead and gave a yelp of pain. Richards knelt beside it, his voice gentle and soothing. 'What's the matter, old lad? Can I take a look?'

The mongrel growled as Richard tried to inspect its leg but the growl died away as he stroked its head. By this time Hilary was kneeling beside him. 'How bad is it?'

As Richards felt the injured leg, the dog gave another yelp of pain. Hilary pushed forward. 'Let me look.' A moment later she glanced round at Richards. 'I think it might be broken.' Then, as she turned back to the dog, she gave a start. 'It's been kicked. Look at these marks on its body.'

Richards saw she was right. 'It's got a collar on. Does it have an address?'

They studied the collar on the trembling dog but could see no identification. Richards straightened. 'We can't leave it here. I wonder where the nearest police station is.' He bent down again. 'Let's get it back to the road. We're sure to meet someone up there.'

As he tried to pick up the dog he caught its injured leg and the animal snapped at his hand. Seeing blood well from the bite, Hilary expected him to drop the animal but instead he wrapped an arm round the quivering body and rose with it. As the mongrel tried again to bite him, Hilary showed concern. 'Be careful, Mark. Those bites could be dangerous. Perhaps we should bring the police down here.'

He was already starting up the steep path. 'He might disappear. If that leg's broken he must be in agony.'

Knowing he was right, she followed him up the path. They found a pedestrian on the cliff top who told them there was a police station, half a mile away. Before they reached the station, blood was seeping from another bite on Richards's wrist but his voice and handling of the dog remained as gentle as before. Hilary's concern was as much for him as the dog now. 'You'll have to have tetanus injections for those bites, Mark.'

On their arrival at the police station, a sergeant promised a veterinary surgeon would be alerted. Like Hilary, he showed concern over Richards's injuries. 'You'd better get them bites treated, sir. You don't know where that dog's been.'

It was only when a veterinary surgeon had been contacted that Richards would leave the dog, which was now lying in one of the vacant cells. As they entered the main hall, the sergeant handed Hilary a first aid kit. 'Will this be any use, miss?'

She thanked him and insisted on bandaging Richards's hand and wrist before going outside. To her surprise she discovered he was trembling but he knew it was not because of his injuries. As they left the station, he glanced back. 'You know what will happen now, don't you? They'll put the poor thing down.'

She hugged his arm. 'You've done all you can. Now you must think about yourself. You must get the station MO to give you those injections when you get back. It's important so don't forget.'

His mind was still on the dog. 'I wonder who kicked it like that?'

Seeing a pub a few paces down the street, she drew him towards it. 'You need a drink and I think I do too. Let's go inside and sit down.'

Inside the pub, sitting at a table with a drink before them, she felt able to bring up the subject of the dog again. 'Have you always cared for animals, Mark?'

Embarrassment made him frown. 'I suppose so. But don't we all?'

'No. The man who kicked that dog doesn't. He probably enjoys giving pain.'

When he frowned and drew on his cigarette without answering, she felt a sudden need to explore his sensitivity. 'It's not just caring for animals, is it, Mark? You hate cruelty too, don't you?'

Long seconds passed before he answered. 'Yes, I suppose I do. But it's everywhere, isn't it? Even in children.'

She leaned forward. 'When did you find that out?'

He drew on his cigarette again before answering. 'There was a kid in our school. He had a cleft palate and all the others used to jeer at him. I tried to be friendly but he got so he wouldn't trust anyone. Then one day he didn't come to school. We got the news the next day. He'd committed suicide.'

She winced. 'I'm afraid bullying is very common, Mark. It always has been.'

Her words opened the floodgates of an emotion that his masculinity had found effeminate. 'Isn't bullying just another word for cruelty? And doesn't that run right through life itself? The entire world's a slaughterhouse. And not only animals kill one another. Who's better at it than we humans are?'

She was already intrigued by the contradiction of the young airman's persona, a hater of cruelty in all its forms and yet a volunteer for a military unit. Now he was revealing deeper, even more private, emotions. 'But you're religious, Mark. You believe in a merciful God. Doesn't that help you to live with it?'

Seeing his expression, she knew it was a cruel question. At the same time his complexity was fascinating her. She did not miss the shame in his reply. 'It should, shouldn't it? But it doesn't. Not when you find cruelty so ugly. It's a paradox I've never come to terms with.'

And I once believed this man just a simple airman who carried out his destructive work without regard to its consequences, she thought. Suddenly afraid she had gone too far, she tried to lighten his mood. 'Cruelty isn't everywhere, Mark. Some people are very kind, like yourself.'

He gave a short laugh. 'They haven't had much influence on world history, have they? It's the war lords who've shaped it.'

'How can you say that? Who founded your religion? The kindest man who ever lived. And what about the saints that followed him. Didn't they sacrifice their very lives for mankind?'

He shrugged. 'Maybe but where did it get us? Just one war after another. Killing the innocents with the rest, just as they did in Guernica.'

She found his bitterness at odds with the man she had seen with the dog but knowing she was the cause, she tried to make amends. 'No. Even I don't go that far. Sacrifices teach us how we can rise above our primitive selves and be an example to those who follow. So how can they be wasted?'

His troubled eyes rose to gaze at her. 'What are you saying? That sacrifice redeems us?'

She paused, then smiled. 'I never thought of it that way. Yes, I suppose I am. What a lovely expression. Did you invent it yourself or was it something you heard in church?' She could not read his expression as he gazed at her. 'What are you thinking now?' she laughed. 'How awful I am because I don't go to church?'

He shook his head. 'No. I was thinking how you spend your days looking after the sick and wounded. Isn't that a form of sacrifice?'

She welcomed the chance to lighten the conversation. 'Me? You haven't seen me in action. I'm one of those bullies you detest, ordering patients around and forcing medicine down their throats. I'm such a bully that Matron takes tips from me.'

To her relief his mood lifted after that and no further clouds spoiled their remaining hours together. It was only after he had seen her back to hospital and she was in bed that she thought again about their conversation in the pub. While it had delighted her to discover he had such complex feelings, she now found a single cell in her mind was giving out tiny alarm signals. Whether it had been something said or some reaction from Mark she could not pin down, but she found herself puzzling about it until tiredness brought her sleep and relief.

CHAPTER 27

CHALMONT DID NOT return to Sutton Craddock that night nor was he present at the briefing for a squadron exercise the following morning. Half an hour before take-off, Harvey called Richards in to his office. In his usual fashion the blunt Yorkshireman came straight to the point. 'Chalmont's AWOL. Where is he? Don't tell me you don't know.'

'I don't,' Richards confessed. 'I saw his sister yesterday and she didn't know either.'

'Sister? You mean you went to his home?'

'No, sir. She's a nurse in York. He'd seen her in the morning but only for a few minutes. After that she doesn't know where he went.'

'Didn't she try his home?'

'I phoned there this morning,' Richards explained. 'But he hadn't been there.'

Harvey's heavy eyebrows drew together. 'So what is it? Did that bridge operation give him the shits? Has the young bugger panicked and done a bunk?'

Richards shook his head. 'No, sir. He couldn't have behaved better. You saw how well he brought our kite down afterwards. I'm certain it's nothing to do with the operation.'

Harvey frowned. 'How the hell can you be certain? I've known men crack up weeks after a prang. Or do you know something you're not telling me?'

Although he had expected far worse from the tough Yorkshireman, Richards was certain he would pour scorn on the real reason for Chalmont's behaviour. 'I suppose it could be some kind of delayed reaction, sir, although I saw no sign of it. Perhaps he's had some bad news from somewhere.'

Harvey's deep-set eyes were searching his face. 'You're not holding anything back from me, are you?'

Richards managed his answer without lying. 'He said nothing to me about going AWOL, sir.' The navigator took a deep breath. 'He's a fine pilot, sir. I'm sure it must be a private problem and he'll be back soon.'

Harvey, who secretly agreed with Richards's assessment of Chalmont's worth, gave a scowl. 'He'd better be, Richards. Otherwise it could be a court martial and that's something this squadron doesn't want. If that sister of his hears from him again she tells him to report back pronto or he'll be for the high drop. You tell him the same if you hear from him. He's got twenty-four hours. After that my report goes in. All right?'

Richards came to attention. 'Yes, sir. And thank you.'

Harvey scowled again. 'Don't thank me, Richards. I'll jump on the bugger with both feet when I see him again.'

Adams received the phone call that evening when he was assessing the results of the squadron's exercise. Sue handed him the telephone. 'It's the guardroom, Frank. They say Joe Kearns wants to speak to you.'

Puzzled, Adams took the phone from her. 'Adams here. Oh, hello, Joe. What can I do for you?'

Kearns's voice was guarded. 'There's something I need to talk to you about, Frank. Can you come over?'

Adams cast an eye at the assessment papers on his table. 'Is it important, Joe?'

'Aye, it is rather, lad. Otherwise I wouldn't bother you.'

'All right, Joe. Give me ten minutes and I'll be over.' Adams replaced the phone and turned to Sue. 'He wants to see me. He says it's important. Can you manage for a while?'

She looked as puzzled as he was. 'Yes, of course. But what's happened?'

Adams shrugged. 'I can't think. But Joe's not the kind to cry wolf. I'd better get over right away.'

Kearns was waiting at the front door of the inn when Adams hurried up the gravel drive. 'Sorry to bother you with this, Frank, but you were the only one I dare contact. He's in my upstairs room.'

'He?' Adams enquired.

'Aye. That nice lad you brought over a few days ago.'

Adams gave a start. 'Chalmont?'

'That's the one. He was in a bad state when he came in. We thought it better to get him out of sight in case any of his senior officers appeared.'

As Adams followed Kearns up the stairs, Maisie appeared at the

door of the front bedroom. She looked flushed and upset. 'Thank goodness you've come, Frank. We didn't want him to get into trouble.'

She led Adams into the room. Chalmont was lying on the bed, his
shirt collar open, his uniform creased and his face unshaven. As
Adams bent over him, he caught the strong smell of alcohol. The
pilot's muzzy eyes stared up at him and slowly recognition entered
them. 'Hello, sir.'

Adams glanced round at Maisie. 'How long's he been here?'

'Since we opened,' Maisie told him. 'He was like that at the time. We
didn't let him have any booze. We brought him straight up here.'

Adams turned back to the pilot. 'Where have you been, Chalmont?'
When the young man's dull eyes gazed at him blankly, he repeated the
question. He had to lean forward to hear the slurred reply. 'Don't
remember, sir. But I did see my sister....'

'Saw her where? At your home?'

'She's not at home.... She's in York. Saw her in hospital....'

Adams turned back to Maisie. 'Can we have some black coffee?'

Maisie nodded. 'Joe's gone down to put the kettle on. He won't be
long.' She nodded at the drunken man. 'What do you want to do with
him, Frank? Do you want him to stay here until he's better?'

Adams shook his head. 'No, as soon as he can walk, I'll take him
back to camp. Otherwise he'll end up in serious trouble.'

It took three cups of strong coffee, a shave with Kearns's razor, and
the best part of half an hour walking the pilot around the bedroom
before Adams felt able to take him back to the airfield. Maisie saw them
both to the door. 'You will take care of him, won't you, Frank? He's
such a nice kid. It must have something to do with that crash he had.
He was looking terrible when we saw him afterwards.'

Although he doubted her reason, Adams made no comment. He
steered the still unsteady Chalmont towards the camp entrance. As the
sentry came to a salute, Adams tried to return it, only to grab
Chalmont's arm as the young pilot staggered away. Not daring to think
of the comments that would pass around the guardroom at a squadron
leader showing such familiarity with a drunken pilot officer, the
sweating Adams got him as far as his billet and thankfully pushed him
inside.

Richards, at his locker writing a letter to Hilary, gave a start at seeing
the odd couple and jumped to his feet. 'Hello, sir. Where did you find
him?'

Breathing heavily, Adams got rid of his burden on the pilot's bed.
'He's been in The Black Swan. Out like a light most of the time. They

phoned me. What's the matter with him, Richards? I always thought him a sensible, level-headed young man.'

'He is, sir. This is something he can't help.'

Glancing at Chalmont, Adams saw he was not sleeping. He jerked a thumb at the door, saying to Richards, 'Come outside. Let's go for a walk.'

Outside the starlight was bright enough to identify the perimeter path of the airfield. Feeling inside his tunic, Adams drew out his pipe and struck a match. He waited until the tobacco was lit and they had walked past his confessional before putting his question. 'Well, what's his problem? Is it girl trouble?'

'No, sir. It's what Air Commodore Davies told him after we got back from the bridge near Antheor.'

Adams stared at him curiously. 'Davies?'

'Yes, sir. Apparently he was congratulating Jerry about his crash landing when he mentioned the French workers we'd killed the other week.'

Adams sucked in his breath. 'So that's it. Davies let the cat out of the bag.'

'Then you know what happened, sir?'

'Yes. We'd been given the wrong information. So we felt it kinder not to let the crews know.'

'It hit Jerry hard, sir. And his sister too when he told her.'

Adams gave a start. 'He told his sister? About a military operation?'

'Only because he was so upset. He wouldn't have done it otherwise. In any case his sister won't say anything.'

'How can you be sure of that?'

'I know her, sir. I met her when Jerry took me to his home. She's a nurse and works in York now.'

Adams began to relax. 'Have you seen her since?'

'Yes. I saw her yesterday. That was when she told me how distressed Jerry still is.'

'Are you friendly with her, Richards?'

On the subject of Hilary, Richards had no way of hiding his enthusiasm. 'Yes, sir. She's a lovely person. That's why I know you can trust her.'

Adams had heard enough to guess his relationship with the girl. 'Doesn't she know where he has been?'

'No, sir. But she said he was terribly upset about the French factory job. He's much more sensitive than he appears to be.'

By this time Adams felt certain he could trust the young navigator. 'He is. Did you know he has an ambition to be a writer?'

'A writer? No, sir. He's said nothing to me.'

'He wouldn't. He's afraid the others might laugh at him. In fact I warned him not to mention it. But he has written quite a number of short stories. I read one a few days ago and it was good. Very perceptive and sensitive. So the massacre at Guernica must have had a profound effect on a young, sensitive boy.'

By this time they had reached the hardstandings of the Mosquitoes. In the starlight they looked like silver birds at rest. As they reached one of the gun posts that ringed the airfield, a torch suddenly shone down on them. Shading his eyes, Adams gave a reassuring shout to the alert gun crew. A moment later the torch went out. The glow of Adams' pipe appeared in the darkness that followed. 'So in your opinion his behaviour is due to the news he got from Air Commodore Davies?'

'I'm certain of it, sir. It had nothing to do with our operation. I gave that opinion to Mr Harvey.'

Adams nodded. 'I'm certain you're right. So you've seen Harvey? What did he say?'

Richards told him. 'He gave Jerry twenty-four hours. Then he said he'd have to report him missing.'

Adams nodded. 'That's Frank Harvey. When we go back I'll let him know that Chalmont's back in camp.'

A silence fell between them. It was broken only by the sound of their footsteps on the concrete path and muffled voices as they passed one of the service huts near a hardstanding. Adams guessed the resident mechanics would be at their usual practice of brewing tea. His pipe glowed again, then moved from his mouth. 'How do you feel about that factory botch-up, Richards?'

Richards turned towards him. 'You mean about the French workers we killed, sir?'

'Yes. You are religious, aren't you, Richards?'

Richards gave a start. 'How do you know that, sir?'

'I've seen you at church service. Don't be ashamed of it. It's not a crime.'

The night hid Richard's expression. 'I'm not ashamed of it, sir. But it's not an easy thing to be in wartime.'

'I'm sure it can't be, Richards. You have my sympathy.'

No words could have touched Richards's vulnerability more. With his father absent in Canada, he had no older man to confide in and Adams had a manner that tempted a younger man's confidences. It was only when Richards remembered Adams's rank and the unsentimentality of the Armed Forces that he resisted the yearning. 'Are you religious yourself, sir?'

Adams sighed. 'I don't know what I am, Richards. I suppose the priests and parsons would say I'm not and probably they'd be right. It's not easy to believe in mercy and goodness in the world we're living in today.'

Adams had to strain his ears to hear the young navigator's reply. 'No, sir. It isn't.'

Adams had already decided that if he had been blessed with sons this man and Chalmont would be high in his choice. 'You were a volunteer, weren't you, Richards?'

Richards gave a half laugh. 'Yes, sir. But don't ask me why.'

'I know why. You hated the Nazis and their bullying. Aren't I right?'

Richards turned towards him. 'How could you know that, sir?'

Adams laughed. 'I have met others like you, Richards.'

'You wouldn't be one yourself, would you, sir?'

Adams's tone changed. 'Come to think of it, I suppose I am. Only I do all my flying behind a desk and on the seat of my pants. So mine was hardly a heroic gesture.'

'One can't help one's age, sir.'

'That's true enough. But it doesn't make one feel any better. The truth is I'd have given my right arm to have been young enough for aircrew.'

'You wanted to fly that much?'

Adams now wanted to kick himself for his admission. 'Yes, but it's probably just as well I was too old. Or God knows how many aircraft I would have written off.' He checked his stride and turned. 'We'd better get back now. I've still some work to do tonight.'

Little was said between them as they retraced their steps although both knew a bond had grown between them. In Richards's billet they found Chalmont was fast asleep. 'Let him be,' Adams said. 'But I want to see him in the morning. You haven't any flying scheduled tomorrow so tell him to come and see me at 1000 hours. In the meantime I'll see Harvey and tell him what's happened.' He paused. 'What will you do now?'

'I'll probably go to the mess and finish my letter,' Richards told him. The sudden impulse that made him hold out his hand was against all military tradition but he could not resist it. 'Thank you for everything, sir. I know Chalmont will feel the same when he realizes what you've done.'

Adams felt the sincerity in the grip of the young navigator's hand.

As he released it, Adams took off his spectacles, wiped them and replaced them. He hoped his voice had some semblance of military countenance when he stepped back. 'Make sure Chalmont sees me in the morning. Any more slip-ups and he could be in serious trouble. Good night, Richards.'

'Good night, sir.' Richards stood for a long moment watching the bulky figure of Adams disappear into the darkness. Then he entered the dark billet, found his writing pad, and slipped out to the mess.

CHAPTER 28

CHALMONT LOOKED PALE and tired when he entered the billet the following morning. Richards, awaiting his return, swung his legs off his bed. 'How did it go?'

Chalmont shrugged. 'All right. He gave me a lecture, said I mustn't be so sensitive about foreign workers, and told me off for telling Hilary about our French raid. You told him about that, didn't you?'

'Yes. I'm sorry. But Adams won't take it any further. Is that all he said?'

Chalmont drew a sheaf of papers from beneath his tunic and threw them on his bed. 'He also said he liked this little piece I gave him. Nothing else really.'

'You never told me you wrote short stories. Can I read one?'

'If you like. Sometime.' Wincing, putting a hand to his head, Chalmont sank down on his bed. 'God. My head's killing me.'

'It's not surprising, You must have had a hell of a skinful yesterday. Where did you go after you left Hilary?'

Chalmont did not reply. Instead he turned towards Richards. 'Adams said Harvey called you in yesterday. What did he say?'

'He asked if I knew why you'd gone AWOL and where you were. I told him I didn't know. Then he said he'd give you twenty-four hours before reporting you. So you can imagine what a relief it was when Adams brought you back from the pub.' When Chalmont made no comment, Richards went on, 'Do you realize he'd washed and shaved you before he brought you over? I hope you thanked him for it. You'd better thank Maisie and Kearns too. If they hadn't put you to bed and phoned Adams you could be in the guardroom today.'

His hands on his head, Chalmont dropped back on his pillow. 'I won't forget them. Does Hilary know I'm back in camp?'

'Yes. I phoned the hospital and left a message. She'll be more than relieved.'

A silence followed, then Chalmont turned towards Richards again. 'How did you feel when you heard about those French workers?'

Richards knew he must not emphasize his answer. 'I was upset, like you. It was a bad mistake.'

'Bad mistake? It was a terrible one. But I don't believe it was a mistake. I think the shift change was mentioned so we wouldn't offer any objections.'

Richards shook his head. 'No. Adams told me it was a mistake. And he's a man I trust.'

Chalmont turned away in contempt. 'Then you're a fool. I don't trust any of them any more. They'll tell us any lies to get their dirty work done.'

The squadron resumed its interdiction activities the following day. With Chalmont morose and moody, Richards was unsure how he would react but to his relief the pilot could not be faulted on his combat performance although once back on the airfield he was a changed man. Until then, while he had never shared the wild parties that many of his colleagues enjoyed, he had nevertheless been sociable enough for his different tastes to be accepted and tolerated by the other crews. Now he displayed an impatient and ill temper that quickly set him apart from the others and, because men tend to believe what they want to believe, it was not long before they found a reason for his behaviour. Hopkinson, A-Apple's Cockney navigator, expressed it succinctly enough to Tomlinson one day, although not in the presence of Moore. 'The bugger thinks that because of his background and his college he's better than the rest of us. Then to hell with the bloody snob.'

All of this was an embarrassment to Richards. Knowing the cause of Chalmont's changed behaviour and wanting to remain his friend both for the pilot's sake and for Hilary's, he found himself defending his pilot against crews who had once been his friends. With Chalmont his own enemy because of his moodiness, it was not long before Richards found he was almost as estranged as the pilot himself.

Because debriefing allowed this rift to show, the sensitive Adams was the first senior officer to notice it and the following week he called Richards to one side. 'What's happening, Richards? Has it to do with Chalmont?'

While not wanting to make the admission, Richards badly needed help. 'He's changed since he heard about that French factory, sir. He does his job as well as ever but something's happened to his mind. He never mixes with the crews and even I have a job to talk to him some-times.'

'And because he's your friend it's affecting your own relationship with the crews. I see. What does his sister say about him?'

'I don't know that, sir. We haven't been allowed out of camp during the last week.'

Adams made a quick decision. 'Don't say a word to him but I'll have a chat with the MO. He might have some pill or concoction to pull him round.'

Chalmont received the order to report to the MO's surgery the following morning. His mood was puzzled and irritable when Richards saw him half an hour later. 'What the hell was that for? Who gave the order I should see him?'

Richards professed ignorance. 'What did he tell you?'

'He didn't tell me anything. He couldn't find anything wrong with me. So why was I sent?'

Adams managed a word with Richards during lunch. 'No, he couldn't find a reason for resting him. The trouble is the MO isn't a psychiatrist. That's what we need but I haven't any excuse yet to send him to one. Try to support him all you can in the meantime and perhaps a chance will come later.'

Adams had little idea when he spoke how near that chance might be. That afternoon, after receiving a coded message, Davies and Henderson were compelled to pay a second visit to High Elms where they received their usual courteous welcome from Simms. 'Good after-noon, gentlemen. Thank you for coming so promptly. As you see, General Staines has preceded you.'

Both men's eyes moved to the American who had arisen from the long mahogany table behind the urbane brigadier. General Staines of the American Eighth Air Force was well known to both men by this time. A big and amiable Texan, Ed Staines had once played football for West Point and it still showed in his huge, granite-hard body although his hair was now iron grey. His face was leathery with bushy eyebrows and a square chin. Returning the two officers' salutes, he held out a huge hand to them both. 'Good to see you guys again. Simms tells me you're knocking hell out of the Heinies' transport system these days.'

Davies grimaced. 'We're doing our best, sir, although in my opinion Typhoons are better equipped for the job.'

Staines grinned. His voice sounded like emery cloth running over corrugated iron. 'You think so? I seem to remember you guys doing a great job over France on Operation Crucible.'

'We hadn't much choice, sir. Jerry's tanks caught us on the hop.'

'Stop being so bloody British, Davies. You've got a hell of an outfit there and you know it.'

While Davies knew the American had a genuinely high regard for his squadron, all his senses were alert now. 'We try, sir. I take it you're here because of this news the brigadier has brought us?'

Staines' expression changed. 'Yeah. You've guessed it. I couldn't believe it when I first heard. It's getting to be a hell of a war, Davies.'

'Yes, sir. It is.'

For a couple of seconds none of the men spoke. Then the American's natural ebullience surfaced again. 'Let's have a slug or two before we get down to the soiled linen.' He glanced at Simms. 'What about a spot of that bourbon I brought for the guys, Simms?' As Simms nodded and pressed a button on the table, Davies was about to protest when he remembered what a hard-drinking character Staines was. His 'Just a small one for me, sir' to Simms was a compromise.

The twinkle in Staines's eyes told he had also remembered. 'Well done, Davies. You'll like it. I had it delivered from the States only last week. And, hell, isn't this a time for a pick-me-up?' When Davies made no comment Staines' eyes moved to Henderson. 'I take it you'll have a wee dram, Jock?'

Relieved of the problem of placating Davies or surrendering to temptation, Henderson nodded gratefully. 'Thank you, sir.'

The speed at which a uniformed girl entered with a tray, a bottle and four glasses told both airmen that act had been prearranged. After Simms had filled the glasses and passed them round, Staines dropped his bulk into a chair and pulled out a cigar case. 'Take the weight off your legs, you guys. They've gotta last you a long time.'

The three men settled down. Simms slid a box of cigarettes towards Davies, who shook his head. He watched Staines apply a match to a cigar as long as a prize cucumber. The American exhaled smoke, examined the cigar affectionately, then fixed his eyes on Davies. The directness of his question was like a sudden rifle shot. 'It's a hell of an assignment, Davies. Are you taking it on?'

To Henderson, watching the scene with apprehension, the temperature in the library suddenly dropped ten degrees. He saw Davies take a deep breath before giving his answer. 'I don't see I've any alternative, sir, if the orders come from the top. But it's the most tasteless thing we've ever had to do.'

Tasteless, Henderson thought. Where the hell did he dig up that word from?

Staines emitted another cloud of smoke before replying. 'You can say that again, Davies.' He glanced at Henderson. 'How are your men going to feel about it, Jock?'

Davies gave the Scot no chance to answer. 'They'll do as they're told. As they always have. That doesn't mean they'll like it but they'll still obey orders.'

Henderson was not going to let Davies get away with it that easily. 'I expect they will, sir, but I can't see many of them getting much sleep afterwards.'

Staines took a deep sip of whisky. 'I don't expect any of us will.' His eyes remained on Henderson. 'You're not happy about it yourself, are you, Jock?'

'Happy, sir? I'm horrified. I find it worse than murder.'

Davies, resenting both the question to a junior officer and that officer's reply, broke in irritably. 'None of us likes it but if it's going to save our armies in Italy we've no choice.' He turned back to Staines. 'I take it you will give us cover, sir? Otherwise I can't see half my aircraft even getting there.'

Staines nodded. 'That's why I'm here. Eaker's as concerned about our Italian armies as you are about yours. Mind you, it would have been tough to rustle up enough ships for a speculative mission like this if we hadn't already planned another attack on Augsberg. As that's on your route, all we need do is change the date.' He glanced at Simms who so far had been silent. 'Even so, it's going to need precise planning and timing to make it work.'

Nodding, Simms drew a folder towards him. 'That's why I asked you all to be here today. Our intelligence is now certain the enemy intends to go ahead with his plan. The one uncertain factor is the date. He has to bring the necessary elements together and because of the danger they represent this will take time. We believe we have a week of grace although it could be less. However, if we make our plans now we will be ready when the green light comes.'

When all the men nodded, Simms pressed a button on his table and two men wearing civilian clothes entered the library. They joined the four officers gathered round the table. While they talked, the evening sky seen through the French windows turned blood red as the sun sank behind the elms. From the grounds a guard dog barked, followed by a man's shout. To Henderson, now divorced from the decisions that were being made, the scene had an unreal and surrealistic quality. Although the Scot had never seen himself as an imaginative man, he could not throw off the feeling he was taking part in a living nightmare.

CHAPTER 29

ENDERSON HAD A call on his scrambler telephone the following morning. 'Jock, I want you to give your boys forty-eight hours' leave. But everyone must leave his address and none must stray far away from it in case we need a quick recall. Is that clear?'

'It's clear, sir, but is it wise? How can we guarantee to get in touch with them quickly? Most of them will be with girls. Some are sure to wander off to cinemas or dance halls.'

'I know that, Jock, but in this case I feel they ought to get the break. Tell them that wherever they go they leave a message how they can be reached. Make it an order.'

Henderson's thoughts were more than bleak when he replaced the receiver. No order Davies could have given could have reflected more the air commodore's views of the forthcoming operation. The job had to be done but the crews needed mentally bracing before being told its nature. Shaking his head, the Scot reached for his standard telephone. 'Laura, put me through to Wing Commander Moore, Harvey and Young, will you, please? In that order.'

Millburn braked his old Morris on the road that ran alongside the promenade, saw there were no girls waiting, and turned suspiciously to Gabby. 'Are you sure they're both back from leave? This isn't just a trick to get a free ride into Scarborough?'

Gabby looked hurt at the suggestion. 'You can't think I'd do that?'

'Think? Boyo, I think you're capable of anything. Gremlins are famous for it.'

Gabby, dressed in his best uniform, bristled. 'If you use that word once more tonight I'll kill you.'

'What word?'

'Gremlin. Just because you're a couple of inches taller than me doesn't mean you have to insult me every time you speak. It's not the size of the package that matters, Millburn. It's what's inside it.'

Millburn grinned. 'And what's inside yours, boyo? I've always wanted to know.'

'A bloody sight more than you have, Millburn. Who persuaded these women to see us tonight? Not you.'

'And why was that? Because you shot a line about being a wounded hero. I've got you taped, boyo. The biggest line shooter in the business.' Millburn's tone changed. 'Let's get one thing straight before I go any further. The tall blonde's mine. Don't pull any more fast ones about your war wounds and your stiff upper lip. Try that and I'll bounce you under the table.'

Gabby sniffed. 'You're all wind and water, Millburn. You ought to be grateful I've fixed things up for you. You've done nothing else but talk about that blonde since you first saw her.'

Realizing it was true, Millburn lit a cigarette before glancing back at Gabby. 'You've never said where we're taking them to dinner. Or haven't you booked a table yet?'

Gabby said something that was drowned by the waves on the beach below. Millburn glanced at him again. 'What did you say?'

Gabby answered without looking at him. 'The Trocadero.'

Millburn's start rocked the car on its springs. 'What! That's the dearest place in town. Who suggested that?'

'Wendy did. But what's your problem? You don't want to look mean, do you? Everyone expects Americans to flash their money about.'

Millburn was breathing hard. 'So that's why you blackmailed me into promising to pay tonight? All the other joints keep to that five shillings a meal restriction. You bloody little show-off. I ought to drive you straight back to camp.'

Gabby knew he was on safe ground. 'But you won't, will you? You fancy that big blonde too much.'

At that moment a taxi drew up and two girls stepped out. Gabby nudged Millburn in anticipation. 'I told you they'd come. Get set for a big evening, Millburn.'

The two girls approached the Morris. One, with cropped dark hair, was slightly below medium height. The other was tall and blonde with hair that fell to her shoulders. The smaller girl smiled at both the airmen, then addressed Gabby. 'Sorry about the taxi, love, but neither of us has any change. Do you mind?'

Under the steering wheel Gabby's knee nudged Millburn. The American gave him a look, then opened his door and went to the stationary taxi. As it drove off, Gabby introduced him to the girls. 'This is Wendy, Millburn.' He turned to the big blonde. 'Joyce, this is Tommy Millburn.'

The blonde appraised the tall Millburn as she held out her hand. 'Nice to meet you, Tommy. You're an American, aren't you?'

Millburn grinned. 'That's what my passport says. Gabby tells me you two are in Naval Signals.'

Joyce nodded. 'We're just back from leave. That's why we're still wearing civvies.'

Millburn ran his eyes down her tall, statuesque figure. 'You're looking good in them too. What would you both like to do? Have a drink first or have one with your meal?'

'You're taking us to the Trocadero, aren't you?' Joyce asked.

Gabby answered for the American. 'That's right. I've booked a table.'

'Then I'd like to go straight there,' Joyce announced. 'I'm hungry and I know Wendy is too. You are, aren't you, love?'

Wendy nodded. 'Yes. I couldn't get any grub on the train. An' they say the food's great at the Trocadero.'

Millburn managed to avoid glancing at Gabby. 'Then let's go and find out.' He gave Gabby a shove. 'You go in the back with Wendy and let Joyce sit with me.'

With some giggling and flashing of knees, the girls took their seats and Millburn drove off. Ten minutes later he parked outside the Trocadero, a restaurant that advertised its menus at the standard wartime rates outside and charged its own rates within. Although its entrance was blacked out, the restaurant inside was all bright lights and glitter. A five-piece band was playing as a waiter led them to a table. Gabby crooked a finger at him and whispered something in his ear. The waiter nodded. 'I think it might be arranged, sir.'

As he hurried off, Millburn leaned suspiciously across the table. 'What might be arranged?'

Gabby's smile was pure innocence. 'As it's a special occasion I thought we'd have a bottle of champagne. He thinks he might get one for us.'

Millburn's glance would have shot a 190 straight out of the sky. 'You're full of good ideas, Gabby.'

Wendy gave a giggle. 'I've never had champagne before. They say it makes you ever so tiddly.'

Gabby gave her a wink. 'What's wrong with being tiddly when you're with friends?'

'I'm not sure I can trust you, Johnnie Gabriel.'

Gabby was in full song now. 'You can't, love. But isn't it more fun that way?'

As both girls giggled again, the waiter arrived with his ice bucket and champagne, filled the glasses, then handed round menus. Joyce's order made Millburn's eyes widen. 'Are you sure you can manage all that, kid?'

'Oh, yes. I've always had a good appetite. And like Wendy I couldn't get any grub on the train either.'

Across the table, Wendy's order was of the same magnitude. Consoling himself that the two girls would be in prime condition for the after-dinner celebrations, Millburn allowed his gaze to wander round the room. No doubt because of the high prices, the only guests were civilians. Three couples were taking advantage of the band and dancing. The rest were chatting and clearly enjoying the food.

At his table Gabby was refilling the glasses of the two girls. The main course came and within minutes the plates in front of them were as bare as if they had been scrubbed. Millburn managed a grin. 'You kids sure have a good appetite. That train journey must have been hell.' Signalling to the waiter, he turned to Joyce and handed her the menu. 'What kind of a sweet would you like, kid? The raspberry pie looks good.'

He received a smile of pure innocence. 'I think I'll have the main course again, Tommy. You don't mind, do you?'

Millburn's start nearly toppled over the table. 'You want all that again? Kid, you'll give yourself a hernia.'

She stiffened. 'There's no need to be rude. You don't begrudge us food, do you? Gabby said you were generous like all Americans.'

Millburn's glance across the table sent another burst of cannon fire at Gabby. 'Yeah, Gabby's a good friend of mine. Always paints a good picture of me.' His eyes moved to Wendy. 'What about you, kid? Don't you fancy the raspberry pie?'

Wendy shook her head. 'If you don't mind, Tommy, I'd like the same as Joyce. We don't get that kind of food up at the house.'

Millburn's face was a study. 'You don't say?' He glanced up at the waiter. 'OK. Give 'em another helping. Only my friend and I will pass. We'll stick with coffee.'

As he was talking, Joyce was whispering to Wendy. As the astonished waiter moved away, the blonde girl turned to Millburn. 'We won't be a minute. We're just going to the ladies' room.'

Millburn waited until they were out of earshot and then leaned towards Gabby. 'Who the hell are these two? Two horses dressed up as dames?'

Gabby, who had looked as surprised as anyone at the girls' second order, attempted defiance. 'They can't help it. They're hungry, that's all.'

'Hungry?' Millburn hissed. 'They've already eaten enough to go into hibernation. Do you realize what the bill's going to be?'

Gabby did his best to soothe him. 'Think of it as an investment, kid. Think how grateful they'll both be in the car afterwards.'

'Grateful,' Millburn snarled. 'When they've had that second helping they won't be able to squeeze into the goddamned car. I'll kill you when this is over, you little cretin. Wring your neck like a chicken.'

The two girls returned to the table a minute later. Neither of the two airmen noticed the two enormous sailors who had entered the room with them and were now standing on its fringe. Noticing the girls' return, the waiter arrived with two piled-up plates. Avoiding Millburn's glare, Gabby managed a sickly smile. 'That should fill the empty spaces. Do you mind if Tommy and I smoke?'

Wendy shrugged. 'No, you go ahead.' She glanced at Joyce, who nodded. Both girls reached down for their handbags and opened them. Pulling out greaseproof bags, they began shovelling the food from their plates into them. Gabby gaped at the scene. 'What are those? Doggie bags?'

Wendy shook her head. 'No. They're for us.'

'You mean you're taking the food to have later?'

Wendy gave him a defiant stare. 'Why not? You don't begrudge us a bite of food, do you?'

'I do.' The growl came from Millburn, who had just noticed the two sailors standing at the edge of the floor. 'I begrudge every goddamned crumb you're shoving into those bags.'

Before Gabby could comment, Joyce turned sharply on the American. 'What d'you mean by that?'

'I mean I'm not paying the bill, sweetheart. Not one red cent of it.'

Joyce glanced at the two menacing sailors. 'You'd better Yank. If you know what's good for you, you'd better.'

Across the table Gabby was looking lost and mystified. Millburn leaned across the table and jabbed a thumb in the direction of the two sailors. 'Don't you get it? It's a scam. The girls give us the glad eye, have a meal on us, then order food for their boyfriends. And we pay the bill. It's a set-up, boyo.'

With his dreams of after-dinner sex in ruins, Gabby was speechless. Across the room one of the huge sailors was talking in sign language to Joyce. Nodding back, she turned to Millburn. 'My friend says you'd better pay or they'll see you outside. You know what that'll mean. You won't just get beaten up but you'll be in serious trouble – two officers having a brawl with ordinary sailors. So one way or another you'd better pay, Yank.'

Millburn was thinking fast as he answered, 'You're a real sweetheart, kid. I could go for you in a big way.' He glanced up at the alarmed waiter. 'Fetch me the bill, will you?'

As the waiter hurried off, Joyce sank back in her chair. 'Now you're showing some sense.'

Millburn shrugged. 'I'm a sensible guy.' He turned to Gabby. 'Put your money on the table, boyo.'

Gabby looked as if he were having a bad dream. 'I can't pay the bill. You know I can't.'

'Put all you've got on the table,' Millburn repeated.

Wendy, her role as enchantress exposed, tittered. 'I would if I were you, Gabby. My boyfriend eats little airmen for breakfast.'

Muttering something, Gabby emptied his pockets on the table. Millburn gazed at the result. 'Three pounds and sixpence! Is that all you've got?' Before Gabby could answer, the waiter handed the bill to Millburn, who looked at it, whistled, and passed it to Gabby. The Welshman's face froze in horror. 'That's terrible. We can't pay that.'

Millburn shrugged. 'It looks as if we must, boyo.' He glanced up at the waiter. 'I'll pay at the desk. OK?'

The relieved waiter nodded and drew back. 'Thank you, sir.'

Millburn leaned forward and swept up Gabby's money. Then, rising to his feet and motioning Gabby to join him, he made for the desk in the hall. As the two triumphant girls followed them, Millburn hissed in Gabby's ear. 'Get ready to run like hell for the car. OK?'

The two sailors grinned at them as they passed by and turned to follow them. As Millburn reached the desk, he suddenly exploded. Swinging round, he smashed a fist in the nearer sailor's stomach. As the man gasped and doubled up, Millburn turned on Gabby and gave him a violent push. 'Go! Run like hell!'

With the stricken sailor already climbing to his feet and the second matelot trying to grab him, Gabby needed no advice. Flinging open the entrance door, he pelted out into the darkness while Millburn slammed the door in the face of the second sailor and ran after him. As they reached the Morris, lights appeared in the restaurant doorway and two huge figures could be seen pounding down the pavement towards them. Yanking on the passenger door, Gabby found it was unlocked and flung himself inside. His yell must have been heard back at Sutton Craddock. 'Get her off the ground, Millburn! Move it!'

The engine fired just as the two matelots reached the Morris and were grabbing for the door handles. Slamming in the gears, the cursing Millburn reversed and then shot forward, scattering the sailors. As yells and threats followed it, the Morris steadied and then accelerated down the road.

It was a couple of minutes later, when the car was threading its way through the narrow streets of the old town and the two shaken airmen had recovered their breath, that the accusations and recriminations began. 'You've done it again, you Welsh moron. Do you realize what would have happened if we'd had a brawl with those matelots? Davies would have had us crucified.'

'Whose fault was that, Millburn? Who pestered me for a jump with that big blonde?'

'How the hell was I to know she was tied up with King Kong and his brother? Don't you do any research with women before you date them?'

'How could I have guessed they'd pull something like that?'

'The least you could have done was check their appetites. Do you realize how much that Joyce ate before she pulled out her doggy bag? A goddamned gorilla couldn't have gotten through it.'

Gabby wasn't prepared to take all the flak. 'What about my money? You never paid the bill but you took all I had. I want it back, Millburn.'

'What if the restaurant want their money? You think I'm paying the full bill?'

'They won't dare ask for it. It'd give away their illegal charges. I want my money back, Millburn.'

'You'll wait for your goddamned money, boyo. It'll remind you not to get me involved with your crooked dames again.'

And so the recriminations and arguments went on, all the way back to Sutton Craddock and even in the billet afterwards. One thing about the affair could be said with safety. It had not been the best of nights for the squadron's leading womanizers.

CHAPTER 30

RICHARDS'S HOPES WERE not high when he phoned Hilary that afternoon. Being close to many airbases, her hospital was receiving many casualties and free time for nurses was at a premium. 'We've been given a special forty-eight-hour pass,' he told her. 'None of us know why but I had to try my luck. Is there any chance of seeing you? Even for a couple of hours?'

Her short silence made him fear the worst. Then he heard her question. 'What's the leave for, Mark? Do you know?'

'No. Nobody does. In a way it's a nuisance. It would have been better if it had come when you had a day off.'

Her voice suggested she had come to a decision. 'All right, Mark, I'll see you. They won't like it but that can't be helped. Meet me at two in the café and if it's a fine day we'll take a trip into the country.'

He could not believe his luck when he replaced the receiver. From his earlier loneliness, Richards was finding life with riches beyond his wildest dreams.

The small Norman church stood at the far end of the village, gazing down benignly on its flock of cottages. As they reached it, Hilary paused. 'We chose well today, didn't we? This is the kind of village one dreams about.'

They had caught a bus in York an hour ago. With no set plans they had waited until the bus had reached a village deep in the country. There Hilary had insisted on Richards having a meal and a drink in the village pub. Now, with the rest of the afternoon and evening stretching before them, they were exploring the village and the country around it.

The age of the church made it look as if it had grown out of the land that bore it. Seeing Richards's interest, Hilary made the suggestion. 'I'd like to look inside it. Do you mind?'

He looked surprised at her request. 'No. I'd like to myself.'

The huge oaken door at its entrance was unlocked. Inside was the smell of stone and old age. Dust motes floated in a coloured ray of sunlight that slanted across the aisle from a stained glass window. The silence was like a cool hand across the forehead, a tranquillity born of age and the acceptance of life and death.

She watched his movements and expression as they wandered past the empty pews, examining the inscriptions on the ancient stone walls. He was showing no undue reverence and yet she felt the depth of it within him. When they eventually walked out into the sunlight again, he turned to her. 'Thank you.'

She pretended surprise. 'What for? I wanted to look round it myself.'

'Did you?' he said. 'Anyway, it was thoughtful of you.'

About to reply, she changed her mind. A few minutes later they were on a country lane that led them through fields growing the crops a besieged country needed for its survival. As they reached a gate leading into a field of young corn, she stopped and turned to him. 'We're lucky with the weather, aren't we? It was like this on our day in Scarborough. Do you think the weather man likes us?'

He smiled. 'He ought to. We're nice people, aren't we?'

'You're nice,' she said. 'But not me. I'm a cold, heartless woman. Jeremy's always telling me that.'

He laughed. 'Brothers never know their sisters. It's common knowledge.'

'No. Jeremy's right. I am cold. Lots of men have noticed it.'

'I haven't,' he said. 'Not since I got to know you.'

Her dark eyes met his and the contact seemed to galvanize every molecule in his body. 'Do you think you know me now, Mark?'

He cleared his throat, knowing there would never be a woman again who could stir such emotion in him. 'I know you're everything I could ever want in a woman.'

Her expression made him realize what he had said. For a moment her laugh teased him. 'Everything? What simple tastes you must have.'

He could think of no words that fitted the moment. As her eyes met his again the only sound was the organ note of spring. A bee flew past them, intent on the contents of the hedgerow. Then, as almost by accident their hands touched, she murmured something and opened the gate. At her glance he followed her, as powerless as a man in a dream.

She laid her coat down behind the hedge and motioned him to join her. For minutes they lay side by side, their eyes on the white puffs of cloud above and neither of them breaking the silence. Then, like a stone shattering glass, the distant drone of an aircraft engine was heard.

She made a distressed sound and turned to him. 'Mark, I'm sorry. I've made you so unhappy at times, haven't I? About things you can't help. Only I can never forget what we saw in Spain. I wish I could but I can't.'

Before he could speak she put her arms around him and drew him closer. 'I hadn't realized until we went to Scarborough just how sensitive you are. I learned so many things about you that day. It made me wish I'd behaved differently to you. So will you forgive me?'

'There's nothing to forgive,' he muttered. 'You couldn't help what happened in Spain any more than Jeremy could. We're all victims of our environment. That's something I've grown to realize.'

Her face was so close to him now that he could see the reflection of himself in her dark eyes. 'You like me, don't you, Mark?'

A shiver ran through him. 'I think of nothing else. I have since we met in Hereford. Do you mind?'

She gave a soft laugh. 'You silly, gentle boy. Why don't you kiss me? I want you to.'

Her lips were the sweetest fruit Richards had ever tasted. Shyness and the fear of rejection prevented his going any further but she would not allow him to stop now. Whispering, encouraging, cajoling, she loosened her blouse and drew his hands and then his lips to her breasts. After he had tasted their nectar, she reached down and liberated the stress that her slender, willing body had engendered in him. When the act was over and tension flooded out, Richards heard himself sobbing. In that cornfield, on that spring day with the woman he adored, Richards knew that no matter what life might offer or deny him in the future, this would always be the sublime moment of his life.

CHAPTER 31

A T FIRST THE atmosphere in the operations room that Thursday morning was no different from other mornings. Men filed in, took their customary places, lit cigarettes, and passed the occasional wry joke. After weeks of their interdiction raids, only a tiny percentage of the crews suspected their recent forty-eight-hour pass had any more significance than being a reward for services rendered. As a consequence, the buzz of conversation was no louder than usual nor was it any quieter. Like many other aircrews in the country, 633 Squadron believed it was going to be briefed for yet another operation in which a few more of them might be killed or mutilated and were accepting the situation as part and parcel of wartime life.

It was only when the stentorian shout of 'Attention!' brought them to their feet that the atmosphere dramatically changed. As cigarettes were extinguished and men jumped to their feet they saw the diminutive figure of Davies leading in the coterie of officers. To older-serving crews, Davies's presence meant one thing: the kind of operation for which the special service unit had been created. When men remembered the code words of such operations, more than one mouth turned dry. Vesuvius, Rhine Maiden, Crucible, Valkyrie. The names beat on the mind like the drums of a tumbrel.

There was a deep hush in the room now as Davies led the officers on to the platform. As they took their seats, Davies moved to the edge of the platform and nodded at Bertram. A second later the command boomed out. 'At ease.'

There were coughs, a shuffling, and a rumbling of wooden benches as the crews resumed their seats. As Davies surveyed them he knew the situation called for one of his best performances. He began it with a grin. 'I know. You haven't seen me up here for some time so you're wondering what the reason is. The answer's simple. Instead of pissing about with trains and bridges, you're going to be given a worthwhile job for a change. Something that'll make you glad you're a member of

188

the best squadron in the RAF. Better still, the kind of job you've been trained for. So sit back, have a cigarette, and relax while I tell you all about it.'

Matches scratched and smoke began rising again to the dangling models above. Younger members glanced at one another, unsure whether to relax or not. Older members had no such problem. Gabby leaned towards Millburn. 'It's a big one, Millburn. The bastard's too chummy for it to be anything else.'

Millburn nodded, his eyes on Davies, who had now lit a cigarette himself before continuing. 'What I like about this operation, and I know you'll like too, is the way it's going to help our troops in Italy.'

There was a murmur from the back of the assembly. 'Italy?'

Seeing Bertram was about to stamp on the interruption, Davies shook his head and used it to his advantage. 'You like Italy, Machin?'

Although caught off-balance by the question, the Irishman was seldom at a loss for words. 'Oi's never been there, sur. But they tell me it's a great country for opera and women.'

Muted laughs broke out among the crews. Davies grinned. 'I take it you'd like opera, Machin.'

'Oi like women better, sur. If you don't mind, sur, that is.'

Davies shrugged. 'I don't mind one bit, Machin. Only I'm going to disappoint you, Paddy. You're not flying to Italy.'

'Thank God for that,' came another murmur.

Holding up a hand to check the buzz of conversation, Davies walked to the large map of Europe at the back of the platform. Picking up a cane, he pointed it at Austria. 'This is where your target will be. In western Austria.'

A sudden silence fell as Davies walked to the front of the platform again. 'I mentioned Italy only because of the effect your raid might have on our troops there. As you all know, the Jerries have established defence lines there that are proving tough nuts to crack. If we could break those defences it would be a massive help to our invasion of Europe, which we all know must come soon. On the other hand, if Jerry were to break out and drive our armies back, it might have a disastrous effect on Eisenhower's invasion plans. So all this makes those Italian defences a key element in the battles ahead.'

Pausing a moment to draw on his cigarette, Davies was weighing up the effect of his words on the audience. Seeing he had their complete attention now, he walked back to the European map. 'This is where Austria comes into the picture. As you will see, a major railway line runs through its mountains and through a complex of tunnels down to

Italy. In fact, it is one of the lines of communication that the Germans use to supply their Italian armies.'

A single muted voice broke the short silence that followed. 'Not bloody trains again.'

Born actor that he was, Davies seized the opportunity for drama. 'Yes, Hopkinson. But not any old train. This one is very special. So special it could have a massive effect on the Italian campaign and indeed on the outcome of the war itself.'

Knowing his man from old, Hopkinson took the opportunity for a piece of cockney humour. 'What's it carrying, sir? Hitler and Goering?'

Davies knew this was his opportunity. Conscious of the effect his revelation would have on his young audience, he braced himself before dropping his bombshell. 'No, Hopkinson. Something that might prove far more effective than either of them. A trainload full of chemical weapons.'

The effect was that of a time bomb. For a few seconds there was no reaction. Then a single, puzzled voice. 'Chemical weapons, sir?'

'Yes, Allison. In other words gas.'

There was a gasp, then a shock wave that ran through the entire assembly. Not a man present had not heard his father or uncle speak of the horrors of a war only a quarter of a century ago when tens of thousands of men had been blinded or choked by poisonous gas. In spite of the squadron's famed discipline, fear for their mothers or sweethearts brought half a dozen men to their feet. On the second bench Chalmont and Richards gazed at one another in shock. Davies pointed at one of the standing men. 'What is it, Jones?'

'What's all this mean, sir? Is it the start of gas warfare? Are the Jerries going to use gas against this country?'

Davies shook his head. 'We don't think so, Jones. To begin with we have larger stocks of mustard gas and phosgene than the enemy has and we've made certain he knows it. We've also got more heavy bombers than he has so he knows we could contaminate more cities than he could. No, the possibility exists that he is sending gas down to Italy because he thinks *we* might be going to use gas there ourselves.'

Another disturbed murmur ran through the assembly. 'Are we going to, sir?' Jones asked.

'Not that I know of. But it could be the rumour has reached their High Command and they've decided they can't take the chance.'

Men began to relax and take their seats again. Only West remained standing. 'Then why is this train so important, sir?'

'It's important because neither the enemy nor ourselves can read the other's mind. It's possible he might be taking his chemical weapons to Italy in the hope it'll prevent us from using ours. On the other hand he might be taking it with the intention of driving our armies back with it and so delaying the invasion. As that is a possibility our High Command can't ignore, we've been ordered to destroy the train and its contents before it reaches Italy.'

West sank back in his seat. 'I see. Thank you, sir.'

Coughs sounded as Davies searched his audience for more agitated members. When no one else spoke he withdrew to the map again. 'So we've had to devise a way of doing the job. It'll have to be in daylight because of the mountains. As most of you know, Austria's full of the damn things.'

The murmur that broke out among the crews this time had a different tone from the one that had preceded it. Recognizing it came from professional concern this time, Davies raised a hand. 'I know. You're wondering how the hell you'll get there in daylight. The Yanks are going to help you again, as they did in Rhine Maiden. They'll make a long-range daylight raid on Augsberg while you piggy-back above them. They'll attract all Jerry's fighters and will also give you radar cover as far as Augsberg. After that you'll be on your own but when we've finished organizing half a dozen spoof raids, Jerry's defences won't know whether they're on their arses or their elbows.'

A hand rose, followed by a gruff voice. 'What about our return trip, sir? We won't have Yanks to give us cover then, will we?'

Although Davies had been expecting Harvey's inevitable questions, he was still unable to suppress a sharpness in his reply. 'We can hardly expect 'em to wait around for us, can we? We get round that by timing. We strike the train just before dusk so we can return at night.'

Harvey sounded puzzled. 'When are we supposed to go?'

'I can't say that yet. We're waiting for agents to tell us when the train is loaded and when it sets off. That's why you're getting the briefing now so you'll be ready when the signal comes through.'

Harvey had not finished yet. 'If we're flyin' out with the Yanks, isn't our ETA going to be a problem? Their cruising speed's lower than ours. And if we should arrive after dark, how can we be sure the train's in the right place for our attack? We can't go blundering about mountains looking for it. It'd be a death trap.'

Although Davies was professional enough to know these were valid questions, it did not prevent him wishing Yorkshire had never existed. 'Do you think we haven't given thought to all that? Your ETA will be estimated on your lower cruising speed while you're with the Yanks.

As for the train, we're lucky. It's due at a station just before dark where it bunkers up with coal. Fortunately this is in a wide valley. That's where you can safely make your attack.'

Harvey was not satisfied yet. 'But if we get this train, what's to stop the Jerries sending another? He'll repair any damage to the track in a day or two.'

As a murmur of agreement ran through the crews, Davies shook his head. 'No, it seems he can't. Apparently it's taken him weeks to prepare the gas shells and distributors for this consignment. He might eventually send another train, of course, but by that time we'll either have got enough gas into Italy to be ready for him or the invasion crisis will be over.'

An Australian voice broke in at that moment. 'You say we hit the train at a station, sir. What is this station? Some place out in the bush?'

Davies switched his animosity to Australia. Although he had known the truth would come out eventually, he had been congratulating himself on concealing it so far. Now Teddy Young gave him little or no choice. 'No, there are a few buildings around it. Houses for the staff, I suppose.'

'How many houses, sir?'

At this Davies lost his temper. 'For Christ's sake, Young, how can I know that? There's a small village around it, that's all I know.'

Sitting alongside Chalmont, Richards saw the young pilot give a violent start. For a moment there was a stunned silence in the room. Then Harvey's brusque voice broke it. 'How many people live in this village, sir? Do you know that?'

It was the question Davies had been dreading and of all men it had to come from Harvey. 'No, I don't,' he snapped. 'A few hundred. Perhaps a thousand. No more.'

'A thousand,' Harvey repeated. 'And that's where we're supposed to blow up a gas train.'

Davies knew he was on the defensive now and inwardly cursed the SOE and all its members. 'We've studied map after map but the mountains and tunnels offer too much cover. We can't afford to half do the job or Jerry will still get some gas through. We're also not prepared to have this squadron scattered in bits and pieces over mountain tops. Yes, if it is to be stopped it has to be there. We're damn lucky it's due at the station at the right time.'

Before Harvey could reply there was a sudden shout as Chalmont leapt to his feet. 'You can't allow this, sir. It's monstrous!'

In his worst nightmares Davies had not expected this. Henderson, watching aghast from the side of the platform, saw his cheeks turn pale and two red spots appear in them. Before Davies could speak, Bertram's voice thundered out. 'Sit down, sir! Sit down at once.'

Chalmont ignored him. 'We can't do this, sir. We'd kill hundreds of civilians. And with gas of all things. You can't expect it of us.'

Sitting alongside him, Richards was suffering a crisis of resolution. Honed by war and its cruel problems, he understood only too well why the agonized decision had been made. But personal factors were in conflict and one of those was Hilary. Taking a deep breath, Richards also rose to his feet. 'I agree, sir. I can't do it either. I'm sorry but I can't.'

As shouts of approval broke out, Davies knew he was on the verge of a rebellion. He swung round on the startled officers alongside him. 'You've no choice, Henderson. Do it quickly.'

Henderson knew he was right. 'Mr Bertram. Put those two men under close arrest. At once.'

Cries of protest rang out as the pale Chalmont and Richards were marched from the room. Aware how close his beloved squadron was to revolt and disgrace, Davies pulled himself together and moved to the edge of the platform again. 'I know how you all feel but you must remember we are at war and these are the unfortunate decisions that sometimes have to be made. If we don't bomb that train and it is the enemy's intention to unleash gas in Italy then we would be directly responsible for the deaths of hundreds, perhaps thousands, of our fellow countrymen. Have we the right to put enemy civilians before them, particularly when one hopes many of them might escape before we attack the train? I don't think we have and neither does our High Command. Think of it that way and you will realize the job has got to be done.'

When no one moved or spoke, Davies had a quick word with Moore then addressed the silent assembly again. 'As we have at least two days and perhaps longer before the operation begins, you'll be given your combat orders later. In the meantime, although all communications are cut and you must stay within the camp, there'll be no beer ration and you can use the mess as often as you like. That's all. Dismiss.'

There were none of the usual jocular and relaxed remarks as the men filed out from the room. Their silence and behaviour brought a worried frown from Henderson as he turned to Moore. 'What do you think, Ian?'

'They'll do it,' Moore told him. 'But don't expect them to like it.'

Henderson searched the pilot's good-looking face. 'What are your feelings?'

Moore's voice was bitter. 'Mine? Much like yours, I suppose. War makes savages of us all. Destroys our consciences and takes away everything that's fine and gentle about us. I've given up trying to make sense of the things we do to one another.'

'But you'll still do it?' Henderson questioned.

A small nerve twitched above the scar on Moore's cheek. 'Of course. It's my duty, as Davies would tell me. In other words I'm as trapped and damned as everyone else in this lunatic world.'

CHAPTER 32

NOTHING SHOWED THE unease that Henderson was feeling at the affair more than the patience he showed Adams in his office after the briefing. 'Do you really believe this, Frank?'

Adams nodded. 'I'm sure of it, sir. Even Harvey does and no one can call him a Nazi lover. I believe those two lads represent all of us to a greater or lesser degree.'

Henderson frowned. 'That's all very well but we are members of His Majesty's Armed Forces. Surely that means we obey our orders however much we dislike them?'

'Do you agree with that philosophy, sir? I mean, would you agree if we were ordered to torture and shoot every German prisoner we captured?'

'That's a bloody stupid question, Frank. You know we'd never be given such an order.'

'Some are. The Gestapo are told to torture and kill certain Allied prisoners. No doubt their oath of allegiance to Hitler appeases their consciences. As we're also sworn to obey every command we get, we'd have to do the same unless we broke our oath.'

With his temper already jagged at the edges by the briefing, Henderson began to lose it at last. 'You know your fault, Frank? You make a debate out of every situation that arises. How the hell can I allow two of my men to refuse an order and then get away with it? I'd not only lose the respect of my staff, I'd also lose my command. Davies would see to that.'

'I know that, sir. I'm only asking that Chalmont and Richards are allowed to use their billet until their case comes up. They'll still be under close arrest.'

'You like those two young sods, don't you?' Henderson accused. 'In fact, you admire them for what they did.'

Adams did not duck the question. 'Yes, I do. As I see it they represent our consciences.'

Henderson swore. 'Our consciences? Do you realize that if we all acted the same way we'd lose the bloody war and let those Nazi bastards take over our country?'

'I know that, sir. That's what keeps me going. But you can't deny they had courage to stand up the way they did.'

Henderson gazed at him, then sighed. 'All right. I'll tell the guard-room to put 'em in their billet. But you do understand it's not going to keep 'em from a court martial? Davies can't afford to have his orders disobeyed.'

'I know that, sir. Thank you.' Adams was at the office door before Henderson checked him. 'Hang on. You're the one the kids feel they can talk to. Why don't you have a word with them and try to change their minds? If you could, I might be able to talk Davies into letting them off.'

Adams hesitated. 'Ian said he was going to talk to them this after-noon. Do you mind if I don't, sir?'

The Scot stared at him. 'Don't you want to get them off a court martial?'

'It would be at a high price for them, sir. I don't think I've the right to ask it.'

Henderson stared at him, then swore again. 'So the rest of us have to stay the villains, have we? Let's hope Moore isn't so bloody high-minded.'

Chalmont and Richards were escorted to their billet half an hour later. Although told an SP would accompany them wherever they went, they would be allowed to resume their normal lifestyle until a court martial was convened. 'I wonder who's behind this?' Chalmont asked as he closed the door on the SP outside.

'Probably Adams,' Richards told him. 'He looked as shocked as anyone when Davies mentioned gas.'

Chalmont threw himself on his bed. 'You shouldn't have got involved. My protest was enough.'

Richards grinned wryly. 'Why should you get all the glory?'

Chalmont turned to face him. 'You had Hilary in mind, hadn't you?'

I have Hilary in my mind all the time, Richards thought. 'Yes, I suppose I had. Along with other things.'

Chalmont's expression changed. 'How can they think of such a thing? There'll be children in that village.'

Before Richards could comment there was a knock on the door. 'Can I come in?'

As both men turned they saw Moore standing in the doorway. As they jumped to their feet, Moore waved them back. 'This is an off-duty visit, chaps. So sit down and relax.'

Richards offered him a chair. Thanking him, Moore drew out a cigarette case and held it out. When both men refused, the young wing commander lit a cigarette himself, then slipped the case back into his pocket. 'I heard the guardroom had allowed you back into your billet so thought it gave us a good opportunity to have a private chat.'

'It won't change our minds, sir.' The comment came from Chalmont.

Moore smiled. 'I don't expect it will. But as you're relatively new to the service I feel it's only fair you know what to expect if you face a court martial.'

'I know all about that, sir. We'll be disgraced and cashiered. We're prepared for it.'

Moore gazed at the glowing tip of his cigarette for a moment before glancing back at the young pilot. 'Are you quite sure, Chalmont? Are you prepared to have your disgrace reported in your town's local newspaper? Because that's what often happens when aircrew are found guilty of lack of moral fibre.' When both men gave a start, Moore's expression betrayed his opinion of the practice. 'Yes, aircrews who refuse to carry out active service duties are deemed to be cowards and it's usually publicized. Disgusting practice, isn't it? But it's only fair you should know it happens.'

Chalmont's face had gone very pale. 'We're not cowards, sir. Haven't we proved that already?'

'I couldn't agree more, Chalmont. You are both very brave men. If it hadn't shown already, you proved it today at the briefing. But the Service won't see it that way. It'll brand you just as guilty as if you refused to fly on one of our train-busting jobs.'

By this time Chalmont had recovered. 'Then it can't be helped, sir. I can't go out and cause the death of hundreds of civilians any more than Richards can. Particularly by burning or suffocating them with gas.'

Moore's eyes searched the young pilot's face and Richards saw the compassion in them. 'Shall I tell you something, Chalmont? I dislike it as much as you do. And although you won't believe it, so does your flight commander, Harvey. Yes, that big tough Yorkshireman told me only a few minutes ago that the job disgusts him.'

'Then why are you both doing it, sir?'

Moore sighed. 'It's because Harvey and I have been in the war long enough to know that peacetime rules don't apply here. It's no longer that two wrongs don't make a right but that one wrong is necessary to prevent a second wrong happening. Davies was correct in what he said this morning. If we allow that gas to reach Italy there is just the chance that thousands of our men might be killed by it. Harvey and I know we can't take that chance. So do our other old sweats.'

In the silence that followed the scream of an electric drill in one of the hangars could be heard. Then Chalmont's face set. 'I'm not blaming you or the other men, sir. I know you are doing what you believe right. But I can't do it. I'd never live with my conscience.'

'That's fair enough,' Moore said. He turned to Richards. 'What about you, Richards? Do you feel the same way?'

Richards was wondering what his decision would have been if he had never met Hilary. 'I'm afraid I do, sir. Why can't the train be bombed elsewhere where civilians wouldn't be at risk?'

'I only wish it could, Richards. What Davies didn't mention at the briefing was the long-range Spitfire he sent from Benson to take oblique photographs of the rail track. Before Adams filed them away, Davies, I and two specialist officers spent half the afternoon searching for another spot where we could safely attack the train. Sadly we couldn't find one.'

Neither of the other two men noticed the change in Richards's expression as he listened to Moore's explanation. 'So the air commodore does realize what a dirty job he's given us?'

'Oh, heavens, yes. He's not a monster, Richards. He's a professional airman who's committed to obey orders no matter how distasteful they are.'

Richards cleared his throat. 'It's good of you to come and talk to us, sir. We both appreciate it.'

Moore shrugged. 'I'm sure you won't believe it but I admire both of you. If I could have talked you round we might have persuaded Davies to drop his charges. As it is you can be sure I'll do all I can to help. Is there anything you need at the moment?'

Although Chalmont shook his head, Richards hesitated. Moore gave him a questioning glance. 'Is there something you want, Richards?'

'Yes, sir. As time's going to drag here until the trial I wondered if we could help Mr Adams again. We did some work for him a few weeks ago and as his assistant has gone on leave he might be able to use some extra help. His old files were still in a mess when we finished the last time.'

Thinking Adams's advice might succeed when his had failed, Moore nodded. 'That's a good idea. Davies is coming tomorrow, so Adams will be kept busy. I'll talk to him tonight. Anything else?'

When both men shook their heads, Moore went to the door. 'Then keep your chins up. In the meantime I'll work on Davies and see if I can help in any way.' Nodding at the two men, he left the billet.

Chalmont closed the door, then turned impatiently on Richards. 'Why did you ask about Adams's files? I can't say I'm in the mood to work on them.'

Pushing past him, Richards opened the door a few inches and saw the SP was chatting to an airman on the path outside. Closing the door again, he turned to the curious Chalmont. 'I've got an idea. It might not work but I think it's worth a try.'

CHAPTER 33

T HE TWO MEN, accompanied by their bored SP, reported to Adams's confessional after breakfast the following morning. Adams, already informed of their wishes by Moore, made them welcome. 'Yes, you can be useful.' He pointed at a package that had arrived the previous day. 'That's your first job. Unless I'm mistaken it's a pile of propaganda posters I'm supposed to pin or plaster all round the walls. Then you can get back to those files you worked on before. They should end up in date order. Neither Sue nor I have had a chance to look at them since those interdiction raids started.'

Had the truth been told, Adams didn't care a fig about the old files. Full of sympathy for the two airmen, he welcomed the opportunity to talk to them and offer some of the comfort he felt they richly deserved. To Adams, a permanent civilian by nature, the punishment meted out to aircrews if their courage became exhausted was disgusting. Unlike many of their countrymen, they had volunteered to serve in a unit that had the highest ratio of casualties in the country's armed forces and to punish them afterwards because their nerves proved inadequate seemed pure injustice. Not for the first time Adams had wondered what the general public would make of such punishment. Many believed their Services were compassionate but Adams, a student of military history, knew the reverse to be true. The British had been the last to use the lash and their treatment of shell-shocked soldiers in the First World War had been nothing but scandalous. To Adams that was bad enough but for these two young men to face punishment not because of failed courage but because of compassion was the ultimate outrage. It had even made Adams consider notifying the press, had not two things stopped him. One was the knowledge that the wartime press would never be allowed to publish such a letter and the other was his own self-admitted inadequacy. If he were caught writing such a letter he would undoubtedly face the kind of disgrace that Valerie, his young and snobbish wife, would never forgive or forget. At the same time his punishment would be nothing compared to that of the young airmen. Which to the self-critical Adams was the final irony.

He was notified by the guardroom just after 1000 hours that Davies's staff car had just arrived. Fifteen minutes later his phone rang. He must report to Henderson's office immediately. Replacing the receiver, he turned to the two airmen who were pasting the propaganda posters to the Nissen hut walls. 'The air commodore has arrived and wants to see me in the CO's office. I don't know how long I'll be but I'll see you have tea brought in. Have a go at those files when you've finished the posters. It would be a help to get them in some kind of order.'

With that Adams left the confessional, nodding at the SP outside who saluted him. His thoughts were bleak as he trod the path to the administration block. Hours spent with senior officers discussing the ways and means of destroying a train that would pollute and ravage a village were not Adams's ideal way of spending a fine spring morning.

Davies picked up his cap from Henderson's desk. 'Then it's settled at last, is it? No more bleats and cavils?'

'Only the wish we hadn't the job to do, sir,' Henderson said.

Davies frowned. 'No need to hammer the point home, Jock. That's all been said before.' His eyes roved round the other men in the office, Moore, Adams, Harvey and Young. 'You're sure you're all satisfied with the details?' When all nodded his eyes fixed on Harvey. 'You satisfied too, Harvey?'

'Aye, sir. I suppose so.'

Davies wanted to say 'that's a bloody miracle in itself' but bit back the comment. He turned to Moore. 'Then you'll brief the boys this afternoon. Stress the importance of wearing their respirators when they make their attack. Hopefully they won't be necessary but it's better to be safe than sorry.'

'Yes, sir. I'll tell them.'

'Good. Then I'll get back to Group but I'll see you all tomorrow. Make sure your kites are fully air-tested before I arrive. Everyone will have an eye on us tomorrow afternoon. We can't afford any cock-ups.'

With that Davies donned his cap, returned the others' salutes, and disappeared. As his short, quick footsteps were heard hurrying down the corridor, the look Henderson gave the others defied analysis. 'Let's be fair to him. He doesn't like it any more than we do.'

'Let's hope that's true, sir.' It was Harvey.

Henderson frowned. 'Don't be like that, Frank. He was as shocked as anyone when Simms told us the job.' He switched his reproving eyes to Moore. 'What time do you want the briefing, Ian? 1400 hours?'

Moore nodded. 'That'll be fine, sir.'

'All right. I'll see everyone's there.' The Scot's tone changed. 'Go easy what you say to them, Ian. Everyone's on edge at the moment.' When Moore nodded he went on: 'All right, you can dismiss now. I'll see you all at the briefing.'

Adams returned to his confessional fifteen minutes later. Almost subliminally he noticed that the SP standing outside the room had been changed. He found the two airmen sitting at Sue's table with files strewn all over it. He adopted a mood he did not feel. 'You two look busy. Well done. It'll be a load off my mind if I know I can trace individual files when they're requested.'

'Have you been with Air Commodore Davies, sir?' Richards asked.

Adams nodded. 'For nearly two hours.'

'Is the operation still on, sir?'

Adams suppressed a sigh. 'Yes, I'm afraid it is, Richards. Wing Commander Moore is briefing the crews on their combat roles this afternoon.'

'Do you think we'd be allowed to attend, sir?'

Adams gave a start. 'Attend! What on earth for?'

With Richards showing intense embarrassment, Chalmont replied for him. 'We've changed our minds, sir. We'd like to go with the others.'

Adams could not believe what he was hearing. 'Changed your minds? But why?'

'We've had more time to think about it. We still feel the same about endangering the civilians but we see now that our own soldiers must come first. So we were wondering if you would speak to Wing Commander Moore for us.'

Adams was trying to come to terms with this astonishing volte-face. His first thought was that both men were afraid of a court martial and its consequences. 'I can speak to him but I can't guarantee what Davies will say. He might still insist on a court martial because of your earlier behaviour.'

'We know that, sir, but if we carry out the operation the air commodore might have second thoughts. But whether he does or he doesn't, we'd still like to fly with the others.'

Adams was baffled by his own feelings. One half of him knew he should be glad of the couple's decision. If they went through with the mission and behaved well it seemed highly unlikely that Davies would proceed with his threat. At the same time another part of Adams was feeling intense disappointment. 'Are you both sure about this?' When both men nodded he took a deep, steadying breath. 'Very well, I'll speak to the CO and Moore. But I wish you'd made this decision yesterday. All you've done is upset the other crews and caused dissension among the rest of us. If you'd made less of a drama of it, all this could have been avoided.' With that Adams picked up his telephone. 'Wing Commander Moore's office, please. Hello, Ian. Adams here. I've something important to tell you. May I come over? Fine. I'm on my way now.'

Giving the couple a look but without a word, Adams left the room. For a moment neither man spoke, then Chalmont rose and walked to the window. 'He's angry and he's disappointed with us. Adams of all people.'

Richards winced. 'I know. And doesn't it hurt like hell.'

CHAPTER 34

MOORE LOWERED HIS pointer from the large map of Europe. 'Remember we'll be coming back at night so it's imperative all navigators keep individual logs. Radio silence will be strictly kept until we break away from the Yanks. Our call signs for the operation are as follows. Ours is Merlin, the station's Lancelot, the Yanks' is Alamo, and the operation's is Round Table.' As men scribbled the words down Moore went on: 'That about sums it all up except for our day out with the Yanks. We'll top up at Manston and then rendezvous with them over Dungeness, as we did in Rhine Maiden. They'll be aiming for 24,000 feet by the time they reach Germany so we'll need to fly at 30,000 to gain radar cover from them. We'll all have an escort as far as our fighters' extreme range, then we'll be on our own. However, as we're hoping to go unnoticed as far as Augsberg, we shouldn't have any interception problems. It'll be the Yanks who'll get all the stick.'

'Poor bloody Yanks,' someone muttered. As a few mordant laughs broke out, Moore's tone changed. 'Remember they're laying all this on for us and their cost will be heavy because Jerry will fling everything at them as he always does. It won't be pleasant to watch and some of you might feel like giving a hand.' At this point Moore's eyes switched to Millburn seated on the second row of benches. 'If you do, you resist the temptation at all costs. We can't afford to be spotted and the Yanks know that. So they won't think any worse of us for sitting tight.'

With that message stressed, Moore turned back to his wider audience. 'The rest you'll get from your executive officers. You'll air test your kites in the morning. Tonight your beer ration will be two pints per man.' As a groan sounded, Moore smiled. 'I want you all bright-eyed and bushy-tailed when we meet the Yanks. I don't want them to think we're a bunch of drunks.' As laughs and catcalls broke out, Moore moved forward along the platform. 'Have any of you any questions to ask before I pass you over to our gen men?'

Five arms rose. Moore pointed to one at the rear of the assembly. 'Yes, Donaldson. What's your problem?'

'You haven't mentioned our stores, skipper. What armament are we carrying?'

'To destroy the wagons – and we must destroy as many as possible – we need something more accurate than bombs. So we'll be using rockets. But as a back-up in case of an unforeseen emergency each kite will be carrying one or two 500lb heavy case bombs. Your armament officer will tell you the number.'

'If we're using rockets that means we'll have to go in low, skipper?'

'Low enough to be accurate, yes. Didn't I make that clear?'

'It's not that, sir. I'd been wondering why we had to take gas masks.'

As a low murmur ran through his audience, Moore knew he was on sensitive ground. 'We probably won't need them, Donaldson. But we feel it's better to be safe than sorry.'

'Amen to that,' a low voice was heard. Picking it up, Moore used it to ease the tension that had arisen. 'You gone religious, Paddy? I never thought you were the type.'

Machin did not let him down. 'Oi aren't, skipper. But Father Clifford wants me to keep on tryin'. He says if I stick at it long enough it'll melt down me badness and maybe make a saint out o' me.'

The laughs and comments that followed were more cynical and mordant than usual and Moore did not need telling why. 'I hope he's right, Paddy. We could do with a saint or two in the squadron.' Moore pointed at a second raised arm. 'Yes, Roberts.'

'What if the train's late, sir? We won't be able to stooge about waiting for it, will we?'

'No, we won't. We've no intention of hanging around for Jerry's fighters to arrive although we will be carrying enough fuel to allow for a delay. The reason we're not expecting problems is because of the train taking on coal and a new crew at the station. As we are told the job takes around thirty minutes, our ETA will be set to get us there halfway through the exercise. That means we ought to be able to attack it straight away.'

As Roberts nodded, Moore moved to the third arm. 'Yes, Baldwin.'

'Am I right in thinking the Jerries might never use this gas, skipper? That it might all be a false alarm?'

'Yes, you are right, Baldwin. It might only be a precaution he's taking.'

'Then doesn't it seem a hell of an operation for something that might never happen?'

Moore nodded wryly. 'Jerry might have been thinking the same thing when he prepared the gas shells and the train. But he's still prepared them. That's war, Baldwin. The safeguarding of possibilities. Neglect one and you might lose everything.' He pointed to a fourth arm. 'Yes, Allison.'

'You haven't given us a take-off time yet, skipper. Is this because the train times aren't known yet?'

'Not yet,' Moore admitted. 'We know it's setting off tomorrow morning but the exact time isn't known yet. It seems agents will be watching and will let London know the exact moment. Train experts will then be able to work out the time it will take to reach the station. From their calculations we'll be given our own take-off time.'

'But what happens if it doesn't arrive at the station before it gets dark?'

'That's another reason we must attack it at the station. If it were among the mountains when we arrived, a night attack would be suicide. Hopefully, however, if the Jerries and our calculations all play their part we should find it at the station before dusk falls. But in case something does go wrong – and I agree it's possible – we'll all be carrying flares for a night attack. All right?'

'Just one other thing, sir. The air commodore mentioned spoof raids. Are we getting any?'

'Yes, you are. The Banff Wing are doing a foray over Denmark and 11 Group are attacking a target in Southern France. So with luck Jerry's controllers will be at sixes and sevens.'

'Thank you, sir.'

A single arm was still raised. Moore pointed at it. 'Yes, Andy. What's your problem?'

The twangy New Zealand voice that answered him made it clear Andy Larkin had no intention of dodging the question other crews wanted to ask but were too British to voice aloud. 'I'd like to know why that couple Chalmont and Richards are here today, skipper. I thought they'd refused to fly and were under close arrest.'

Moore, who had noticed the curiosity the crews had shown earlier when the two men were seen in the briefing room, was tempted to stamp on the question as being out of order. Then he realized it could be used to advantage. 'It's none of your business, Andy, but this much you can know. Chalmont and Richards have realized our servicemen in Italy must be protected and so have changed their minds about the operation. Personally I congratulate them and I hope you'll all do the same. Any more questions?'

No more hands were raised. Instead, men were showing relief that the breach in their ranks had been closed and those close to the two embarrassed airmen were seen chatting to them. Catching Henderson's eye, Moore saw the big Scot was also showing relief and pleasure. It was a moment when none of the men present had the slightest idea of the drama that would unfold on the morrow.

CHAPTER 35

SUTTON CRADDOCK WAS a beehive of activity that night and the
following morning. Although Simms had told Davies the train
was almost certainly not due at the Austrian station until the late
evening, Davies was taking no chances. By this time reports of the
threat it might present to both the Allied armies in Italy were causing
near panic among Eisenhower's planners and rumours were already
circulating that retaliatory gas shells were being rushed into Italy to
combat the threat. But as the weight of supplies for such a project
could only be supplied by sea, it was clear to all and sundry that there
was a frightening time gap between the arrival of the rogue train in
Italy and the arrival of the ship hastily loaded and dispatched from
Britain. Moreover there was no guarantee it would survive the enemy
aircraft and submarines that still infested the Mediterranean.

With all these imponderables, the British and the American High
Commands had considered launching high-density raids on the train
with their Lancaster and B–17s but the preparations for such a raid plus
the distance and the mountains had been the deterrent. Mass raids by
heavy bombers could never be hidden from the enemy and once their
target became apparent it would be simplicity itself for the train to take
shelter in one of the many tunnels along its route. A surprise attack by
fighter bombers would have a far greater chance of success if it were
well planned and led. Should it fail then heavy raids on the supply
bases in Northern Italy would need to be carried out although without
any guarantee the gas shells would be destroyed.

With 633 Squadron in its role of a special service squadron being
chosen for the vital attack, Davies was under massive pressure.
Henderson had hoped he would stay away while preparations were
being made but soon realized the air commodore's highly strung
nature would allow no such thing. Returning to Sutton Craddock that
evening, Davies was here, there and everywhere, out on the hardstandings where mechanics worked all night on the Mosquitoes, in the

hangars where minor repairs were being made, and in and out of Henderson's office until the Scot wanted to shoot him with the Smith and Wesson he kept for emergencies.

There was not much rest for the aircrews either. With no illusions about the dangers of the operation ahead, many sat up late talking or writing to parents or girlfriends. Others, inveterate card players like Hopkinson, Larkin, Machin and Baldwin, played their usual game of poker under the mordant reasoning that money was only of use to survivors. To be fair to the crews, with the operation not scheduled until the afternoon, all believed they would be allowed a late call in the morning. When Davies decided around midnight that he wanted air tests carrying out before breakfast so that any latent faults could be found and corrected before lunch, curses flew like angry bees around the airfield. One way and another it was perhaps a miracle of a kind that Davies survived assassination that night.

Morning came and with their eyes encrusted with sleep the crews carried out their air tests. Most were able to sign their clearances to their NCO flight mechanics; a few reported minor faults that brought a rush of attention to their aircraft. When the minor faults were corrected and the deafening roar of Merlins was silenced, armourers arrived with their trolley lines of weapons. Rockets were slid beneath Mosquito wings, 500lb bombs and flares were stored in bomb bays, and 20mm cannon magazines clipped into sockets. Spring-loaded panels were opened and belts of .303 shells fed into Brownings. By the time the panels were replaced, the bomb doors closed, and the trolley lines driven away, the sixteen Mosquitoes on the Sutton Craddock airfield had been turned into sophisticated and deadly machines of war.

Now, for the crews, the worst part of the operation began, the waiting. Lunch came as a relief but it was over quickly and no alcohol was allowed afterwards to wash it down. Some men read what they had written the night before, tore the letters up and started writing another. Some played darts in their flight offices. Some read newspapers or magazines. Others tried to sleep and failed. The card party counted their winnings or losses and decided to try their luck again. In a deckchair out in the afternoon sunlight, Richards decided to pen yet another letter to Hilary. Alongside him Chalmont had put down his book and was gazing at the Mosquitoes as if he were in another world altogether. Moore, walking out of the administration block with Harvey, stopped and pointed at the two men. 'What made them change their minds, Frank?'

The Yorkshireman shrugged. 'You don't think it's the reason they gave?'

'I don't know, Frank. I just don't know.'

'Maybe it was that talk you gave 'em. You said you mentioned the lack of moral fibre bit.'

'It could be. But I wouldn't have thought those two would scare that easily. They must have known the punishment they'd get.'

'Then perhaps it's what they say. Adams seems to think so.'

Moore gave a half laugh. 'You know I'm sorry for Adams. He admired the stand they made.'

Harvey's grunt was affectionate. 'Poor old bugger. He'll never get used to war, will he?'

While the two men were talking, a teleprinter had begun clicking in the signals room. When it ceased a Waaf grabbed the tape and ran from the room. Five minutes later a tannoy boomed out. Men filed into their locker rooms and returned to the field with their pockets emptied of personal effects but equipped with gas masks, revolvers, survival kit, German and Austrian money, compasses, maps and parachutes. All men knew from experience that some of them would almost certainly die that day but being young most of them believed it would not happen to them. Nevertheless, men found their hearts beating faster as the afternoon wore on and were glad when Waafs brought out tea and sandwiches.

The teleprinter began clicking urgently again when the sun, no longer at its zenith, began to cast longer shadows across the waiting airfield. A minute later the tannoy boomed out again, sending a flock of starlings high into the air. Shouts were heard and mechanics and aircrew raced towards their Mosquitoes. Merlins coughed and fired, jetting smoke from their exhausts. Operation Round Table was under way.

CHAPTER 36

A T 30,000 FEET the sixteen Mosquitoes were yawing slightly in the thin air. Led by Moore, they were flying in five ranks of three aircraft apiece. Six thousand feet below, in tight boxes, ninety B–17s were pouring out condensation trails and exhaust gases that merged together into a white landscape. In the brilliant sunlight of the stratosphere the effect was stunning, like that of flying over some Arctic landscape with its ice flows stretching back to the far horizon.

Gazing down through his smoked goggles at the stupendous sight, Moore was reminded of a fact he had once read in a military magazine, that on each of the heavy bomber raids the British and the Americans were now carrying out, a greater weight of weaponry was involved than by the Grand Fleet at the Battle of Jutland.

A sudden voice on a low signal strength broke into his thoughts. 'That's our stint over, Alamo Leader. We'll buy you a warm beer when you return home. Over to you.'

A reply with an American accent followed. 'We love your warm beer, Limey. Thanks for your help.'

Hoppy, a grotesque gnome in his tight-fitting oxygen mask and pressurized waistcoat, glanced at Moore. Altitude made his voice sound tinny. 'It won't be long now, skipper.'

Moore nodded. With the escort of Spitfires and Thunderbolts forced to turn back because of their limited range, German controllers would already be alerting their defences. Although the 'spoof' raids of the Banff Wing and 11 Group would be diverting some fighters towards them, enemy controllers were experienced enough to know that the B–17s' assembly point over Dungeness meant their target was some-where in south-eastern Europe and would have kept a reserve of fighters to handle the threat. With Allied fighters withdrawn, those fighters would already be scrambling to attack the B–17s.

Flak had been bursting around the bombers since they crossed the Channel coast and more than one B–17 had been hit and forced to turn back. To their crews, however, the bursting shells were almost welcome because their presence betrayed the absence of enemy fighters. It was when the shells ceased blasting out their steel shards that gunners adjusted their flak jackets and goggles and searched the pitiless sky for the darting, murderous fighters.

The warning came fifteen minutes later. Suddenly the B–17s were no longer rocked and threatened by the ugly black explosions. Pilots gave warning to their gunners who crouched behind their heavy duty Brownings. 'Watch out, you people. Any minute now.'

The attack came from the front and could be seen clearly by the Mosquitoes above. Although well defended by their thirteen guns per aircraft, many of the B–17s still lacked a 'chin' turret and earlier that year the Focke-Wulfs of Jagdgeschwader 1 had exploited the weakness with great success. With all enemy squadrons duly informed, the fighters below made full use of the new tactic. Instead of attacking from behind or from the side they headed straight at the leading B–17s as if intending collision. At 900 metres they released their 21cm rockets and at 700 metres they opened fire with cannon. With tracer streaking out before them, they kept firing until the last moment before collision, when they dived beneath the B–17s and swung sharply away to dodge the B–17s' side and ventral gun positions.

The effect was painful to see. Two Fortresses received direct hits from rockets and reeled helplessly away like blinded animals. One collided with an undamaged aircraft alongside it and the two huge bombers went spinning and twisting down into the haze below. Another B–17 was struck by cannon shells that ripped and exploded the full length of its starboard wing. As the wing tore away, the asymetrical remains toppled over, fell a few hundred feet, and then exploded in a massive ball of fire.

As the boxes of B–17s closed their ranks more tightly, another *gruppen* made its attack. From above, the scene resembled a huge flock of birds being attacked by vicious hornets. With their homeland threatened, the German pilots were displaying the same courage and self-sacrifice as their British counterparts had shown during the Battle of Britain. Equally the American crews of the B–17s were showing the same discipline and dedication. Fire from their Brownings was threading luminous patterns in the war-torn sky and fighters could be seen exploding in mid air or spinning downward leaving a trail of smoke and fire.

Six thousand feet above, the Mosquito crews could hear the sound of battle as the American crews fought for survival. 'Keep it close, you guys. Keep formation.'

'Watch it, Mac. Five o'clock high.'

'Put that fire out, Lejinsky.'

'Bail out, you guys. For Christ's sake, bail out.'

For the Mosquito crews, many of whom had suffered the same situation during the Rhine Maiden operation, the effect was painful. Every man knew he was in an aircraft that even with its present weighty armament could probably outfly the German fighters, and the imperative need not to interfere made more than one crewman resent his orders. For Millburn, aggressive by nature at the best of times and now forced to watch his countrymen suffer while he had a grandstand seat, the order was agony to obey. Every time a B–17 was hit Gabby feared the temptation to plunge down and defend his countrymen would be too much for the American.

There was one other Mosquito in which emotion was playing a dominant part. In S-Suzy, Chalmont and Richards were gazing down at the battle with the same dismay and fascination as the rest of their colleagues. But it was not intervention that lay behind Chalmont's question when he glanced at Richards. 'Are you certain that's the right time?'

Richards nodded. 'It has to be. Otherwise, if the squadron hasn't been spotted yet, we might give its presence away.'

'So we do it after Augsberg?'

'I think so. Soon afterwards anyway.'

The battle below raged for another ten minutes, then suddenly the sky was empty of fighters as pilots withdrew to refuel and restock with ammunition. Bursting shells began rocking and threatening the B–17s again but to the crews it was a respite, giving them time to jab morphia into wounded or dying colleagues and drag more belts of .5 shells to their Brownings. Novice crews began to believe the worst was over, older colleagues knew better. Deep into Germany as the B–17s now were, enemy controllers would know they had a target of prime importance and so would call up all available fighters to repel them.

The second attack came fifteen minutes later. This time the *gruppen* were a mixture of day and night fighters. Once more the sky became laced with tracer and smoke and the airwaves sounded to the cries of warning or the screams of pain. It was painfully obvious to the Mosquito crews that the Americans were paying a heavy price for the protection they were giving.

The second ordeal ended when flak began bursting round the B–17s again and an American voice came over the R/T. 'Alamo to Merlin Leader. Augsberg coming up. I guess that's it, you guys. Good luck with that magic wand.'

With radio silence no longer valid, Moore's voice sounded in reply. 'Many thanks, Alamo Leader. We appreciate the job you've done. Good luck.'

A couple of minutes later the B–17s began releasing their clutches of bombs. Beneath the haze that lay over the city, flash after flash showed as the bombs rained down. Although high above the carnage, Chalmont found himself unable to look down and turned to Richards. The navigator shook his head. 'Give it a few more minutes.'

Ahead Moore was setting the squadron's course a few degrees to starboard. Invisible from the ground below because of their great height, the Mosquitoes followed him. Richards waited five more minutes then braced himself. Seeing his nod, Chalmont cleared his throat, then addressed his R/T. 'Red Four to Merlin Leader. I've got engine trouble, skipper. Can I abort the mission?'

Before Moore could reply a gruff voice broke in. 'What sort of trouble, Red Four?'

'I'm not sure, sir. It's my port engine. The revs are dropping.'

'I don't bloody believe you, Chalmont. Stay on course.'

Moore's impatient voice silenced both men. 'Red Four! Is this a genuine emergency?'

Chalmont glanced at Richards, who nodded. 'Yes, Merlin Leader. The engine temperature's rising too.'

'Then you can abort. Go home and good luck.'

'Thank you, Merlin Leader.'

In D-Danny, Harvey watched S-Suzy bank and swing away. His curse rattled radios. 'They're quitting again. The young bastards.'

Moore's reproving voice brought order back. 'Settle down, Red Zero. These things happen and we've a job to do.'

With most men disbelieving Chalmont's excuse after his earlier behaviour, the incident unsettled crews and brought arguments between pilots and their navigators. Guessing this if only from Hopkinson's caustic comments, Moore had a quick word to calm them down. As usual his personality had its effect and as S-Suzy disappeared into a cloud bank that had appeared to the north, men put their minds back to the task ahead. They were only too aware that now their cover had gone, enemy radar controllers would be asking frantic questions and trying to guess the nature of their target.

*

Hopkinson tapped Moore's arm and then pointed to the map strapped on his knee. His high altitude equipment distorted his voice. 'Can't be far away now, skipper. But I don't like that mist.'

Moore glanced down. The evening mist the cockney referred to, although as yet thin and patchy, made some of the mountains below look like islands in a crimson-tinted sea. Mountains that looked innocuous from the height the Mosquitoes were still flying yet every crewman knew their aspect was illusionary. Down at ground level they would be massive peaks of rock that would smash to pieces any aircraft foolish enough to fly among them.

For long minutes Hopkinson had been tracking the hair-thin rail track that threaded its way through the mountains. According to his chart the squadron had struck the railway a degree or so too far to the south and a couple of minutes had been wasted correcting the error. Now, as a wide mist-filled valley drifted into sight, he lifted his binoculars. A moment later he gave an excited shout. 'That's it, skipper. The station and the village. At ten o'clock.'

Moore took the binoculars and gazed down. Through a thin mist a railway station with bunkering facilities and a water tank swam into view. Moving the glasses Moore saw a large cluster of buildings and farmhouses spreading out on both sides of the track. 'You're right. It must be. But where's the train?'

Hopkinson took the glasses again. To the north, pools of mist were deeper between the mountains. 'It's either late, skipper, or our experts got their timing wrong. Or maybe, if it's late, it's going through a deep valley or a tunnel. There must be plenty of 'em down there.' Hopkinson finished on a negative note. 'On the other hand perhaps it's been cancelled and won't be coming at all.'

If the train was on its way Moore knew it must not spot them or it would certainly take cover in a tunnel. Nor must the refuelling station detect them or a radio warning would go out. 'I'll send the boys lower but keep them out of sight. You and I will stay up here and keep a watch for the train.'

Hopkinson showed unusual misgivings. Mosquitoes crews felt relatively safe at the height they were flying. If detected by radar, it would take enemy fighters long minutes to reach them even if equipped with nitrous oxide to boost their performance. Medium or low level was a different matter, as Hopkinson pointed out. 'It'll make it easier for Jerry's fighters to find and reach them, skipper.'

Moore issued his orders before answering the cockney. 'I know that but it can't be helped. We haven't unlimited fuel and if the train does come we can't waste time making our attack.'

Five minutes later the squadron was down and orbiting behind a range of mountains that Moore hoped would hide them from the village and station. In the meantime, hoping his height kept him invisible and equally hoping the German controllers had not yet guessed the Mosquitoes' target, he and Hopkinson kept watch on the mist-shrouded mountains and village.

It was a watch that grew more perilous as the minutes ticked away. Marauding German fighters could not be far away and the feeling was growing in all the waiting crews that the operation was a total failure. Either the train had been cancelled or it would not arrive until fuel supplies became dangerously low or fighters found them. In truth Moore was about to abort the mission when Hopkinson caught his arm. 'What's that, skipper? At two o'clock?'

At first Moore could see nothing for drifting banks of mist. The he saw faint streaks of light lancing through it. Puzzled, he addressed his R/T. 'Merlin Leader to Red Zero. Something's happening north of the station. Take Millburn and see what it is.'

Unable to see the two Mosquitoes because of distance and the fading light, Moore waited for news while he kept his eyes on the northern mountains. The flashes of light had ceased and his hopes they might have come from a locomotive began to die. Then he saw them again and with the sight came a shout that almost destroyed his radio. 'Moore, it's those two kids, Chalmont and Richards. They're here and they're attacking the bloody train.'

CHAPTER 37

H ARVEY COULD NOT believe what he was seeing. A thousand feet below, like an enormous anaconda, the longest and most formidable train he had ever seen, was snaking its way along the confines of a steep, rocky gorge. Powered by two huge locomotives at front and back and guarded by two flak wagons also at either end, it consisted of twenty tanker wagons painted an ominous yellow. Two wagons were showing damage and one was trailing yellow fumes. As Harvey dived lower he saw a single Mosquito circling to attack again. As it swung round to dive into the perilous gorge, looking as small and frail as a moth beside the train's enormity, Harvey's shout rang out. 'Chalmont! Abandon your attack! This is an order. Abandon attack until you receive support!'

S-Suzy showed no sign of hearing. As it launched another rocket, Harvey's shout rang out again. 'Damn you, Chalmont. Abandon your attack. At the double!'

The two flak wagons were in action now. Formidable steel structures that contained braces of pom-poms and LMGs, their firepower could be devastating at close quarters and because of the narrowness of the gorge S-Suzy had to fly right over the rear one. As the aircraft vanished into a net of tracer Harvey's eyes closed for a moment. But when he opened them another tanker was streaming out yellow liquid and fumes and S-Suzy, followed by spears of tracer, was climbing to escape the flanking mountains that lay ahead.

Inside S-Suzy Richards was trying to regain his breath. 'Give it a rest now, Jerry. Now Moore knows what we're doing he's sure to bring the others here. And they can take care of the train.'

Out of breath himself, Chalmont needed a moment to recover. Below, urged on by their foremen, the two drivers were fighting for their lives. Both knew that a mile past the station where they were supposed to restock with coal, was a long tunnel. If they could reach and hide there they would save the train. As they rammed regulators

forward to their furthermost limits, pressurized steam thrust the locomotives' giant pistons even faster and sent blackened smoke billowing
into the gorge. As long as the track remained intact, both drivers
believed they had a chance.

Alerted by Harvey, the orbiting Mosquitoes had cleared the mountain range and were now skimming the mist towards the gorge. In
A-Apple, also diving down to the scene, Moore's emotions were
mixed. With the train still protected by the mountains, his crews would
be in far greater danger than if they attacked it at the station. At the
same time, now the train was under attack, it most certainly would not
halt there to present an easier target. Mountains or no mountains,
Chalmont and Richards had cast the die, and in his heart Moore knew
he was glad.

Circling the train, Harvey glanced at his navigator. 'How do you
feel? Shall we give it a try?'

Lacey swallowed once. 'If you feel we should, skipper.'

Harvey nodded. 'Good lad. But we'll leave the gas wagons until the
boys arrive. I want the front engine.'

As he circled to attack there was a yell from Millburn. 'Hold it,
Frank. Let me go for the rear flak wagon. OK?'

Harvey adjusted his gas mask. 'Good idea, Yank. We'll attack 'em
together.'

Thirty seconds later the two Mosquitoes dived into the gorge at the
rear of the train. As the flak gunners hastily lowered their guns,
Millburn released two rockets. One struck the massive steel structure
obliquely and ricocheted away but the second scored a direct hit.
Although it did not wound or kill all the gunners, the explosion was
sufficient to daze them and allow D-Danny to pass overhead and fire
two rockets at the foremost locomotive.

But luck was not with Harvey. At that moment the track was curving
around a mountain spur and the diversion was just enough to throw
the rockets off course and miss the engine. As the cursing
Yorkshireman heaved back on his column to avoid the mountains
ahead, a hail of shells from the foremost flak wagon made D-Danny
shudder. Tearing off his gas mask, Harvey glared at Lacey. 'Sod these
mountains. How the hell are we going to prang the bloody thing while
it's weaving through them?'

A calm voice came over the R/T. 'Bad luck, Red Zero. Now it's our
turn to try.'

With Moore now united with the rest of his crews, a sustained assault
would have been possible had not the train been speeding down the

gorge. As it was, only one or at the most two Mosquitoes could attack simultaneously. Had the distance to the village been greater and the night calm, Moore might have waited until the train emerged into the wider valley ahead and then made his attack. But with gas fumes pouring from its ruptured tankers and the near certainty that once the gorge ceased to contain them the prevailing wind would drift them over the village, common humanity seemed to give only one answer. After a brief hesitation Moore gave orders to attack.

As always he went in first. His rockets struck another of the tankers, causing another eruption of liquid gas and fumes, and a second struck the leading flak wagon although without inflicting serious damage. As A-Apple came climbing away Hopkinson looked shaken as he pulled off his gas mask. 'I reckon they've got both phosgene and mustard gas in those tankers, skipper. God help those villagers if the stuff ever reaches them.'

C-Clara, flown by Morris, was next to go. He was unlucky. A 37mm shell from the front flak wagon scored a direct hit on his cockpit, shattering both men and mangling their bodies together. C-Clara reared up like a speared animal, cleared the rim of the gorge, but then went spinning down the mountainside, turning into a fireball as it went. A few seconds later it disintegrated in a huge explosion.

Van Breedenkamp went in next and managed to blow open another tanker before a shattered aileron forced him to climb gingerly from the gorge. Martin followed him fifteen seconds later. He destroyed a tanker, only for a hail of tracer from the front flak wagon to shatter both propellers and engines. His flying speed allowed him to escape from the gorge but with no engine thrust he could not sustain height and crashed down a nearby mountainside in a vain attempt at a crash landing.

Ordered that the train must be destroyed at all costs, Moore had no choice but to continue the attack. Young, Baldwin and Machin survived their ordeal and three more tankers were ripped open. Yet all the damaged wagons remained on the rails and the two locomotives, protected by their flak wagons, were still driving the train forward and fast approaching the wide valley.

By this time Moore had decided the locomotives rather than the tankers should be their target. If they and the surviving flak wagon could be knocked out, the intact tankers would be at his mercy unless enemy fighters arrived. But then, with the gas wagons so drastically reduced, it was highly unlikely they would have any impact on the Italian stalemate even if they ever reached that country.

But there was another factor in Moore's decision and it was not missed by Chalmont and Richards, who were circling above. Until now, shaken by the fury of the defence they had encountered, the two men had watched the battle almost in a daze. It took Moore's calm voice to his crews to alert them to the new danger that had arisen. 'Merlin Leader here. I don't know why but those drivers seem determined to reach the valley and with those leaking tankers the results could be vile. If we can knock out or derail an engine or that flak wagon, we'll have the rest of the tankers at our mercy. If I make it, Red Zero, finish the rest off. If I don't make it, take the boys home. By this time bandits can't be far away.'

Harvey's fierce protest distorted earphones 'No, Ian. That flak wagon isn't damaged. If the drivers are such bloody fools to risk the village we're not to blame.'

'No argument and no heroics, Red Zero. If I don't make it, you've got your orders. Whatever happens I can't see those remaining tankers getting to Italy.'

Chalmont, his face marked by the earlier tightness of his gas mask, looked incredulous as he turned to Richards. 'You hear that? Moore's going to risk his life for those villagers.'

Richards was looking equally pale. 'I know.'

Chalmont gazed down at the smoking train that was still thundering through the gorge. 'Can we let him?'

Only the young know the sweetness of life when sacrifice means its finality. For a moment Richards saw Hilary as clearly as if she were in the cockpit with him, offering him her arms and her love. To give his consent, to lose her for ever, was like having his heart ripped out. As the two men's eyes met and Richards reached into his soul, the young pilot took a hand off the control column and held it out to him. A second later, when Richards nodded, S-Suzy dipped her nose and went down.

Moore saw the diving Mosquito as he was circling to attack. Guessing its intention, his urgent voice rang out. 'Get back in orbit, Chalmont. On the double!'

There was no response from S-Suzy. Levelling off only to establish its position, it dived into the gorge and in seconds was lost in the mist and billowing clouds of gas from the stricken tankers. Ahead the crew in the flak wagon had already laid their guns on it and were now pumping out sheets of tracer. To the crews above it seemed impossible any aircraft could survive and Harvey's hands on his control wheel turned white and bloodless. A couple of seconds passed and then there was a massive explosion. As pieces of wings and fuselage were seen in the mushroom of fire and smoke that erupted from the gorge, the astonished Lacey turned to Harvey. 'They didn't fire their rockets, skipper. They dropped their bombs instead.'

A sob had broken out from Harvey when the bombs burst. Now, to cover his embarrassment, the Yorkshireman let out a curse. 'The young fools. What the hell did they achieve but to kill themselves?'

But Harvey was wrong. When the smoke cleared away the smoking, shattered locomotive and the flak wagon were both seen to be lying on their sides. Behind them, looking like toys thrown awry by an irate child's hand, the gas wagons were piled up on either side of the track. From the yellow fumes that were escaping it was more than clear that neither the German villagers nor the Allied troops in Italy faced any further danger from them.

With Mosquito crews momentarily stunned by the suddenness of the attack, it took a moment for them to understand what had happened. Nose fused bombs burst on impact, meaning certain death to a low-flying aircraft but ensuring great accuracy. Between them Chalmont and Richards had made very certain the trainload of leaking gas would never reach the village.

Moore broke the silence of the circling crews. 'Aircraft left with rockets finish off any undamaged tankers. Then we'll call it a day and go home.'

The dawn was long over when the last crewman left the confessional and Adams was able to sink back in his chair and remove his spectacles. Although the last surviving Mosquito had still needed the flare path to complete its landing, Henderson, who had gained a full report of the operation from Manston, had decided to allow the weary crews to breakfast first before submitting their report to Adams.

Now, with the confessional empty at last, Adams was wishing Sue was back. Not for the first time after operations that had cost many lives, he found comfort in her presence and sympathy. This morning he needed it as never before.

As he fumbled for his pipe he heard the clink of metal and the shouts of NCOs as mechanics worked on the surviving Mosquitoes. Hardly a machine had not suffered some damage, the only fact that day from which Adams could find any comfort. At least it would be some days before Davies could find another mission for the exhausted crews.

The sound of footsteps outside made him replace his glasses. When he saw Henderson outlined in the doorway he suppressed a groan. Adams liked the big genial Scot but he was not the man he would have chosen as a confidant at that moment.

Henderson approached his table. 'You finished, Frank?'

Adams indicated the file of folders on his desk. 'For the moment. I still need a longer chat with Moore but he's occupied at the moment with all the repairs to be made.'

Nothing more was needed to release Henderson's resentment. 'What a disaster it was, Frank. Do you realize how many crews I've lost?'

Adams knew only too well. 'Yes, sir. I know how you feel.'

'Do you? Does anyone? Christ, Frank, I had to put up with it when we've had definite targets like Rhine Maiden or Valkyrie. But this was only a precaution. Jerry might never have intended to use that gas. Yet look what the cost has been. Not just to our crews but to the Yanks as well.'

Only too aware how futile words could be at such a time, Adams made no attempt to answer. Henderson pulled out a cigarette packet from his tunic, then dropped on the bench opposite. As Adams offered him a light, the Scot sucked in a lungful of smoke. His words were more of a challenge than a question. 'But there's a lot more to it than that, isn't there?

Knowing it had to come out sooner or later, Adams did not attempt evasion. 'Yes, sir. I'm afraid there is.'

Henderson leaned forward, his voice hoarse. 'Why, Frank? Why did they change their minds like that?'

Adams sighed. 'I don't think they did, sir. They just thought of a different way of achieving their ends. I suppose it was partly my fault. I shouldn't have let them work in here and I certainly shouldn't have left them alone. They found the photographs the reconnaissance Spitfire took and they planned the rest.' Adams removed his glasses again and began to wipe them. 'We should have guessed what they were up to but I suppose we were so glad they might avoid a court martial we didn't take it any further.'

'But Moore says it wasn't just an attack on the train. They chose suicide to make sure it didn't reach the village. Why would two young-sters with everything to live for do such a thing?'

Adams sighed. 'Apparently if the train hadn't been stopped then it would have entered and contaminated the valley. The very thing the youngsters wanted to avoid.' He rose and went over to one of his cabi-nets, returning with a file which he laid before Henderson. 'These are short stories Chalmont wrote and allowed me to read. It was his ambition to be a writer one day and he had the sensitivity to be one. I think when you've read them you'll understand the effect Guernica had on him.'

Henderson gazed at the file, then up at Adams again. 'But what about the other lad, Richards? He'd flown with us before Chalmont appeared and he'd never seen Guernica. Don't tell me Chalmont dropped those bombs at low level without consulting him?'

Adams shook his head. 'No. Chalmont wouldn't do that. Richards had a different reason. He wasn't only religious, he'd met and fallen in love with Chalmont's sister, Hilary. And she was more affected by Guernica than even Chalmont was.'

Henderson was looking puzzled. 'How do you know all this? The boys don't share their love lives with you, do they?'

Adams leaned down and opened a drawer. 'When the SPs were cleaning out the missing crews' billets this morning, these letters were found in Richards's locker. One is from Hilary. The other, not quite finished, is a reply from Richards. I was given them because the guardroom knew the boys had worked for me.'

Henderson took the letters. Watching him, Adams believed he saw moisture in the big Scot's eyes as he scanned them. 'So you could say it was Richards's love for this girl that killed him.'

Adams gave a slight start. 'You know, I never thought of it that way. Yes, I suppose you could say that.' Then, as an afterthought: 'Although I think his previous experience with a dying pilot had some effect on him.'

Nodding, Henderson pushed the letters back across the table. The silence in the confessional was louder than a cry of protest when he ground out his cigarette, rose, and went to the doorway. He stood there a long moment, then turned back to Adams. 'I think I'm going to get drunk tonight, Frank. And I'd be obliged if you'd join me.'

Adams nodded. 'I will, sir. But, you know, there is one thing of comfort in all this.'

Henderson's laugh was pure sarcasm. 'There is? Then for God's sake give it to me.'

'Those two boys had everything to live for. And yet they gave their lives to save hundreds of their enemies from dying a hideous death. Isn't there a hopeful message in that somewhere?'

Henderson frowned. 'Is there? Even though those villagers will never know about it?'

'That's true but I think you know what I mean.'

Henderson stared at him, then the professional airman's mask of unsentimentality dropped back into place. 'You always were a deep bugger, Frank. Don't forget that drink tonight. You always explain yourself better after you've had a few drams.'

Adams watched him disappear, then picked up the letters. As he gazed at them he realized his glasses needed wiping again. Dropping back into his chair, Adams wished once more that Sue was back from leave.